I0685955

PROPHECY OF FIRE

MICHAEL G. THOMAS

© 2014 Michael G. Thomas

The right of Michael G. Thomas to be identified as the Author of the Work has been asserted by him in accordance with the Copyright, Designs and Patents Act 1988.

First published in the United Kingdom in 2014 by Swordworks Books.

All rights reserved. No part of this publication may be produced, stored in a retrieval system, or transmitted in any form or by any means, without the prior permission in writing of the publisher, nor be otherwise circulated in any form of binding or cover other than in which it is published and without a similar condition including this condition being imposed on the subsequent purchaser.

All characters in this publication are fictitious and any resemblance to real persons, living or dead, is purely coincidental.

ISBN 978-1-911092-38-4

Typeset by Swordworks Books
Printed and bound in the UK & US
A catalogue record of this book is available
from the British Library

Cover design by Swordworks Books
www.swordworks.co.uk

PROPHECY OF FIRE

MICHAEL G. THOMAS

CHAPTER ONE

The heavy fighter losses sustained during the Great Uprising served as a reminder that the fighter program needed improvements. The existing stocks of Lightning and Thunderbolt fighters would be retained for years to come, but even the new Hammerhead couldn't match the power and expendability of cheap robotic fighters. Though too late to participate in the fighting, the first squadron of X57 Avenger combat drones was activated aboard the newly commissioned Conqueror Class battlecruisers to serve alongside exiting fighter squadrons. Finally activated in 361CC, just a week after the Zathee standards were raised over the capital buildings on Helios, they would see action in their first few months of service.

Robots in Space

The battle of C34A should have been nothing more than a routine operation; instead, it became a watchword for one of the greatest military disasters in the history of the Helion military. It wasn't even supposed to have been a battle, and in hindsight should never have been suggested. Even the name was itself something as a misnomer, as the Helions themselves were the agent of their own destruction. If superior forces had engaged the ships, it might have been inexcusable. As it happened, so the loss of every single soul spared them from the indignity at having been defeated by an inanimate object.

Twenty-one of the most advanced and powerful ships in the vast Helion Navy arrived at the allocated area with perfect timing and were well equipped and prepared for battle. As well as the ships, they were also accompanied by a dozen smaller vessels and over a hundred heavy fighters. Instead of glorious victory, the entire force was lost in the vain attempt at intercepting the deadly comet as it hurtled through space. The battle marked the lowest point in the Helion military for generations and was the greatest loss of military ships since the defeat of the Biomechs hundreds of years earlier.

The operation was conducted with a degree of planning and coordination that might be expected from the Helions. They approached the comet from the rear so that they might match its speed rather than smashing through it, something that would result in catastrophic damage as well as the loss of many, if not all the ships. Now traveling at nearly two hundred and fifty thousand kilometers per hour, the hunters and the hunted were finally in range, and the mission moved to the next phase.

Under the protection of a great cloud of fighters, a dozen large craft were launched to attach devices to parts of the comet. Each of these was at least five times larger than a fighter and carried the parts to assemble a complete gravity generator that would help move the comet off course. None had made it anywhere near the object before vanishing in a series of fireballs. There were no signs of debris that might cause the impact other than tiny particles of dust and ice that trailed the core. This immediately halted the plan to deflect the course of the comet by even a few meters using non-violent measures. This should have been enough to warn the Admiral and his captains that a new and more considered approach needed to be taken.

This time the fleet adjusted its course to avoid potential damage from the vast debris cloud that moved with the object. This meant the force of ships had to spread out by hundreds of kilometers. Weapon systems on the ships targeted floating debris that followed the comet like parasites. It took almost a full day for the fleet to pick its way through the deadly cloud so that they were position directly in front of swirling maelstrom. Once in front, it took incredible skill and bravery by Helion fighter pilots and the warship gunners to keep chunks of rock and ice from striking the ship. This was the only success in the entire operation and resulted in the entire group of ships being placed safely in the path of the blue orb.

Comet C34A didn't appear to be anything more interesting or unusual than any other comet. It showed up as a glowing blue sphere on the dark background of deep space. It was the largest known comet in the system with a nucleus of over eleven kilometers in diameter. A light blue coma expanded around it like a shimmering cloud, and its trail extended millions of kilometers behind it. At the heart of the comet was a dense core of dust, rock, organic compounds, and ice that might have made it a rich target for mining and exploitation.

With the failure of the initial mining and explosives operation, the Helion flagship Horizon moved into weapons range and unleashed over a hundred atomic missiles. They rushed out from the missile tubes and covered just a short distance before each detonated prematurely, sending their cargo of fissionable material into the swirling cloud that was the coma of the comet. Thirty second later, every single ship opened fire with kinetic weapons. It was a hopeless attack and could be expected to achieve nothing more than adding a few more craters to the comet. In the middle of the onslaught, they suffered their first casualty. Horizon split in half, and a dozen blue explosions ripped through her superstructure as she was torn into fragments. The remaining ships were unable to change their course, so opened fire at whatever targets their scanners could identify. Some of their missiles locked onto their own ships and IFF systems failed. In a matter of minutes, the fleet and the comet became one, as chunks of debris, missiles, and pieces of rock moved about. The last phase of the battle for Comet C34A was over in less than six minutes, leaving the shattered hulks of the ships and over five thousand Helion dead.

* * *

"Gentlemen, I don't have long. The stories of this impending doom are starting to unnerve the public, and the President wants it squashed, fast. What is the problem that you want brought to his attention so urgently? Has something happened on the Helion colonies?"

General Rivers, the Chairman of the Joint Chiefs shook his head in reply.

"No, Mr. Secretary, our operations are continuing as planned. I asked you and the Joint Chiefs to come together to listen to something of much more concern. I have received a number of disturbing reports from the Helion Naval Institute, as well as from Naval operatives via Admiral Jackson, of a potentially devastating threat."

He looked at the officer who waited patiently around the table along with the others.

"These reports could indicate a threat even larger than the current insurgency we are helping to eradicate. If I may?"

The Secretary of Defense sat down and sighed.

"Go on."

All it took was a quick signal to the pair of scientists, both in their fifties and who were waiting patiently next to the display unit. They wore smart, though ill-fitting suits that suggested they were not their usual clothing.

"Doctor Steiner, if you will."

The senior scientist nodded politely and then pressed a button on his personal secpad, and a video stream appeared. All of those present looked at it with a mixture of intrigue and surprise. The video shuddered and flickered before finally freezing to a still image of the massive comet. It was very grainy and to most of them was nothing more than a blue blob on the screen.

"Now, if you look here you will see the object," said the senior of the two.

There was a deathly silence in the large briefing room. It was easily capable of seating nearly thirty people, but on this occasion less than a third filled its space. The ceiling was low, yet the inlaid sculptures throughout the room gave it a feeling of ancient opulence, almost decadence. All of the imagery documented the colorful past of Terra Nova, dating back to its first colonies and its struggles in the Great War and the Uprising. A slightly lighter section of wood showed the most recent artwork, one of the Fall of Terra Nova, a key event that saw the agents of the Biomech enemy driven from the capital world of the Confederacy and the founding of the Alliance, and the modern age. The room was windowless and only one door provided access. Two Marine Guards waited with their carbines resting up against their shoulders. They all watched the video stream as the comet continued on its path before it vanished with a white light.

"What exactly is that?" asked General Hammerstein, the Chief of Staff for the Colony Guard, the new military force that operated defense forces on each of the colonies. The scientist tapped several buttons. The comet shrunk in size and moved back to its initial point. The man pointed at a dark shape to the left of the comet. Admiral Jackson stood up and walked to the screen.

"Alliance ships have already charted this section of space during our patrols near the Black Rift. At first glance it looks like a piece of debris, flotsam if you will. In reality, however, this is actually the abandoned Helion remote outpost that used to provide long-range support for fleet operations near the Black Rift. It was being used to store materials and supplies but luckily was unoccupied at the time of the impact."

The video stream continued, but this time at a much slower pace. The quality was still grainy, but it was possible to make out the shape of the orb and the spot that marked the station. The comet moved though the black dot and continued on its original course, with nothing but a bright white flash to indicate the fate of the station. The General gasped, but the others remained completely still. Admiral Jackson moved back to his position and sat down. The chief scientist continued.

"Our long-range scientific scanners indicate there is nothing left of the station, and the comet has continued on its path."

The scientist paused and looked at the group of older men and women. All were military, apart from the Secretary of Defense who wore his civilian suit.

"Go on," he said.

"Well, if you look at our projected trajectory, you can see the comet will pass through the orbit of the outer moons of Helios before striking the planet itself."

"I don't understand. You said just a few kilometers. It doesn't seem that big, are you sure this is as significant as you say it is? We have enough problems, what with the Helion insurgency, and this political stand-off with the other aliens."

The image on the screen was evidently insufficient to show the sheer potential destructive energy of such an object, and it clearly frustrated the senior scientist. He looked about at the group, rubbed his forehead, and then repeated his earlier summary, but in a language he hoped the Defense Secretary would actually understand.

"Defense Secretary, you recall the massive asteroid impact that was responsible for a planet-wide mass extinction of dinosaurs back on ancient Earth?"

The look on the man's face was clear enough, and rather than wait the scientist continued.

"This is one of the most famous impacts in our history and was responsible for a shift in ecology, as well as in the biology of Earth. Hundreds of thousands of species were wiped out, and if there had been cities and humans, the casualties would have been catastrophic. We know with certainty that in exactly one hundred and twenty-four days and seven hours, the planet of Helios will face an unavoidable extinction level threat."

The Defense Secretary seemed to take this description as a personal affront.

"Doctor, I am well aware of what happened to the dinosaurs. I need to know how this will affect the security situation with regards to Helios and to our treaty with them. I am briefing the President in ten minutes, and I need everything we know."

"The Helions are aware of this threat, I take it? Why can't they put asteroid defense measures in place for something like this?" asked General Cornwallis, the Chief of Staff for the Marine Corps.

Admiral Jackson nodded.

"Indeed they are aware, General, but this isn't an asteroid. This is a comet."

The General shrugged as if it made little difference.

"So?"

"Well, for starters, comets are made up of ice, dust, and rocket material and follow extended orbits. This one vanished from sight a long time ago, and the Helions are not sure why they missed it."

"Why can they not do something about it?" asked General Rivers.

Admiral Jackson pointed at the object.

"As you know, the Helion military is fractured, and many of their commanders took their ships away after the collapse of their military government. Even so, their basic apparatus still exists. One of their regional commanders took a small force of about twenty ships on an intercept course a week after the base had been destroyed."

"Now we're hearing about this?" complained the General.

As the Chairman, General Rivers took this question with the usual ruthless efficiency he exhibited in political situations.

"Yes, we may have a treaty, but that doesn't mean they pass on all information directly to us. The Helions are a proud people, General. They don't want to come crying to us with every single problem they have at their back door."

General Cornwallis said no more and waited as Admiral Jackson continued.

"One of our Crusader class ships detected the object in Helios space and notified the regional commander. We assumed that was it until in the last hour we received the news."

"Go on, Admiral, give us the details. What happened?" goaded the Secretary of Defense.

"The Helions set an intercept course, with the initial plan of placing explosive weapons at key points to break up the object. This failed for unknown reasons, and so they resorted to placing a single gravity well generator or a similar type used on our ships for artificial gravity."

The look on the faces of the Chief of Staff for the Marine Corps and the Colonial Militia suggested they had no idea what the Admiral was saying. The Naval officer considered trying to explain but motioned for the chief scientist to do it instead. The man nodded and wiped his brow before starting.

"At the start of the twenty-first century, an aerospace engineer on Earth suggested making use of ballast to alter an object's center of mass, so the object could be moved safely from the intercept course."

"But this didn't happen?" asked General Cornwallis.

"Exactly," Admiral Jackson answered. It seems this also failed, so they resorted to assaulting the object from space with heavy weaponry. Now this took place six days ago and without informing us. They were a day away from making contact before they lost communication."

He paused for a moment while long-range imagery loaded on the viewer. It didn't show much, and the small dots had to be highlighted with bright circles.

"According to the Helions, each of these dots is the shattered wreckage from their fleet. They lost the entire fleet, including the flagship Horizon with all hands. It was veteran of the war with the Biomechs."

General Rivers looked at the man who had now sat down with a grim look on his face. The Admiral was of a similar age to him, and like most of the High Command, a citizen of Terra Nova. There was always a degree of professional courtesy but no friendship between the two. The Great Uprising had reinforced the differences between many of the military families, and they were still resentful of those from the worlds of Proxima Centauri that had brought fire to the planets of Alpha Centauri.

"I see, well this is something the President will need to be briefed upon. General Rivers and I will bring these details directly to him. Is there anything else?"

Admiral Jackson indicated for the chief scientist to continue. As the man loaded up more imagery, General Rivers looked at the new Secretary of Defense. Sam Mithy was one of the new intake of politicians, following the recent Alliance elections. He knew the man by reputation only, and although he had some experience in the Confederate Army as a junior officer a generation earlier, he understood it to have been on stations or barrack moons with the reserve fighter squadrons that had seen no actual combat in the war. It didn't impress the General at all, even less when after just a few days in office, the man had laid accusations of incompetence at military commanders that seemed to be prevalent with the new regime, one that was on a personal mission to rebuild the Alliance military around a rigid core of politically reliable leaders. It made him uneasy.

"Well, this object could potentially wipe out all life on Helios, what else is there to know?" answered General Rivers with an irritated tone.

"This is serious, of course, and we will do what we can to help. The President has to answer to our citizens, however, and there is a growing weariness of the strain on our colonies at our involvement in the affairs of these alien worlds. We will endeavor to assist them in any way we can, but not at the expense of our own national interest."

General Rivers shook his head angrily.

"What do you mean? We are already committed to action on a number of fronts," he snapped.

The others were stunned by his lack of diplomacy, but the General continued.

"We have only just helped them win their fight for freedom on their world, and now you say there are more pressing concerns than the wiping out of all life on Helios?"

It was clear from the expression on the Secretary of Defense's face that this was exactly what he was thinking.

"We benefit greatly from our contact with our comrades in Helios, as well as the other worlds. Don't forget the

Biomechs intervened politically and technologically in our last internal conflict. We cannot adopt an isolationist viewpoint right now, if ever," General Rivers added quickly.

The Secretary of Defense moved his head slowly as though he was disgusted by what he had heard.

"General, do not suggest this regime will abandon its friends. Trade is booming between our colonies and these new regions. The number of ships moving through the Prometheus-T'Karan Rift is in the hundreds a day now. That is why we have started construction work on a whole new layer of support Rifts that will link every colony world in less than a decade."

All of them waited for the 'but'.

"Even so, based on recent events, it is imperative that our military capabilities are prioritized, and it is the view of the President that the top-priority for our entire military effort should be on one place."

The conversation was already starting to drift off-topic, and it led General Rivers to think the Secretary of Defense had an ulterior motive in bringing it up.

"The Black Rift, Mr. Secretary?"

The room fell silent once more.

"Yes, that is correct. The Black Rift is the elephant in the room. With the increasing trend in newly discovered Rifts and isolated occurrences of Biomech warships, our citizens are becoming concerned. Helios is important but is irrelevant when compared to the great threat of the Biomechs themselves. Does the lack of this supply base cause us additional problems at the Rift?"

Admiral Jackson shook his head.

"No, we have the 4th in the Helios system with ample resources coming through the Rift to T'Karan. Our remaining Strike Groups are undergoing deployment or taking part in a number of exercises. We've never been stronger."

"We said the same in the Uprising, and it went on for years," General Rivers hissed through his teeth.

"The fact of the matter is that the Black Rift is more than just a Spacebridge to what we are told is the home system of the Biomechs. It is the longest range Rift we have ever come across, one that we cannot begin to match in terms of our own technology. From the information given to us by the T'Kari, it would take over a millennia to build enough conventional Rifts in sequence to get from Helios to the Biomech homeworld. Because of this vast range, the Rift generator equipment requires vast reserves of power to open, and is incredibly volatile. It can only be opened within a short range of the guard station, and with the express permission and access data from one of the five Powers."

Admiral Jackson ignored the General's previous retort.

"On top of that, the defensive measures are impressive. Any Rift within a light year can be collapsed in less than seven seconds, with the destruction of anything in it. According to the logs of the Helions, the Biomechs have never attempted the creation of a Rift back to Helios.

The Secretary of Defense seemed a little more relaxed at this information, but General Rivers couldn't see why. None of it was new, other than the comet and the threat it presented.

"Why not? Surely it would be worth trying from time to time."

General Rivers lifted his hand slightly.

"If I may," he started. "The T'Kari say the station build by the Narau is more than just a way of controlling the Rift to the Biomechs. It is a doomsday weapon, one that has never been used. It can render the area of space useless for at least a millennia if they choose to trigger the device. This is the threat that stops the Biomechs from coming."

Admiral Jackson nodded in complete agreement.

"This is true. The Biomechs are an ever-present threat. Their ability to encourage support from many directions is impressive. We have seen ships in other parts of space that are loyal to them, and this comet has arrived at just the time when the Helions prophesied the return of the Enemy. This is the matter that concerns me the most, and I feel the comet and the safety of this sector are the same thing."

The Secretary of Defense looked at his watch and sighed before looking back at him.

"Yes, why?"

"What if this prophecy isn't the Biomechs, but instead is for the comet itself? It could potentially destroy Helios and with it the only military power in this sector. If Helios falls, a Biomech assault could soon follow, and can we rely on the others to help?"

Even as he said the words, it was clear this was what the man had been thinking about all along. He gave a grim, barely visible smirk as General Rivers finished making his thought known.

"So why did we only just hear about this threat, if it was so important? Surely your commanders in the Navy are capable of spotting dangers in space, isn't that what we pay you for?"

Admiral Jackson rose to his feet, but General Rivers lowered his hands to get him to remain seated.

"I think we all know the value of the Navy, Mr. Secretary, and technically only the private sector workers pay for our armed forces. We are all public servants, paid for by the public purse."

He walked over to the image of the comet.

"I'll answer you again, Mr. Secretary, but the facts haven't changed. Everybody, including us, missed this object, but all of this is irrelevant. We are here to discuss the security implications for Helios, the Orion Nebula, and the Alliance, and I think it is clear from the thoughts of the Joint Chiefs that the comet is a clear and present danger."

The Defense Secretary rose to his feet to leave without saying a word. He moved to the door, turning back to look at them.

"General, it is time. The President awaits our briefing and neither this comet, nor the Black Rift itself, respects our schedules."

The two men left the room, and the two scientists followed shortly after, leaving the three Joint Chiefs behind on their own. General Hammerstein was the first to speak as the three considered what had been said.

"Is it me or is the Secretary of Defense becoming a little obsessed over just one point in space?"

Admiral Jackson smiled curtly.

"Well, he does have a point. If what the Helions and the others say is true, the entire might of the Biomechs is waiting on the other side. Even a comet would pale to insignificance compared to the threat something like that could offer."

It was a thought none of them seemed to relish.

"What about the fighting on the moons, how is that progressing? I thought we were winning this war?" asked General Hammerstein.

General Cornwallis seemed to almost shudder at this question, as though a cold wind had just touched his skin.

"It's progressing. We helped the Zathee and their allies win, and win quickly. This insurgency is unexpected, however. We are unable to fight them head on, and they are resorting to asymmetric tactics to nullify our edge in manpower, weapons, and mobility."

"The home front isn't much better,'" complained General Hammerstein.

"How so?" asked the Admiral.

"For starters, there are rumors in the Guard that when the Biomechs arrive, they will be the cannon fodder. You can imagine the quality of the people that are left. Recruitment for the Corps or the Navy isn't a problem, but the Colonial Guard gets none of the glory. If you want to travel and see alien worlds, you don't become a part-time soldier on Terra Nova, do you?"

General Cornwallis looked unimpressed.

"The Colonial Guard is not a frontline unit, you know that, General. What does this have to do with the Biomechs?"

"The Guard is becoming less and less popular on the homeworlds with the Doomsday Prophecy. The rise in apocalyptic cults is rocketing, and some have turned to violence. We clamp down on them, but we always seem to come out as the bad guys."

Admiral Jackson finally understood the man's concerns.

"General, in the end it isn't up to us to be loved. We have a job to do, and if we don't do it, you know the consequences. We weren't prepared the last time, and I'll be damned if we'll let it happen again."

"What are you suggesting?" asked General Cornwallis.

"I don't know, but the arrival of this comet is no coincidence, and apart from the actual threat it brings, I strongly believe there could be something much worse on the way. I see no reason to disbelieve the warning from the Helions."

General Hammerstein was unimpressed; at least that was how it looked.

"What if you're wrong?"

Admiral Jackson grimaced.

"What if I'm right?"

CHAPTER TWO

The capabilities of a warship can only be replaced by technology and equipment to a point. Ultimately, a ship can only be in one place at a time, and this is where the small fleet strategy of the early Alliance began to unravel. Luckily, the resilience and power of the new Heavy Strike Groups would show how a small group of advanced ships could hold their own against greater numbers. In time, the number of Crusader class Heavy Cruisers and its larger brother, the Conqueror class Battlecruiser would come to dominate Alliance affairs in a way no other ship design had.

Naval Cadet's Handbook

The highly reflective clouds of sulfuric acid that shrouded Venus were a welcome sight for the tired eyes of Spartan. The T'Kari ship's scanners brought up pages of data, but he already knew the planet he was staring at was one of the most inhospitable places in the Alliance. Its surface was a dry, barren desert, interspersed with rocks and volcanoes. Its dense carbon dioxide-filled atmosphere made viewing the surface impossible from this distance, but Spartan knew the world's reputation. Even though it was useless to them, he still felt a rush of relief at seeing something, anything that was familiar to him.

"Look," Khan said in a dull tone.

Spartan watched as the pale orb finally moved out of sight and was replaced by the wondrous blue sphere that was Earth.

"Have you ever seen it before?"

Spartan was surprised at the low tone of reverence his friend used. The old warrior looked exhausted, yet the relief at being in Alliance territory was clearly visible on Khan's brow. Spartan took a slow breath to avoid the pain that still spread around his ribs. The injuries he'd sustained in captivity were far from healed, and the escape through the Rift and the space battle had done little to improve that. He looked to his friend and shook his head.

"No, not in the flesh. Well, not until today. You've got to remember, Khan, until we built the Rifts; it used to take decades to make the trip between Sol and Alpha Centauri. The colonization fleets that went first were on a one-way mission. Lots didn't even make it there because of the long journey."

Khan looked to his friend with a single raised eyebrow.

"It's true. There are stories of some ships with thousands of people on board vanishing on the trip. It took decades with the engines permanently on full burn. Any kind of technical problem, and they were left stranded."

"So why not stop and pick them up?"

Spartan smiled.

"You never studied, did you?"

Khan snorted.

"And you did? I thought you spent your early years dodging axes on the arena circuit?"

Spartan had to concede that point. He had indeed spent some time on the illegal pit fighting circuit. It wasn't quite about killing each other with axes. Although people did die, especially in the illegal fights, it was very rare. It was something he hadn't thought of it for many years, and the images of his last fight on the space station orbiting Prometheus was a painful one. Luckily, Khan's attention had moved on to their current predicament.

"What about the people on Earth, do they still live there? I heard it was a dead world."

Spartan looked at the blue shape with a mixture of fascination and foreboding. Earth was a wondrous sight to see. Even though the planet's surface and oceans had been plundered for millennia, it still looked calm and rich when viewed from space. Its toxic clouds were barely obvious, but he knew full well the planet's dark past.

"Yeah, Earth is still populated. In fact, I think this

entire Solar System is still populated, but it ain't nothing like where we're from Khan."

They both watched the blue orb move from view as the T'Kari ship continued to drift in space.

"Remember why our people left this star in the first place; resources, habitable worlds, and a new life. Just look at her."

He pointed at the shape of Venus as it drifted passed their view once more.

"Venus is a no go area, always has been, even without our help. Only the planets of Mars and Earth have populations still on them. Mercury is suitable for industrial machines robotics, and the others are gas giants; they're only useful for harvesting."

He moved his head a little, thinking a little more on it.

"Plus the moons, of course, and then the space stations."

Khan grinned as Spartan realized he was rambling.

"Look, let's just say there are still people out in this wasteland. Okay?"

Something struck the ship somewhere very hard. The impact was powerful enough to send a jolt through its structure and forced Spartan and Khan into silence.

"What is that?" asked Khan.

They both looked in the direction of their three T'Kari comrades that were busy managing the ship. None of them paid any attention to them and continued with their work.

Another great impact shook the vessel, and then the vast glass window flashed and changed to show a magnified image. Spartan blinked, his brain temporarily confused at the change in the visuals. The glass gave the impression of being a window, when in fact it was a cleverly designed piece of display technology.

"Who are they?" asked Khan; his right arm extended and pointing at the bottom right of the window.

Spartan followed his gaze and spotted the shapes moving toward them.

"Ships! Great, I thought we'd given the Biomechs the slip!"

Thoughts of the planets quickly vanished as they turned their attention to the new threat. They had only just entered the safety of Alliance territory, and already they were in trouble. The escape from Biomech captivity and the collapse of the temporary Rift should have been the end of Spartan and Khan's troubles, but it seemed their arrival was to be yet another problem waiting to be resolved with violence. Spartan checked his targeting system and tried to return fire. He didn't want to destroy the attacking ships, but he had to do something, and a burst across their bows might be all that was required.

"I've got nothing, what about you?"

Khan smashed his fist onto the display for what must have been the tenth time.

"Nothing. These ships are finishing what the Biomechs

started. We need to get off this ship!"

Another heavy impact smashed into them. It was powerful and reminded Spartan of the numerous times he'd been aboard ships when they had been struck by heavy ordnance.

This is strange though. We're in friendly territory and already ships are upon us. The odds of a ship being even within a few days' range of us are minuscule.

"Who the hell are they?" he growled.

Spartan tried to get a response from the computer system, but it refused to respond. He had only just about managed to work the gunnery system thanks to Khan's intervention. Trying to get anything more constructive out of the alien technology was proving impossible. He looked at the T'Kari, but no matter how much he shouted, they ignored him. The three aliens seemed to need all their attention focused on trying to get the spacecraft as far away from the attackers as possible.

"You're wasting your time, you fools," he snapped and looked back to Khan.

"Those are our ships, Spartan. Don't you recognize the markings? They look like orbital barges to me, and we're flying in an unmarked T'Kari Raider. Are you really that surprised?"

Spartan gazed at the fleeting image of the ships that were firing. They didn't look like current designs, but they had been away a long time, and now they were orbiting

Earth, a place he'd never visited before.

Maybe they are using wrecks for defense.

Another group of hardened metal armor piercing projectiles rushed ever closer, each of them traveled at incredible speeds after being hurled into space by the Alliance warships. Spartan finally got a decent view of the ships, and once he could see them in a profile position, he knew what they were. He was used to the newest vessels, having spent so much time out on the T'Kari frontier. These were not the large capital ships of the fleet. They were the protective barges dating back over seventy years that were still in use as orbital defenses. The magnetic railguns that had fired them were simple technology, perhaps even primitive by modern standards. Even so, there were fewer more destructive weapons in space.

"War barges, I thought they had all been scrapped after the Uprising."

Khan shook his head and laughed.

"Really? I think the three out there would say otherwise."

The warbarges were an old concept, and one that had fallen out of favor as the human empire expanded out to the stars. Back when the colonies had numbered just a few worlds, it had proven useful to construct large, slow moving vessels with thick armor and bristling with weapons. They usually stayed in orbit and were more like armed satellites than space faring ships. Though they were capable of interplanetary travel, they were not generally equipped or particularly suitable for it. The ships around Earth were third-rate at best. A single turret from the T'Kari ship finally activated, and Spartan watched dispassionately at its rounds embedded ineffectively in the thick armor of the barge.

"Yeah, that's about right."

The barges may have been primitive, but they had always been constructed to take a heavy beating. Dozens of white flashes ran about the turrets of the Earth ships, and Spartan felt his body tense.

"Incoming!" growled Khan while watching his gunnery screen.

Lines of projectiles from the medium-caliber railguns slammed into the forward armor of the T'Kari ship, despite the best efforts of her crew. An undamaged ship such as this might stand a chance in a fair fight, but this vessel was barely operational. Her hull was pockmarked with a hundred holes, and missiles had ripped plating and weapon mounts off all along her frame.

"Can't you reach them with the comms?" asked Spartan.

As if to answer his question, the computer monitors all switched off. Even the emergency lights vanished, leaving the control room in complete darkness.

"Oh, great, this is just what we need."

A final volley tore a hole the size of a man in the portside armor, and in seconds the breach alarms were sounding. Spartan tried to pull the belt back on where he sat, but he was too late. The ship was already spinning out of control, and he flew across the open space and crashed into the ceiling. He didn't even have time to see what Khan was doing before he blacked out.

* * *

Eos had more in common with a conventional planet than that of a moon. It was a barren, rocky world with dozens of industrial sites and shielded cities littering the moon. Though protected by the massive gas-giant planet Gaxos' magnetic field, it carried only a trace atmosphere and below average gravity. Unlike Helios, most of the structures were low, and many were built directly into the ground, with some even deep below the surface. A formation of three Hammerhead fighters moved at low altitude, scanning for signs of insurgents, and a column of five Bulldog vehicles made slow progress across the dusty surface. The armored vehicles kicked up a dust cloud that could be seen for kilometers around them.

"Keep your eyes open, marines. You saw the reports," said Sergeant Stone.

The eight-wheeled Bulldog shook violently as it bumped over the rough road surface. No matter how many times Jack traveled about in these vehicles, he found himself constantly amazed how small they were internally compared to the large bulk on the outside. He looked at the Sergeant with a mixture of awe and amazement. It was only seven months earlier that they had been fighting on Helios against Animosh paramilitaries and their allies. Jack swallowed, doing his best to hold back the cold knot feeling in his stomach. The vodka from the previous night burned inside him, and he had to tense his entire body to avoid vomiting inside his helmet. He looked sideways and took a sip of tepid water from the tube near his mouth. The feeling in his stomach subsided for a moment.

Get a grip, Jack. You've got a job to do.

He'd been granted only a modest amount of leave, prior to being sent on the four-month trip to the moon of Eos. That meant it was almost seven months since he'd witnessed the flags of the Zathee being raised over the capital of Helios. They weren't his people, and he felt no great affection for them, apart from those he'd been in immediate contact with, like the Helion synthetic named Vadi. But the length of the journey to the moon did leave him with a feeling of unease. They were far from home and little help could be sent if it was needed, certainly not in time.

The fact that there was no Rift anywhere near the planet surprised him until he'd seen the remains of the space platform that orbited the moon. Animosh sympathizers had shattered it, presumably in a vain attempt to seize control of the moon before the Zathee could do anything about it. That didn't concern him anything like as much as the thought of his family back on Terra Nova. He felt a growing pain in his stomach and took another sip of water.

Easy now, you don't want to throw up in your suit!

That thought seemed to sober him up faster than anything else. The thoughts of his mother recovering in the military hospital nearly put a smile on his face, that was until he recalled the arguments and shouting with his siblings. It started to fill him with a rage he could barely suppress.

"I hate this place," muttered Private Callahan, voicing the thoughts of the majority.

He was easily the largest built of the entire group, now that Wictred had been transferred to assist in the training and command of the heavy units being added to the battalion. His complaining turned Jack's attention from the events of Terra Nova, and he was thankful for it. He would have plenty of time for silent reflection after this operation.

"Son, you're not here to like this place; it's just a moon, like any other," snapped back the Sergeant.

There were no windows inside the vehicle, but the small number of display screens allowed them to see what was happening outside via the camera feeds. The computer system may have screwed things, but from what Jack could see the place was an arid, gray looking environment with no large structure of note.

"Why are we here, Sarge, can't drones do this?" asked Corporal Frewyn in his common sounding accent.

The tall and obviously attractive Private Riku laughed.

"Of course not, drones are expensive, marines are cheap."

Now the Sergeant was angry. He leaned into the middle of the squad and scowled at each of them. His eyes moved from one to the other until he stopped in front of Riku.

"Marines are the most expensive asset in the entire Corps. Your training, equipment, supplies, medical gear, and retirement rack up to millions. Now you secure this crap and concentrate on your job. Understood?"

The marines replied quickly and without hesitation. Stone moved back to his seat and pulled on his harness, just as they struck another rut in the dirt track.

"There might be peace on Helios, but this ain't Helios, is it?" he asked rhetorically.

With a clenched fist, he pointed to the side of the vehicle. The effect was slightly spoiled by the fact he was wearing the dark PDS Alpha armor that exaggerated the size of his body and fingers.

"This is one of the richest industrial sites run by the Helions under the control of the Irkerk corporation. This world's output is greater than Kerberos, Prime, and Terra Nova combined, and that's just on a moon. They have shipyards, fuel processing plants, and engineering sites are all over this moon."

Another rut would have broken their necks had the marines not be strapped in. Instead it bumped and slid for a few seconds before righting itself. Sergeant Stone called out angrily through his intercom. The visor was open, and the other marines could easily see his face.

"Watch your driving. Last thing we want is an upturned Bulldog out in the middle of this place."

They continued onward; each watching through the view screens for signs of the elusive enemy. Every small settlement or factory site seemed deserted with only the occasional engineering vehicle using the same roads. The slightly lower gravity than they were used to making the dust clouds they kicked up even worse than normal. By the time they had moved through the fifth factory district, the marines were becoming agitated. The inability to move about inside the vehicles was physically uncomfortable as well as claustrophobic.

"Sarge, what are they even doing here? I though the fighting was over?" asked Private Riku.

Stone looked at her without moving even a single muscle on his face. Jack watched, waiting for his reply and noted how hard and disciplined the man was.

Just like Spartan, all military, he thought distantly.

"The fighting on Helios might be over, but Justitium Lyssk is still at large, along with the Animosh that escaped. They have resources, money, and plenty of people who don't like what's happening on Helios."

Jack nodded as if the Sergeant was actually answering him. He was correct. There were many on Helios from the previously powerful cultures that had lost power in the revolution.

"It's true. Helios is a complex place. The main three pureblooded groups are hardly the greatest of friends, but they are at least equals. The Sh'Dori control most of the money and hold the greatest power."

What about others?" asked Riku.

Sergeant Stone noticed her leaning her head toward Jack. He grinned but not enough for anybody else to notice.

"Yes, Private, explain it to us. I'm sure we'd all like to hear your insight on the ethnic and political makeup of the Helions."

The sarcasm was clear, but Jack didn't care. Talking took his mind off the swirling cocktail of alcohol in his body and forced his mind away from his demons.

"Okay, well, as I understand it, the Irkerk and Yuulen were the original people, one being industrial and the others coming from agricultural stock. The Sh'Dori were warriors, but I don't remember where they came from."

"Aliens?" asked Riku with a forced smile.

Jack smirked.

"No, I just mean I don't know where on Helios they came from. This was millennia ago, don't forget."

"Ah...if you say so. Go on."

Some of the other marines seemed to be taking an interest in Jack's little lecture. He opened his mouth to continue when he spotted the hastily repaired damage marks on Sergeant Stone's chest. He'd been hurt several times in their last engagement, but as always, the tough as nails Sergeant was back in the fray. Jack had seen a lot of violence in his life so far, but it was the brutal slaying of his friend Hunn, and the torn up bodies on Helios while fighting machines, that had pushed him too far. The combat two months earlier had been on an even grander scale, and he was now at the stage where he needed drugs or drink to sleep.

"Jack?" asked Riku.

He looked at her, a glazed expression showing through his eyes. She checked Sergeant Stone wasn't looking before hitting him on the side of his armored helm. The impact shook him, and his eyes flickered before returning to something approaching normalcy.

"Jack! Snap out of it," she said as quietly but firmly as she could manage.

He stared into her eyes before remembering where he was and what he was doing.

"What about them?"

"You were telling us about the Helion factions."

He remembered and inhaled slowly, trying to remember how far he had reached.

"Okay, yeah. Well, the Sh'Dori, right?"

Riku nodded quickly.

"Right, they moved into and took over all the major institutions. The other two stayed but specialized. Over time this became exaggerated, and now the Sh'Dori have the same population as the other two combined."

Sergeant Stone must have been listening because he decided to wade in.

"The Private is right. The Sh'Dori are the ones with the most to lose by the rise of the Zathee. They are producing the money and support for the Animosh and Justitium Lyssk.

Jack thought of the Zathee and how so many of them had risen up to overthrow their so called 'pureblood' oppressors. Few would publically question the right of the majority class known as the Zathee to be treated fairly, but nobody would relinquish power voluntarily, certainly not the Sh'Dori.

"And that just leaves the Zathee, how do they fit in?" asked Private Jana Jenkell, the unit's medic, who had remained silent until now. Even inside her helmet, her eyes seemed to almost glow bright blue. They were unlike anything Jack had seen before. Private Riku spotted him looking at her and shook her head in annoyance.

"Are you going to tell us then, or is it a secret?"

Jack looked back at the screen nearest him and spotted something on the ridge to the right. This part of the moon looked the same as every other section they had patrolled so far. The road was wide enough for three Bulldogs side-by-side, and there were ditches each side below the raised roadway. The low rolling hills filled the background, but it was the sprawling shape of a dozen factory structures with their towers, spires and, warehouses that was most noticeable.

"There," he said without thinking.

Sergeant Stone leaned over to look at the screen.

"What is it?"

Jack pointed at the shape he'd seen move on the ridge near the closest building, a two story storage complex. They stared for what seemed like an age, and then a black smudge appeared and vanished again.

The Sergeant nodded and leaned back.

"Good work, Private."

He started to speak with the driver over the intercom. The other marines checked their own displays, looking for potential targets. As usual, the hexrotor drones buzzed overhead looking for signs of the enemy. Though on old piece of technology, the reconnaissance and communications of the past were being rectified, by fitting control nodes and flight packs on most vehicles in the Marine Corps inventory. A red blip appeared on the right of the screen, indicating a potential drone problem.

"Drone down, possible enemy action," said a spotter in the lead Bulldog.

Jack felt the shockwave slam into his chest, and the

Bulldog veered off the road. The level of skill shown by the driver was impressive. Jack reached out and grabbed one of the many grab rails inside the vehicle as they careered from the track and off into the ditch on the right-hand side. One wheel tore clean off as they hit a mound of jagged rocks, and then they were through and bouncing across the flatland, finally bogging down in the thick dusty surface layer.

"Dismount!" growled Sergeant Stone.

The doors hissed open just like in their training exercises, and the marines poured out. Three seconds after the doors opened, a rocket exploded ten meters from the Bulldog's hull. To untrained eyes it looked as if the vehicle had been struck, but Jack spotted the yellow flash from the topside mounts just before the missile struck. It was the Bulldog's set of advanced reactive armor. A brief moment before the rocket struck, it fired a stream of disruptive shards as a cloud in the path of the missile to detonate it prematurely. Nothing more than broken fragments bounced from its hull. The entire squad was now free, and Jack could see marines flooding from the other three Bulldogs until the platoon was out and taking cover.

"Stay down!" snapped Sergeant Stone as he moved about the defensive laager created by the four vehicles. The fifth Bulldog, and the only mobile gun unit, still burned on the dusty highway, all of its crew dead and the wreckage spread for meters in every direction.

"Sergeant, six hundred meters to the east!" Jack shouted as he checked the tagged targets on his helmet overlay.

"Good eyes, son."

Each of the marines lay face down in the dirt, doing their best to provide the smallest possible target. That didn't mean they had been rendered useless though. As they waited, they trained their carbines and rifles at in the direction of the enemy force as identified by the drones, Bulldog defense scanners, and information from each of the individual marines.

"Sergeant, what do we have?" asked Lieutenant Daniel Elvidge, the platoon's new officer. He'd been transferred to them direct from the Marine Academy, along with dozens of other marines to replace the casualties from the operation on Helios. His roundish face, light brown hair, and calm persona could be misinterpreted by some as one of the many privileged citizens that had joined directly as an officer. Sergeant Stone spotted him moving toward him and nodded, avoiding signs that could be identified by the enemy.

"Sir, we've got seven targets tagged at long-range."

"Why are we not being hit?"

"My guess is they are lacking heavy weapons."

The new Lieutenant lifted his hand to wipe his face before striking the visor. It was a simple gesture and easily made, yet it did little to instill confidence. It wasn't helped when he moved to hit the release toggle to open it up. The

Sergeant grabbed his hand.

"I wouldn't do that if I were you, Sir."

The Lieutenant looked to the Sergeant with a sheepish expression on his face. It was his first combat mission, and already he'd lost a vehicle and crew. He thought of his training at the academy, and it flooded back to him.

"Comms, appraise command of our situation. I want one squad to stay here. Check the Bulldog for casualties and prep for evac. The rest of you are coming with me."

"Lieutenant?"

He turned and looked to the Sergeant.

"The hostiles are all in the industrial site, is that correct?"

"Yes, Sir, all seven."

"Then we need them neutralized."

The Lieutenant had already moved away and was rounding up the other two squads of marines before Sergeant Stone could try and stop him.

"Lieutenant, it might be wiser to stand off, watch the enemy, and bring in air support to finish them off."

The new officer nodded smartly while directing the others.

"True, but don't forget the mission, Sergeant. This isn't Zathee territory. This sector is mainly heavy industry and engineering with a mixture of pureblood Irkerk and Yuulen. We have few friends here outside of the habitation districts. We need to find, capture, or kill these insurgents face to face. If we cause excess damage to their property or hurt their civilians, we might as well hand the victory to the enemy."

Jack could hear them speaking over the open marine channel. It was strange it had taken so long for the replacements to reach them. They'd already conducted six patrols on the ground in the last week. The reinforcements had been delayed a week, so they had managed by transferring existing officers to temporary positions.

I wonder if we've drawn the short straw with this new and very green officer.

"I want air support on standby, should we need it," said the Lieutenant.

Jack watched him go toward one of the other squads. It was clear to him that Sergeant Stone wasn't too sure either. The two marine squads were already moving now, and Sergeant Stone moved with them but stayed close enough to the Lieutenant in case he needed assistance. The level of gravity was lower than the Earth standard amount, but at least it was only slightly lighter. They moved further and faster here but so did the enemy, and they would be used to it. Sergeant Stone's first impression had been a confused one.

The man is certainly green, and no doubt he comes from a privileged background. Even so, he was decisive, and his primary concern was for the mission. I just hope he has as much concern for the men and women under his command.

Two fireteams led the way, with Jack and his comrades

forming the unit to the right. He scanned the open ground and felt a chill through his chest. The open space was nearly two hundred meters of killing ground, and nothing but the odd rock for cover.

"Corporal Frewyn, get your fireteam forward and secure the vehicle pool. Everybody else maintain your progress. Check your fire, all targets must be clearly identified."

The remaining two fireteams of eight marines moved at a quick walking pace. The hexrotor drones buzzed in front of them at a height of no more than a hundred meters. They provided top down reconnaissance, but even more importantly, they were able to detect mines and explosives; a weapon the Helion insurgents, under the training of their Animosh masters had turned to in a matter of weeks, following their defeat on Helios.

"Come on, move it!" said Corporal Frewyn.

He might have been the oldest and perhaps even the wisest member of the four-man fireteam, but Jack could never take his rural accent seriously. As far as he was concerned, it was like a farmer trying to give him orders. Even so, he knew the man understood his job. If it hadn't been for his drinking problems, the command of this team might have been his. They moved a good distance away from the other marines and ran into the vehicle pool. It was of modest size with a low concrete type wall around the perimeter, and five large-wheeled earthmoving vehicles waited under a layer of dust. Frewyn and Riku slid down behind the first vehicle. Jack and Callahan ran further to the left and dropped down behind two large storage sheds. No sooner did they reach cover than they were hit by the staccato sounds of automatic gunfire.

"Get a drone over there, now!" shouted Corporal Frewyn.

Jack had already selected the nearest three of the eight hexrotors in the area and gave them orders to advance on the direction of the gunfire. One was destroyed almost immediately, but the others used their speed and agility to avoid the fire and move around the site, pinpointing the enemy position. As each target was spotted, it was tagged, and the details uploaded to all Alliance units in the area.

"Good work," said the Lieutenant, as the rest of the marines moved off to the left of the motor pool in a head-on approach to the structure. They were still a hundred meters further back than Jack's unit.

"Drones show seven targets, all biological and at least one heavy weapon emplacement," Private Callahan said, checking the data as it came in.

The marines spread out behind the small outbuildings and low wall two hundred meters from the compound being used by the enemy. It was a three-story structure that lacked windows. The walls were sturdy and a low meter-tall wall protected it. Lieutenant Daniel Elvidge looked up from behind the storage unit at the target. Off to his right he could see the four dark shapes of Corporal

Frewyn's fireteam. According to the stats on his overlay, they were carrying three L52 Mk II carbines and a single L48 sharpshooter support rifle.

"Corporal Frewyn, I want your team to provide sniper fire, as and when you have eyes on the target."

He then looked to Sergeant Stone.

"I won't risk any of our marines. We will use fire and maneuver with the remaining fireteams to get into position around the compound, understood?"

"Yes, Sir," he snapped back smartly.

He moved to the other marines to move them on to their objective, allowing himself the briefest of moment to look back at his new Lieutenant.

He might not be much to look at, but he respects the men and the mission. How bad can he be?

The return of machine gun fire from the top floor of the structure sent some of the marines scurrying for cover, but it wasn't being aimed at them. It was against Corporal Frewyn's unit off to the right.

Good, that's what they're there for.

"Marines, move out!"

CHAPTER THREE

The coming of the great comet was seen as the final stage by many of Echidna's followers. Most had vanished or lost their faith following defeat at Terra Nova and Hyperion. The news of Biomech ships on the increase, and the mysterious comet, gave new impetus to a growing group of neo-Echidna cults. Rumor had it that the faithless would be punished, especially those that had turned from the cult. The more the Alliance clamped down on each group, the greater the resistance and desire to protest.

Holy Icons

Admiral Lewis took a long draught of coffee and looked back at the new imagery from Terra Nova. It showed an extremely grainy image of an astronomical object named C34A. It was hardly worth of such a major object, but that was its current designation. The data wasn't particularly interesting to him, but the target was.

So, this thing is heading for Helios, and it just so happens it will be passing by us in less than two days. If only we were closer, we might be able to help.

The information on the loss of ships in the Helion taskforce was of concern, though he had little, if any respect for the Helion military command. The fact he had now been assigned the job of cleaning up after their failure rankled him. They might have been crippled by the period of infighting on Helios, but the revolution had been won, and from what he could see, the space forces of theirs were far more numerous than those of the Alliance.

Yet they continue to fail, and now I have to risk our ships for them, again.

The reports from the ships in his fleet were already there, and he was satisfied all his captains were ready for what he had in store for them. The list was impressive, especially with the arrival of ANS Valor to replace the heavily damaged ANS Savage from the battle with the automated fleet near Helios itself. His Strike Group had been expanded, thanks to the intervention of Admiral Anderson. Six more Hunter class frigates ships had joined the recently promoted Commodore Hampel to give the fleet a more substantial escort. Even better was the replacement of one of his Crusader class with a brand new Conqueror Class Battlecruiser, ANS Royal Oak. She wasn't the first ship to have used the name, and as befitted her ancestors, she had been optimized for fleet defense as a fully-fledge fleet carrier.

Just look at those hangars, he said to himself with a smile.

Like all the new generation of warships, the Crusader and Conqueror class were built around the principle of a universal design. The basic hull was the same, but the mission units could be changed in dock to optimize the designs for different roles. His own flagship, ANS Conqueror was a general-purpose warship, much like the standard Crusader design. All the ships in the fleet could operate small groups of fighters and also carried Marine units on board. ANS Sentry and ANS Valor were equipped with marine transport mission units to allow the transport of more warriors. ANS Royal Oak, on the other hand, only had the space for a single company on board; the remaining space was used for hangar space and point defense units.

The first carrier of the Alliance, and she's mine!

He took another sip and checked her statistics. They were impressive. Automation had reduced the total crew to just under one and a half thousand personnel plus an air group of six hundred. She could carry a tailored air group of up to forty aircraft, including all the current fighters, plus the new X57 Avenger fighter drones. After gazing at the units and spacecraft aboard the ship, he tapped his communication unit. With just a few presses, he started a video communication file.

"This is Priority One message to Admiral Anderson, commander of the outer territories and regional governor."

He paused for a moment, composing his thoughts.

"I have checked the data sent via your office and that of Terra Nova High Command, and had my staff cross-reference it with our scans in this area. I can confirm C34A will arrive at the calculated hour. The distance from my current position will make interception impossible by all but a single frigate on patrol."

He went to continue, but then spotted something very strange about the data that had just arrived from the T'Kari surveying ship that was halfway between the moon and the C34A. The more he looked at the data, the more he couldn't believe his eyes. He reached out and hit the pause button on the device, retuning his gaze to the image of the comet and the projected path. It would pass nearby to the moon and then on for its rendezvous with Helios. All of this was known and confirmed, except that something in the last six hours had changed. Instead of continuing the message, he hit the button to Captain Shaw, his adjutant.

"Get the senior commanders here; I want a war-briefing in fifteen minutes."

He didn't even bother to wait for an acknowledgement. He moved back to the video communication and restarted it while grabbing for his jacket.

"New information has just arrived on my desk and is on its way, along with this message. I had been preparing the fleet for an operation to deflect the object, but something is different...according to the T'Kari surveying ship, C34A has altered its course by three degrees."

He stopped for a moment, still not quite believing what he was seeing.

"The comet is on an approach vector for Eos and will be here in six days."

He had to stop and think for a moment. Even as he had been speaking, the pages of assessments from the tacticians on the ship had arrived, and it all made for extremely uncomfortable reading. He slowed his breathing, calmed down, and continued.

"My officers are already assessing this data, but based on a first look, the comet will be able to enter orbit around slingshotting past us and on to Helios."

He lowered his head and rubbed his brow.

This can't be, surely not?

He lifted his head and looked into the screen, now wishing the distances were much shorter and that he could speak with Admiral Anderson in real-time. With the local Rift generator station destroyed, he was months away from either Helios or the Rift back home, and it suddenly filled him with a feeling of distance and loneliness.

We're out here on our own. We have to help ourselves.

"This is no normal comet. It is under the guidance of a third party, one with vast resources, skills, and incredible technology. It is heading for Helios, and for some reason is going to perform an orbit of Eos before continuing on. I can only think this is for one reason."

Again he stopped, his heart pounded in his chest.

"Admiral, there's a reason why the Helion fleet was smashed so easily. There is more to this object than we were led to believe. In six days, it will be close enough to Eos...close enough to..."

To do what? You can't be serious? He thought, barely believing what he was saying.

"...to potentially launch an attack on the moon itself."

He leaned back in his tall chair.

"Either way, the 4th Heavy Strike Group will prepare for all eventualities."

* * *

They inched forward from the first industrial vehicle and took up position behind a stone-faced bunker. It was open on the one side and filled with spare parts and heavy tooling. A thick layer of dust ran around all of it, cleared only by the heavy boots of the small group of marines. There was no more cover from the vehicle pool to the low wall running around the refinery plant storage blocks. Further back, the rest of the platoon spread out and inched forward in pairs, two covering while two moved. It was slow work, not helped by the sniper fire coming from the balcony on the third floor.

"Down!" Jack shouted.

He might not have been in charge of the squad, but the others listened to him. There was no time for worrying about seniority in a situation like this. Worrying about a rigid command structure would get people killed. The timing was perfect, as a volley of close range gunshots came in from the right. Jack dropped to one knee and twisted about his waist at ninety degrees, taking aim down the sight of his carbine. Through the low-magnification scope on his weapon, he could see the shape of an Animosh fighter. The cloak was the same as they always wore, but this one had his head covered in a sand colored scarf and wore thick goggles to protect against dust. He aimed at the fighter's chest and squeezed the trigger. Three small red puffs marked the impacts, and the fighter was down.

Damn drones didn't spot him!

He looked at his Corporal, who nodded a silent thanks before accessing the communications channel.

"Lieutenant, we've just been hit by a sniper on the right flank. Private Morato brought him down, but there might be more," said Corporal Frewyn.

"Understand, Corporal, good work. Keep them busy. We're moving in."

Jack looked at the stonework in front of him that blocked his line of sight to the enemy in the multi-story building. The tagged overlay showed their seven outlines, but technically he could not see them. As he moved his muscles in his left leg, another burst of gunfire ripped into the small amount of cover he'd managed to find.

"Corporal, what's the plan?"

The older man threw him a short glance.

"You heard the Lieutenant; we provide covering fire so the other squads can get closer to the building."

Another burst of a dozen rounds shattered the stonework above their heads, sending chunks of masonry down on them. It wasn't sporadic gunfire but targeted and precise shooting designed to suppress them.

"Yeah, right!" snapped Jack, and he dropped down even lower.

"Looks to me like the only one getting any covering fire is them."

Frewyn checked the drone information and noted no more targets had been identified in the area. Jack could see the concern on his face. The man might have been the most experienced in terms of training and age, but the command of a small squad seemed to confuse him. Finally, he looked to his squad mates.

"Be careful and try and pin them down. The others need our help, and right now we seem to have their attention."

Jack reached out and grabbed his arm.

"Frewyn, are you sure? What about that guy back there? There could be more the drones didn't spot."

More fire clattered about them, and even Jack flinched at the fire. As before it was coming from the building, yet it was sporadic and wild.

"I don't have a choice, now do it!"

The Corporal had finally found his voice, even if Jack found it hard to accept such foolhardy orders. He inched around to the left of the small structure and waited with his carbine up to his shoulder. Private Riku did the same on the right-hand side, but she had the larger bulk of the L48 rifle. The two looked at each other. Riku nodded first. They moved just a few centimeters around the cover and took aim with their weapons.

"Wait," said Jack, a sly grin on his face, "I have an idea."

Riku shook her head. She was all too familiar with Jack's cunning plans and amazing ideas. In her experience, they tended to revolve around doing the unexpected and getting bruises at the same time.

"Well, what is it?" she asked.

Jack lifted a hand, telling her to give him a moment. He used his computer to select two of the nearest hexrotor drones. One was only a hundred meters from the building, doing its best to avoid the odd stray shot fired by the insurgents whenever they caught a glimpse of its small frame. Jack gave it a tactical order and then called out to Frewyn.

"Corporal, I need a drone override!"

Frewyn didn't even check the order. He acknowledged the request and authorized it. Whether it was simply down to trust or just not knowing what to do, the order went through, and the drone twisted in the air as if an invisible hand had reached out, grabbed it, and then hurled it toward the ground. Just before it hit the dusty surface, it lifted up and rushed toward the balcony. Jack watched the view from one of the other higher drones with a look of nervous excitement on his face.

"Go, do it!"

The mechanical unit traveled at almost fifty kilometers per hour when it shattered through the double-sized window frame where the insurgents were sniping.

"Uh...Jack...what the hell?" chortled Private Riku.

All of them were now watching as the drone smashed its way inside and crashed into the room. The drone was no larger than a family dog, yet the speed of its attack and the fragments breaking off from the six ducted fans sent chunks of metal and plastic in all directions. Jack could barely contain his glee at the violence and destruction it caused.

"Now!" he cried.

Private Riku's shot moved first from her weapon, but it was Jack's that reached the target quickest. The muzzle velocity of the L52 carbine was higher than any other marine weapon in the inventory. Three magnetic projectiles struck the window frame around the enemy position on the top floor to no effect. Private Riku's much larger explosive charge ripped through the wall and exploded in a small puff inside. A single body was blown from the window and dropped the three stories before crashing to the ground. One more came up as a KIA, and suddenly they were down from seven fighters to five, and the room had started to burn.

"Nice covering fire!" laughed Jack.

His amusement was short-lived though as dozens of rounds came from a balcony ten meters to the right of the original one. It was filled with the insurgents.

"They bugging out!" said Frewyn with a sense of relief and excitement.

Two handled what looked like a heavy machine gun, but rather than stopping, they moved in the opposite direction to what looked like a fire escape, except it ran around the rear of the building. In seconds, the enemy had vanished, and there were no obvious threats in front of the marines. That was the moment when Jack's Corporal finally understood what he had to do.

"They're getting away, follow me!" he cried.

Without even considering his own safety, he leapt up from the cover of the stonework and ran out into the open. Jack and the others didn't wait and chased after their Corporal. With the lower gravity than normal, they ran and bounced in a slightly elongated arc that seemed almost comical. They were quickly over the perimeter wall and halfway to the building. Jack spotted a face looking toward them that vanished in a cloud of blood from a carbine shot. He didn't even bother checking who had fired and kept moving ahead. As they reached the dusty wall of the three-story building, a flight of Hammerheads screamed overhead and moved out of view, leaving nothing but their roaring engines for them to even know they'd been there.

"All here?" asked Corporal Frewyn.

He looked at them, making sure Jack, Riku, Callahan, and Jenkell were all there before leaning out and checking the building.

"Looks clear to me. The drones show a doorway at the rear, lower level."

In the distance, the rest of the marines continued to inch forward and made up half the distance before the clatter of machine gun fire forced them to take cover. The automatic weapon's rate of fire was much lower than equipment used in the Alliance, and the thermal charges burned black holes in anything it struck.

"Nasty," Riku muttered.

Frewyn looked at each of them and thumbed toward the building.

"We need to fix this and fast."

Jack checked the ammunition marker on his overlay, and he still had an almost full magazine. There was no need to change it, certainly not when in such an exposed and dangerous position.

"Get in and rush the place before they can cause any more trouble. Now!"

There was no time for discussion, as once again their

Corporal led from the front and along the side of the building. The gunfire continued, but it didn't stop him. The man didn't even wait for the drones to move into a better position. As they moved closer, Riku pulled out a stun grenade, one of the three types each of the marines carried. It was smaller than the usual fragmentation grenades and colored with yellow and black stripes along the top and bottom. She threw her body around the corner after the others and hurled the grenade with perfect precision. It spun through the air, landing right in the small doorway fifteen meters away.

"Flash!" she shouted, but Frewyn was not holding back.

The other marines were already around the next corner right on the heels of their Corporal and heading for the small doorway, when the metal door flew open and out ran a trio of Helions. All carried weapons, and their heads were covered in thin helmets with a ventilator unit that looked more like a gas mask on their faces. One spotted the marines and opened fire as the grenade activated. A bright white flash pulsed and blinded anybody not looking away or wearing the marine helmets. Like welding equipment, the visors blackened for just long enough to beat off the flash. In less than half a second, they returned to their normal slightly smoked look. Jack lurched to the left, hugging the wall and ran at them with all the speed he could muster.

"Spread out!" shouted Frewyn, but it was much too

late. The first two rounds hit his collar and bounced off the armor. The third and final round struck his arm in the joint and managed to penetrate the outer layer before embedding in his bone. He cried out and dropped his carbine. Private Jana Jenkell dropped down next to him, covering him with her carbine while the others continued forward. Callahan and Riku automatically moved to one knee and opened fire on the group, keeping their fire to the right to avoid striking Jack who was almost upon them. One was killed outright, and another of the Animosh staggered about, temporarily blinded. The Helion had already turned away from them, and instead of running, aimed his gun in the direction of the marines and held down the trigger. Thermal rounds clattered everywhere, and then Jack was amongst them. He ducked under the blow of the last remaining insurgent and struck with the butt of his carbine. Incredibly, the lithe and agile fighter pulled back his torso to avoid the strike and fired a shot at Jack.

"Bastard!" he cried, stumbling back.

The burning round left a scorch march along his flank where it had almost burned through. Another few centimeters, and it would have stuck his chest straight on. Even so, he stumbled and found himself falling before crashing onto his back. The insurgent was on him in a flash, but even he wasn't quick enough to avoid the charge by Private Callahan. The man was like a bull and shoulder barged the alien. His bulk and strength sent the Helion flying through the air and crashing onto his side in the dirt.

"Stay down!" snapped Riku. She chased after him, her weapon pointing at his head. Only then did it occur to her he probably had no idea what she was saying.

Callahan helped Jack to his feet and looked over to Riku.

"Don't worry, he understands. And if he doesn't, you know what to do."

Frewyn groaned from the pain of his injury, and Private Jenkell was already busy seeing to the damage. That left just the three of them plus the two prisoners waiting outside the doorway. Movement came from the corner of the building, and three marines charged around it with their weapons raised.

"Lieutenant," Jack said with a slightly raised pitch to his voice.

The adrenalin was now pounding through his body, and he could feel a violent rage starting to build up inside him. He tried to focus on the data from the drones, anything to try and stop his blood from boiling inside.

"There are more inside the building. We need to secure it, and fast!"

Lieutenant Elvidge nodded in agreement.

"Good work, marines," he said, turning to speak with Sergeant Stone who had only just arrived with another four marines.

"Sergeant Stone, secure this position and the prisoners. Guard this door, and make sure they don't double back. Morato, Riku and..."

"Callahan, Sir," answered the marine.

"Yes, the three of you come with me. We have work to do."

Jack was surprised to see the green officer to be so fit and keen to get stuck in. The run across the open ground from the ambush location had been significant, yet the officer showed no obvious signs of fatigue. Even better was the fact the man stopped at the entrance and checked carefully before entering.

So, he isn't just a pretty boy from Terra Nova, he thought optimistically.

Then they were inside and moving through a narrow corridor. There were no lights, and so as not to give away their position, the four marines used their thermal and infrared overlays to allow them to see in the darkened structure. Callahan went first with Jack following. The Lieutenant came next, and Riku brought up the rear with her L48 rifle now slung on her shoulder.

"Can you hear that?" asked Jack.

The sound amplification unit built into their suits was capable of identifying discrete sound and located them in both direction and distance. His suit had amplified part of the sound, and he could hear what sounded like something heavy being dragged across a floor.

"I hear it, sounds like equipment," suggested Riku.

"Maybe, it could also be an attempt to barricade themselves in," Jack added.

The Lieutenant cut them off.

"It doesn't matter either way. We have to get in there and stop them. The last two ambushes failed, but they still managed to escape. We need prisoners and a successful counter-operation. This will be it."

Jack wasn't so sure, but they moved on until the passageway widened the split with the hall on one side and a staircase leading up on the right. Callahan lifted his carbine slightly and aimed up the staircase.

"Up, Sir?"

"Affirmative."

It didn't take long for them to reach the next level up in the narrow stairwell. The doors were all missing, and refuse and debris filled the hallways. They ignored it all and moved on to the next and final level. Halfway up the stairs, Callahan stopped and lifted his hand. The group stopped and automatically dropped down to one knee.

"What is it?" asked Riku.

There was silence for perhaps three seconds, and then an insurgent appeared and looked down at them. The breathing apparatus hid his face, but his body language suggested he'd been caught by complete surprise. Even the Helion's rifle was hung low as though he had not expected to see a threat on the stairs at this point. Jack leaned forward, grabbed his lead arm, and yanked down. The insurgent lost his footing, and they stumbled down the steps until he reached Riku. Although slight, she had no problem in dropping her knee down onto his chest and pinned him to the step.

"Stay," she whispered.

Callahan moved his carbine around the corner at the top of the steps and watched the video feed from the sight directly on his helmet overlay. It showed a short passageway of six to seven meters and then a broken doorway leading to a long passageway that must have run for the entire length of the building. He nodded and went ahead with Jack and the Lieutenant right behind. Their footsteps crunched on the flaked paint and dust that seemed to litter the place. Jack slowed his breathing, but his pulse continued to race as he watched for signs of the insurgents. He spotted the green shapes on his overlay; it was a group of Hammerheads that had landed near the Bulldogs.

Good, the Medevac teams are here.

There was little worse than the idea that you might be left injured on a battlefield, with no chance of help. They reached the broken doorway and fanned out, but it was clearly almost entirely deserted, but for one place, a large room with two doors that looked like a machine room. The door was missing, and Jack could see large pieces of machinery lined up, presumably refinery machines or tooling of some kind. He almost missed the twinkle of a gun sight and then dropped to the floor.

"What is.." started Riku, but a large caliber round burned a fist-sized hole in the wall exactly where Jack's head had been.

Lieutenant Elvidge ducked to the left away from the doorway and toward the smaller entrance off to the left and further down the passageway. Riku followed in the same direction and was about to enter when Jack spotted something like a fine, silvery line, almost like a spider's web.

"Stop!" he cried.

The gunfire from the machine room was light, but every single round was aimed through the larger doorway.

Yeah, they want us to take the other door.

"Looks like a booby-trap, Sir."

Riku squeezed past the officer and bent down to check. It only took a few seconds for her to confirm Jack's fears.

"Yeah, you're right, it's a trap all right. Tripwire and a thermal wall charge, we were lucky!"

The Lieutenant nodded politely to Jack, a modest gesture but one that meant a lot under the circumstances. He pointed to the doorway that Jack and Callahan were watching.

"Yours?"

Callahan was on his knees and checking the frame but staying back to avoid defensive fire. He finally lifted himself back up and spoke quietly.

"This one's clear."

Lieutenant Elvidge inched back with Riku in tow.

"Very well," he considered his options for just a few seconds, "we have to clear this place. Suggestions?"

"Stun and run," Jack said without even thinking.

Callahan looked at the Private, nodding in agreement.

"Yeah, it worked outside. They're not prepared for a direct rush."

"Okay, good. Two grenades, then we move in and fast, but I want prisoners. Shoot to wound, not kill."

Callahan looked at Jack incredulously.

"Understood?" repeated the Lieutenant.

"Yes, Sir," they answered in perfect unison.

Riku and Jack each pulled out a stun grenade and activated the timers. With a nod from Lieutenant Elvidge, they tossed them inside at opposite sides of the room. The countdown progress indicator showed up inside their helmets, so they could time it to the second. One second before the charges activated, they moved. Jack was through first, and then Callahan, and the rest close behind. As Jack passed through the doorframe, the grenades burst, and for a brief moment he lost his vision as the visor blackened. Then he was moving along the right-hand side of the machine room with his eyes wide open and his carbine at his shoulder and ready. Riku followed behind, and the others took the left-hand side of the room.

"Move it!" growled the Lieutenant.

An insurgent appeared ahead of them and opened fire. The stun grenades had done their work, and he sprayed gunfire in the rough direction of the doorway. Jack rushed to his side, slamming his carbine into the Helion's chest. With a groan, he fell down. Riku knelt beside him to bind his hands. Two more insurgents remained, and both were waiting behind a long machine with dozens of static robotic arms extending upwards. Bronze colored rust covered the edges, and like the rest of the place, a thick layer of dust covered the rest. One pointed at Jack, and the second lifted up a heavy weapon onto the machine and opened fire.

"Watch out!" screamed Riku.

Both rolled to the ground and vanished from sight among the myriad of machines and pieces of heavy equipment. At this height, it looked more like a maze than a workshop or refinery, and they were able to crawl along the floor while the heavy weapon continued to tear chunks from machines and the thick walls. Jack and Riku stayed down low. Callahan and Lieutenant Elvidge tried to move around the left flank.

"Morato, can you flank them?" asked the Lieutenant.

Jack crawled a meter and looked around the base of the machine. Another identical unit, turning ninety degrees back in the direction of the insurgents obstructed his view.

"Maybe, see what we can do."

He slipped around the corner and slid along the floor. The slow thump of an L52 carbine firing came from the other side of the room.

Good work, Callahan, keep them busy.

It seemed an age before he reached the end of the next machine. Jack pushed out his carbine, using it as a viewing device to see around the corner. He could see the two remaining fighters loading a box onto the mounted weapon.

I have to go for it!

He didn't bother with a grenade this time and instead lifted himself and hurled forward. His foot caught on the base of the machine, and he stumbled at them. He was on them before Riku even knew what was happening.

"Jack!" she shouted and chased after him.

Jack crashed into the nearest insurgent; the second flipped out a sidearm and shot twice. All three fell to the ground in a heap. Private Riku was on them as the second lifted to his feet. The other continued to grapple with Jack, but this fight was between the masked insurgent and her. He fired a shot with his sidearm that struck her carbine and tore off the pistol grip. She looked down at it, swore, and then threw the shattered frame at the Helion. He beat it aside; firing another shot that glanced off her armored pauldron. Her fist struck him in the chest, and she grabbed his arm. It was a classic lock, and although the Helion was strong, he was betrayed by the slight physiology of his race. Riku was also no weakling and twisted his arm so that he cried out in pain as she forced him to the floor.

"Got you!" she said triumphantly.

Callahan and the Lieutenant were now there and moved in to secure the prisoners. Meanwhile, Jack and his opponent were engaged in a violent fight and had moved from the floor and toward the open window.

"All units, building secure, hold your fire!" called out Lieutenant Elvidge as the two crashed out onto the balcony. The Helion was surprisingly quick and a good bit taller and larger built than the average. As they fought, the insurgent seemed to have even greater speed than Jack. They pushed apart and circled each other, just out of striking distance. The Helion muttered something and pulled back his cloak, revealing a gold colored armored breastplate with unusual marking running down it. Jack found himself staring at the design while his hooded opponent moved around him. The cloak remained around his head and shoulder, and the plated respirator and mask covered the alien's face, making it impossible to make out any kind of facial expression.

"If you're trying to sound tough, you're wasting your time!" laughed Jack.

The alien struck three times in quick succession and managed to hit Jack on the shoulder blade with a hammer strike that dropped him to a knee. It wasn't enough to slow the young marine down, and he locked the Helion's arm and hurled him past. Anybody would have fallen, but not this one. Instead, he hit the ground, rolled, and landed back on his feet.

"Impressive."

The other marines had already secured the machine room, but no one intervened with the personal fight between the two of them. Even so, Riku and Callahan kept their carbines ready, just in case. Jack would win one way or another. Now it was Jack's turn to launch into a flurry of attack. He kept his guard close and his elbows tucked in while closing the distance. Each time the alien tried to defend himself, Jack struck out at his opponent's limbs. It was slow, almost mechanical work but in less than thirty seconds, the alien fighter was suffering from the strikes to his unarmored arms. Finally, he managed to kick against Jack's stomach and separated for a few seconds.

"Not bad, I think you can give up now."

The alien simply laughed at his words, clicked his neck, and stretched. Jack's face changed from amusement to annoyance, and then they were back at it. This time the alien was much more cautious, and Jack was forced to not over extend and leave himself vulnerable. The two moved about each other as they tried to strike with their hands and feet. Jack managed to land a number of blows, but each time the Helion leaned away and hit back. After a particular heavy miss by Jack, the alien slammed his knee into Jack's stomach and followed it up with bringing his arm down onto the marine's back.

"Enough!" roared Lieutenant Elvidge.

The Helion looked at the human officer with confusion, and Jack took the opportunity to jump back up and deliver a single powerful uppercut into the Helion's chin. This time the alien staggered and collapsed to the ground. Jack pounced on him and rested his knee on the alien's throat. Within seconds, the Helion was unable to breathe. Riku moved in beside him and fitted the bindings to his wrists before he could try to escape.

"Good work, everybody. Look what they were doing here," said their Lieutenant with a measure of pride in his voice. It was only then that Jack, Riku, and Callahan gave the room a good look. Crates containing small metal devices were stacked inside, and the broken frame that would have supported a ground–based missile system lay twisted to one side with two missiles on the floor.

"What the hell is that?" asked Riku.

Callahan ran his hand along the frame, sighing to himself.

"This looks like a surface-to-air missile system to me."

"And that's bad, because?"

Jack closed his eyes and inhaled slowly, doing his best to calm himself. It took a few moments before he could open them.

"It's bad because if it had been working, it could have shot down our Medevac Hammerheads."

"Yeah," Callahan agreed, "this place wasn't just an ambush site. It was here to get us to abandon our vehicles and encircle the place. When support came in, they'd hit our air cover and then finish off our people on the ground."

Lieutenant Elvidge stepped out onto the balcony and noted the smashed stone and metal from the impact of the drone Jack had sent directly into the building. There were also the bodies of the Helions that had died in the battle itself. He could see the rest of the marines in the open ground helping their own wounded and continue checking for signs of any more insurgents. Off in the distance, the shapes of the Bulldogs were slightly obscured by the recent arrival of the Hammerheads and their small units of marines and medical teams. He turned around to look at the three marines.

"Great work today. You stopped the loss of our air units and even better, by taking these guys without a major firefight, we avoided setting off of these weapons."

He pointed at the rockets lying broken on the ground. It hadn't even occurred to him that the rolling fight with the insurgents might have triggered the devices. The idea of them exploding with him and his comrades made him retch, and it took all of his self-control to not throw up in his helmet.

"Okay, bag them. The engineers are going to come in and sweep the area."

CHAPTER FOUR

Ship boarding actions became commonplace in the Great Uprising, and though no particular action stands out, there were over two hundred recorded operations conducted in the first year of the War alone. Many of the advantages of the marines, such as their superlative mobility, were lost. These actions proved to be some of the deadliest during the War and were instrumental in creating better armor and rapid firing weapons. The Alpha variant of the PDS armor and the L52 carbine both came out of experiences learned in these bloody boarding actions.

Great Battles of the Confederate Marine Corps

Teresa was in trouble, and that had nothing to do with the fact she was low on ammunition. The crash landing had killed every member of her platoon, and now she was the last marine left atop the snow covered Atoll. The burned wreckage of a crashed Marine Corps landing craft lay broken in three large sections. Around the spacecraft were scores of Biomech creatures of every shape and size. They hacked at the dead marines as if they expected them to jump to their feet at any time. One group had spotted her, and no sooner had one moved, and the rest were hurling toward her. She took aim and fired, each projectile killing one of the things with incredible precision.

Come on, die!

A dozen fell, yet more clambered over the bodies of their comrades and moved in for the kill. Her carbine seemed weak and ineffectual as she stepped back toward the edge. At this distance, she could see those at the front were identical to the beasts she had faced in the Uprising. As large as a bear, but grotesquely formed, she knew they were constructed from the shattered remains of human prisoners.

"Get back!" she screamed, but no sound left her mouth.

More of the smaller Biomechs swarmed like bugs, and she was forced to fire from the hip in a long burst that emptied her magazine. The weapon was now dry, and she hurled it at the nearest monster. The weapon struck the thing just a meter away, and again she moved back only to feel the edge of the Atoll. She glanced back and saw nothing but the great drop to nothingness.

No, not yet! I'm taking you with me.

She ripped out her knife from her side. It should have

been a Marine issue combat blade, but inside it was long and curved, like the tooth from some monstrous beast. She looked at the object with fascination. It was smooth, yet the tip and edge seemed coated in a sharp layer of silver. Only the approach of more creatures tore her gaze from the object.

"This is the end!" hissed a voice from somewhere further back.

The mechanical voice sent a shiver through her body as though somebody had gently run a finger down her spine. She shuddered and adopted a solid fighting stance. Her left foot forward, knees bent, and both hands lifted as though about to box. The blade hung down in the classic ice pick grip favored by many knife fighters.

Not yet!

Two more creatures launched at her, and she hacked and stabbed, throwing their bodies over the edge. A third followed behind, but this one avoided her blow and struck her leg. The armor tore off as if only attached by thin straps, and a streak of blood appeared. The cut was deep, and it continued to strike at her with its pincer-like arms and foul head. She was close enough to see the expanded ribcage, thick muscles, and exaggerated teeth. It was like a biblical demon intent on tearing her apart.

Stab and don't stop stabbing till its dead!

She remembered her Marine Corps training, the voice of her instructors repeated over and over in her head.

Her movements and stance altered as she moved into a machine-like state where her reactions and muscle memory took over. First of all, she slashed at its neck and then as it pulled back, she sidestepped by swinging her left leg back behind her and to her right so that she twisted around. With a single firm motion, the blade stabbed backward and into the thing's chest. That was far from the end, however, and in less than three seconds, she'd stabbed it another seven times in the same place. Her training worked well, and it was on the ground, blood oozing from a dozen wounds.

"Is that it?" she asked bitterly.

She was granted a short respite as the greatest of the beasts arrived. As came nearer, the smaller ones scattered, out of fear or reverence she couldn't tell. This one was massive, like a demon from hell and larger than any Biomech she'd ever seen. It moved on a pair of short robotic legs and trailed a lizard like tail. Its multiple arms were spiked and barbed, and its head shrunken down and protected by metal plating. It clunked toward her with all manner of soul-destroying sounds moving with it. Teresa lifted herself back to her feet and somehow found another of the blades in her left hand. Both dripped black blood into a growing pool on the ground.

"What are you?" she tried to call out, but again there were no words.

The machine monster continued forward until it was a few meters away and then stopped. For a second it seemed the thing had broken down, but then it lowered itself by bending its legs in an impossible fashion. The center of its armored carapace opened wide, revealing a tortured human figure inside. She gazed at its blood-covered flesh until she could make out its eyes. For a second, she didn't recognize the person.

Me?

Teresa stumbled back, one foot sliding off the ledge, and then she was falling. She looked up. The machine did nothing more than look down at her as she vanished into the blackness, her limbs flailing, and again she tried to cry out. This time a muffled sound managed to make it out, and her eyes opened to blackness.

What the hell was that all about?

The imagery was already starting to fade, and as she sat up in her bed and wiped her sweat-covered brow, the thoughts of the massive machine and its cohorts of terrifying biomechanical creatures faded from her conscious mind. She rubbed her eyes and waited for a second as they adjusted to reveal the small, very dark room. It was her quarters and once again, she had been dreaming of the creatures and monsters of her violent past.

This has got to stop. Why can't you dream of something else for a change?

With effort, she leaned over and slid her feet out of the bed and onto the cool floor of her temporary quarters.

The cold ran up through her limbs, and she shuddered before realizing she was naked bar her nightclothes. Ten minutes later, she had showered and changed into her regular Marine Corps clothing. The room was lighter now, but the lack of windows made the place feel like she was on board some ship rather than on the surface of Terra Nova convalescing. Teresa's quarters were modest and sparsely equipped with just four rooms and little space for entertaining, not that she knew anybody on Terra Nova that she particularly wanted to spend time with. Not even General Rivers had the time these days for a few hours with an old friend. She didn't blame him. With his promotion to Chairman of the Joint Chiefs, he was busier than ever, but she suspected he would rather be leading marines into combat, even at his advanced age.

Ah, well, what about the war?

There was, of course, no war right now, but that didn't stop the Alliance getting involved in ground and space battles just the same. She sat at her desk and poured a glass of juice, selecting one of the many Alliance news feeds. It was her normal routine each day, and she sat there, checking on the public face of the difficulties the Alliance faced. The scrolling ticker mentioned Eos, and she selected it. The video footage of the fighting was always presented to make the events seem as exciting and sensational as possible. In this particular story, a group of marines were chasing an insurgent through rubble. A man leapt from a building, in what seemed like an impossible maneuver, and crashed into the suspected bomber. The two tumbled to the ground, and in seconds the others had reached them and hastily slapped on a set of shiny steel cuffs.

Yeah, that didn't look staged at all.

As she watched the footage, it did make her wonder though. She was a marine and had been since her recruitment at Prometheus at the outbreak of the Uprising. She had seen combat against terrorists, war machines, and Biomechs but never had she seen the aerobatics shown on the video feed. Even the equipment being used seemed to be different. The weapons carried by the marines looked like altered thermal shotguns used by private security units. The more she examined the details she realized the video had absolutely nothing to do with marines. She shook her head, gulped down some water, and moved to another feed that showed trouble in space. The events around Helios were much worse than she had expected, especially as the revolution had been won.

What's this all about then, more enhanced military antics?

This particular one concerned a hijacked tanker. Music in the background added a sense of drama to the occasion, as the large vessel seemed to spin out of control through space. The story announced it was hot news, and Helion militias had retaken the ship with the assistance of Alliance Marines.

Militias? How could they mount an operation like that?

The video report showed a group of Alliance fighters dispatching marines in zero gravity. They were the new Hammerhead models that had proven so effective on Helios. They looked ugly to her, but their record couldn't be ignored. One by one, the marines moved away with small puffs coming from their jet nozzles as they moved in to the ship. For those with no military background it might be interesting, but for Teresa it was simple routine and nothing she hadn't seen before. Even so, the fact the mission was successful and without the loss of a single marine helped her mood, even if just a little. Then the feed changed to show a trio of marines being spoken to by a civilian Helion who seemed happy at their apparent rescue. It reminded her of her three children. Just thinking about them sent a chill through her bones.

The part worrying her most was that all three of them were now on the frontline. They had all finished their training and been posted to military fronts or ships. Jack was busy with his unit on Eos fighting insurgents; her other two children from her previous marriage were preparing to leave with the newly assembled 3rd Heavy Strike Group. Although she was proud of every one of them, the strain was beginning to show. There was always the terrifying thought in the back of her mind that something deadly could occur, and she would be left without any of them.

Most of my family is dead. Spartan is still missing, and all my children are out fighting the wars of the Alliance. Just show me something, anything positive.

She shook her head, trying to cast the thoughts aside.

That's enough...what now?

Her diary showed a number of meetings with the commander of the newly raised Marine battalions and a PT demonstration in one of the many barracks on Terra Nova. None of it really needed her presence, but it was the best she could do until she was given the okay from the medics to return to her own unit.

Okay, you have forty minutes before the introduction to the rookies; let's burn off some of this fat.

She was out of the room and in the gymnasium in less than ten minutes. It was a circular hall filled with weights, training mats, and machines for the military personnel to make use of in their off time. Like every one of the other marines, she had changed into her regulation physical training gear. It was nothing fancy and consisted of a plain green cotton t-shirt, green nylon shorts, black socks, and running shoes. Without giving the other marines a second look, she went through her warm-up and then moved to her exercises with the kettle bells. They were traditional training tools from Russia made from cast-iron and resembled an ancient cannon ball with a handle. They were heavy and different weights. She used the twenty-four kilo kettle bell, the standard heavy model used by the experienced marines. She had been working with it for fifteen minutes before stopping for a breather. Her body dripped with sweat, and she ached from head to toe from the exertion. It was the group of eight marines watching her that stopped her in her tracks. All were dressed the same as her, and none could have been older than twenty.

"What is it, marines?" she asked sternly.

"Sir, you're Major Morato, second-in-command of the 17th?"

She wiped her brow with the towel and then nodded.

"Haven't you seen the news?" asked one of the women, a scrawny-looking thing with short cropped blonde hair.

"What do you think? I'm kind of busy."

She might have been forty-eight, but years of physically training with the Corps, a healthy lifestyle, and access to the best medical facilities in the Alliance had helped her maintain a toned body of a thirty-year-old woman.

"Crews are being rushed to their ships. We thought you might know what's going on," the woman continued.

Teresa walked to the water dispenser, took several sips, and then looked back at them. The look on their faces was an odd mixture of concern and also reverence. It was something she came across all the time on Terra Nova. The adulation of new recruits was a problem she and the other veterans of the Uprising were forced to endure on a daily basis.

That's right; to them you're some kind of hero. Fools.

"This is the first I've heard of it. Check with your

sergeant. You might be needed."

Teresa was back at her room in half the time it had taken to get to the gymnasium. Everything was as she had left it, and then she saw it. For an outsider, the sight of her could easily have been a painting as she stared at the screen in her temporary office, her face showed shocked disbelief. She had been so busy at the gymnasium, she had forgotten to take her secpad with her; no wonder she had received no emergency messages. The message must have arrived at least half an hour earlier, and she cursed herself for missing it. She sat down and poured herself a glass of water while she waited for it to decrypt to her personal space. Teresa selected two separate video feeds, one for the Alliance News Network that was running a piece of a small space skirmish, and the second the official announcement channel of the Alliance High Command. She spotted several messages regarding unit activations. She only managed to get through two of them before the sound alerted her to the completion of the communication decryption; finally it was ready.

Why is Earthsec contacting me?

She looked into the face of a blonde intelligence agent, a face that she had never seen before. In fact, the patch of the agency on the ancient planet and home of humanity filled her with an odd feeling of nostalgia. Teresa found herself trying to look behind the woman, to get a glimpse of the old, dead husk known as Earth.

"Major Morato, this is a rather unusual request, but we have just made contact with a number of individuals on board a military vessel that breached Sol space."

Sol, so why contact me?

"A Rift opened up less than a day ago, and unidentified ships in the middle of a violent exchange entered. It was a violent space battle, but we were too late to stop the first ship coming here. The pursuers were destroyed in the Rift's collapse, but we were unable to identify them."

The image now changed to that of an unknown T'Kari ship. She recognized the sleek lines immediately as being one of the vessel types used by their newfound allies in the Orion Nebula. The ship had clearly been involved in major action, as she was damaged from bow to stern from a hundred impacts.

"We have contacted our agents in T'Karan for information on this model, but we are still waiting. According to the files here, it shares features with T'Kari patrol ships."

He paused as though uncomfortable with the next part.

"I appreciate this is somewhat sudden, but we have two humans here, both of whom match our DNA and dental records on file. I believe you may know them."

Spartan? she thought desperately.

He'd been gone for so long she had all but given up hope of ever seeing him. All her remaining assets had been sold off to spend on a hundred leads even though

Alliance Intelligence had promised her they were doing all they could.

"If you are okay to proceed, please authorize the attached stream that has been supplied along with this video message."

Teresa found it hard to speak and simply stared at the screen for a moment. It was a one-way message, and if she responded it would continue, but for the time being it froze to a still. She wiped her dark hair back and rested her forehead in her left hand.

You have to know, just do it! A voice said in her head.

She shook her head free and reached out to strike the button. The video continued while a secondary stream appeared. The material in front of her was a tracking shot of the interior of a T'Kari ship. The interior corridors and passageways were identical to T'Kari ships that she had been inside before Spartan's disappearance. Then the footage cut to a gray room where a number of Intelligence agents waited quietly. Each wore a dark suit, and one waited in the corner with a long black trench coat that almost touched the floor. The view tracked to the left until it reached a row of medical tables upon which were the shapes of the humans in question. They were of unequal sizes, with the larger being almost double the total size of the other.

Here it is.

She gasped, but it wasn't the vessel that had stunned her.

It was the close-up of two faces. One was of a battered and scarred Jötnar that she instantly recognized as that of Khan, one of her and Spartan's old friends. The next face however was pale and bruised but unmistakably the face of her husband, Spartan.

It can't be, can it?

The image shifted to one side and was replaced by that of a blond-haired Alliance Intelligence agent. He looked for a moment at her, but it couldn't have been to wait for her to speak; the delay for the signal traveling through multiple Rifts to Sol was a long one of nearly an hour.

"We believe this man to be Spartan, formally an officer in the Alliance military and an executive of the defunct APS Corporation," the man stated in a dull, monotone voice.

Teresa looked at his features and felt a sickening feeling in her body. The man in front of her was breathing, but his eyes were closed, and the marks on his face suggested he had been through some kind of horrific ordeal.

"From an initial assessment, it appears the two individuals have suffered numerous external injuries, including multiple limb factures, broken ribs, and in the case of this individual, the violent amputation of a forearm."

He said more, but Teresa heard none of it. Instead, she watched as the camera moved about his body and showed a myriad of cuts, bruises, and burn marks. His body looked more fragile than she'd ever seen it before. A rough beard filled his face, and his hair was longer and messier than ever.

"...the injuries to the legs are far less important than..."

The image cut and was replaced by a temporary still frame with details of the lost connection.

"Damn it!" she snapped and hit the button on her video communicator built into the desk. The face of her newly assigned Captain who waited at the desk just outside her small office appeared; he seemed almost flustered at her appearance.

"I've just lost communication with Earthsec, what's happening?"

His face vanished though as an emergency override replaced him. Instead of the Captain, the face of the Chairman of the Joint Chiefs, General Rivers appeared. The message wasn't directed specifically at her. It was an emergency communiqué to all high-level commanders.

"This is a Level One strategic alert. In the last seventeen minutes, we have lost contact with three of our newest Rift stations. These are the Gliese 876, Procyon, and in the last few seconds the Ganymede Rift at Sol."

Teresa first thought was that this meant she was once more cut off from Spartan, but the stern expression on the General's face allowed little time for that kind of concern. She knew him well, and he looked worried.

"Three minutes before we lost contact, we received

tactical area scans that showed small numbers of Biomech ships. One was stopped at Epsilon Eridani by Alliance frigates, but the others were breached before we lost contact."

Breached? That means they were heading through the Rift, but where to?

The question was futile, however, as the Rifts were simply doorways in space that connected two points together. If Biomech ships had left Sol, Gliese 876, and Procyon, they could only heading in one direction.

"They are coming here!" she blurted out, but nobody could hear her.

"I have given orders to our commanders in the field to mobilize our forces throughout the Alliance. The 1st Heavy Strike Group is assembling at Prometheus in case they attempt to access the Orion Rift. The 2nd is already here at Terra Nova to protect the bridge between Alpha Centauri and Proxima Centauri. The 3rd is only partially complete and will wait as planned for us at T'Karan to give support as required. All other ships and patrol vessels are hereby brought to Condition One."

What about me?

It was as if the General could hear her every word as he answered.

"As well as the fleet, all Marine and Colonial Guard units are to report to your respective barracks."

She tapped a button to look at video feeds but stopped

at the site of the massive comet being shown on one of the many news networks. It looked like a ball of plasma to her, but that wasn't the concern; it was that the feed was being transmitted directly from the bridge of the Alliance flagship, ANS Conqueror, and the ticker line said fleet action in Eos.

Eos, that's where Jack is fighting!

* * *

The massive bulk of ANS Conqueror moved effortlessly through space as it made for its interception vector of Comet C34A. There were some in the Alliance press establishment that had started to nickname the comet as the Doomsday Comet, but it was a term that had been actively discouraged by the top brass, something that was apparently making it even more popular. They had already started to decelerate and had matched the elliptical trajectory of the object so that they would move alongside it in the next hour. The rest of the fleet was spread out, with half the ships maintaining an advance defensive screen near Eos along with the newly arrived ANS Royal Oak.

"Anything?" he asked his second-in-command, Captain Marcus.

The executive officer shook his head.

"Nothing, Admiral, the fleet is in position, and the

comet is maintaining its course. All fragmented debris is accounted for, and the escort wing under Commodore Hampel has intercepted anything coming close. So far he has destroyed seventy fragments with no loss or damage."

Admiral Lewis moved his head ever so slightly in acknowledgement. It was that time that occurred on every operation, the waiting game, and it never became easier. He took a sip from his flask of water and checked the tactical screen for the hundredth time.

So this is what the press calls a planet-killer. Not on my watch!

The emergency alerts blasted through the CIC warning every officer of a serious threat. It wasn't the usual warning from an individual system, but the full battlestations that was activated during an incoming threat or emergency.

"What the hell is going on?" demanded Admiral Lewis.

He was busy watching the comet on the mainscreen, but the data he had been presented with suggested he could expect to face no potential threat until they moved in closer to the object. The scattered debris field was well out of range, and the escorts were doing their job screen the fleet. Nonetheless, the alerts were proximity and thermal signature alarms designed to warn of approaching weapons or ships.

"Uh...Admiral, this...this is..."

He twisted around and threw a bitter look at the tactical officer that he immediately regretted. All he could do was blame it on the situation.

"Snap out of it, man, what is the problem?"

The man had only just joined the crew of the Battlecruiser and lifted his shoulders as he took in a deep breath. There had been many crew changes following the battle against the automated fleet due to casualties, but most had been moved to other less experienced ships to try and boost the overall quality.

"It's the comet, Admiral. Our sensors are detecting objects detaching from it."

"Objects...as in fragments? Is C34A breaking apart?"

His immediate thought was that these chunks could potentially be a navigational hazard for his ships. It was unlikely, as the amount of open space between them and the comet made the odds of an impact almost impossible.

"No, Admiral. Sensors show active weapon signatures on the objects. So far there are forty-one...no, forty-five."

He turned about in his seat to look at him, a look of horror on his face.

"Admiral, these are not chunks of debris. The threat assessment is of a large number of capital ships of unknown origin. It looks like a fleet, and they are moving to an entry vector for Eos."

Admiral Lewis was stunned. The reports and plotting data for the comet had implied something unexpected, and he had assumed the object was being directed as a weapon.

It would seem there is much more to it than meets the eye.

Without even checking with the rest of the senior commanders, he grabbed the intercom and hit the emergency broadcast button.

"This is Admiral Lewis to all captains. Operation Inferno is aborted. Break off immediately and reform in a defensive posture around ANS Royal Oak. This is not a drill; every single ship is at risk. This is a threat Level One warning. Get out of here, now!"

He intended on calling out to General Daniels, but the man was already there, waiting along with his own executive officer, Captain Marcus who had recently transferred from the Titan Naval Station.

"Admiral, these ships are showing weapon signatures as well as extremely heavy armor. They are definitely not civilian. This is an attack, it has to be," suggested the Captain.

General Daniels took another step forward so that he could get a better view of the large images on the mainscreen. It showed the shapes moving from the comet that was already getting smaller and smaller. He could see the list on the right as each of the objects was scanned, tagged and then sent to the rest of the fleet. What really caught his eye was the rising number of ships.

"Eight-two ships...and rising? We have a big problem," he said more to himself than the others. He then turned and looked at the young Captain.

"Of course it's an attack."

The Captain, however, was a master of diplomacy, at least that was the impression given. He nodded, saying nothing but he looked less surprised than the Admiral. The ship groaned as the helmsman forced it to start powering up its engines to alter course. The emergency alarms blared their warning.

"We need to strap in," said Captain Marcus.

The other officers didn't need reminding and quickly moved to the nearest seat and pulled on the straps. The ship's computer began a loud, audible countdown from ten as the engines built up. At the same time, the retro thrusters twisted the massive vessel about to face its new vector.

"Seven...six..."

Admiral Lewis looked at the mainscreen again and was shocked to see the number had just moved past one hundred. What really sent a chill through his body was the magnified view from one of the many long-range scopes fitted to the Battlecruiser. It panned past a group of armored capital ships and toward a large formation of smaller vessels. The camera locked onto one and zoomed in to the target vessels. The image continually moved in and out of focus before it finally settled. The computer started a detailed analysis immediately and put the size at about half the size of an Alliance cruiser, except that this ship was odd, like nothing he'd seen before.

"What is it?" he asked.

The ship shook again, and then a powerful drone spread through the hull. All of them were familiar with the powerful engines, but the fact they were being used to get out of danger sent a palpable feeling of concern through the vessel. Everybody from Admiral Lewis down to lowly ensign knew something was going wrong.

"Look at the configuration," said General Daniels as he studied the craft.

"What about it?" asked Captain Marcus.

"Well, for starters the shape of the bow and underside suggests it is designed for atmospheric entry."

"The General's correct," called out Lieutenant Vitelli, "The craft's configuration is similar to that of our marine landers like the Mauler, except this thing is much bigger. Look at the bow."

They looked for just a moment, but Admiral Lewis could already see the section the Captain referred to.

"I see it. The craft looks heavily armored on the bow."

General Daniels and Admiral Lewis' eyes met across CIC. Lewis spoke first.

"That thing is designed to get to the surface in one piece."

The General nodded in agreement.

"The question is, are they orbital weapons, or something much worse, like landing craft?"

The mention of the possibility the vessels intended to land people on the surface was something of a shock to them all. Then an image appeared on the mainscreen that stopped them all from speaking. It was a black shape that was emblazoned like a piece of heraldry running along the flanks of the ship. As the camera moved, it showed the same symbol on every single one of the other vessels.

"What is that?" asked the executive officer.

"Echidna," hissed the Admiral between his teeth.

Admiral Lewis and General Daniels knew exactly what it was, and the mere sight of the metal serpent sent a chill through both of them. Admiral Lewis had already hit the emergency broadcast button when General Daniels started to speak.

"We're in trouble, what's the plan?"

"You know who they are. I need to contact High Command before they hit us. This could be over in minutes."

General Daniels nodded grimly and walked back to his command room adjacent to the CIC. He had his own, much smaller staff to help coordinate Marine operations in this sector. There were only three people there, including Colonel Horst Brünner, the commander of the 4th Marine Heavy Battalion. The rest of senior commanders were on the surface of Eos helping with the Helion efforts against the Animosh insurgency.

"It's true then?" asked the Colonel.

Daniels looked at his with expressionless eyes. He had seen plenty of battles, but the sight of so many ships filled him with an emotion he hadn't felt for a long time. It was an odd mixture of worry, dread, and hatred combined into an unreasoning desire to strike out.

"Colonel, this is the largest Biomech fleet we have ever seen. Over a hundred capital ships, and they are coming this way."

He was no great fan of Colonel Horst Brünner, but even he could see the flicker of fear show on the man's face. He was used to seeing argument for no reason from the man, but in that instant the Colonel changed.

"We've never come across the Biomechs in large numbers before. They always attack us via third parties. Are we ready?"

The General shook his head.

"Not by a long shot. We have a dozen capital ships and nine frigates. That puts us at odds of at least five-to-one."

"What about our boys on the ground?"

General Daniels smiled at the question. He had always considered Brünner to be a self-righteous and bitter man, one concerned only with self-promotion and advancement. Now that it came to the real test, and the man thought only of their marines.

Maybe he isn't the man I thought he was?

"We'll get them all to safety, and fast. If those are landing craft of some type, we could see a full-scale Biomech assault on Eos. We have to save as many as we can and prepare for the worst."

"General!"

The Admiral shouted from a dozen meters away. He stepped to one side to look back at the man. The look on his face had altered slightly to one of grim determination. The ship had stopped its maneuvering now and was accelerating back to the ships closer to Eos. The image of the Echidna stylized force was showing on every screen, and all he could think about were the Biomechanical monstrosities he'd faced on so many occasions before.

"Yes?"

"Your people have three hours. If I can't stop this fleet, they will face the full wrath of this attack. Get them ready. This will be a battle unlike anything any of us have ever seen."

CHAPTER FIVE

The Zealots and their Biomech influenced masters were one of the greatest mysteries of the past. Their uprising started with suicide bombings and assassinations and soon spread to a military resolution with support, technology, and resources far outweighing what should have been possible. Only in the following decades would it become clear how far the Biomech influence had been in both the supply of technology and their political manipulation. The cunning of the Biomechs was second only to the Byzantines of ancient Earth.

A Brief History of the Zealots

Fort Macquarie was the primary base of operations for the Marine Corps and its auxiliary units supplied by the Alliance Navy. It had been constructed in less than a month and was now the logistics hub for operations carried out by the Helion security forces and their Alliance comrades.

Self-replicating technology was one of the advances now being used by the Marine Corps to great effect. In the past, it might have taken years to create such a site, but a large force of drones and hundreds of supply crates had been installed within a week. Left to their own devices, the autonomous machines were able to assemble the buildings, towers, and bunkers on their own and at an exponential rate as they assembled more drones actually on location. The building materials were harvested directly from the ground itself by robotic mining and refining drones at the now shut down assembly plant in the corner of the site.

With over eight thousand personnel in total, it was the largest base outside of Alliance space. The entire 17th and 8th Marine Battalions were there in force, with an equal number of Helion troops being mentored by specialists from Terra Nova. Two landing strips had been marked out, as well as eighteen individual landing pads for vertical takeoff craft. The site included prefabricated barracks, a large field hospital, and a five-meter tall wall that ran in a giant square around the entire base.

"I hate this moon," grumbled Colonel Gun.

Like all the marines on Eos, he had to wear his enclosed suit of armor to protect him from the lack of a breathable atmosphere and the changeable temperatures. The radiation from the primary star was also a big problem, but his armor was more than enough for modest exposure. In any case, Gun was starting to enjoy wearing his JAS armor, even when inside Alliance buildings. His was the close assault model and featured retractable serrated blades in the arms and a single shoulder-mounted weapon system. With the extra armor and weapons, it made him feel like a God, something he greatly appreciated. An alert sounded inside his helmet, and again he found it uncomfortable relying upon using his eyes to select the message.

What now?

It was a flash message of few words from the fleet. He looked up to the sky as if expecting to be able to see the formations of ships. Even if they were in orbit, they would be far too small to see. Even so, he couldn't help himself. It was shorter than expected and from the communications officer of the flagship. All it said was that the fleet had engaged the Biomechs.

Lewis can make them suffer!

He marched past a sunken structure protected by two missile defense systems. It was in the center of the base, and to most people would have looked liked the command bunker or headquarters. Gun entered an adjacent, far less imposing structure built from six trailer sections fitted together. He was forced to stoop, as always, as he entered. Inside were three open plan rooms and a dozen guards spread out. In the center of the largest room were dozens of computer displays. The holographic tactical unit, a large table-type device showing a three-dimensional model of the surface of Eos, dwarfed them. As soon as the entry airlock sealed, he activated his visor, and the front of the helm opened up from both the top and bottom to reveal his large head.

"Ah…" he sighed, breathing in the air inside the structure.

Lieutenant Martinez approached him, stopped, and saluted. She was short for a marine and like a child next to the armored form of Gun. He looked at her inquisitively and tried to remember what her job was there.

"Colonel, the patrol under Lieutenant Elvidge is coming in within the hour. They have prisoners."

Gun shook his head in annoyance at the marine.

"I know that. The news came in twenty minutes ago. Bring them here when they arrive."

"As soon as they land, Sir?"

Gun looked at the tactical map, trying to hide his frustration. He always kept his orders short and simple, yet he was constantly being asked the most insignificant questions, and it was beginning to try his patience.

"Yes, of course now. We are at war on this world, and I need information fast. This is not the kind of war we trained for."

A critical flash message alert sounded on the secpad fitted into his armor. He bent down before remembering the unit was connected to the computer-controlled visor in his armor.

Yeah, it's all good, till it stops working.

It took a few seconds for him to find the correct way to answer it. It flashed once, and then an image of General Daniels appeared. The expression on the man's face was stern and concerned, and surprisingly it sent a rush of excitement through Gun's body.

"General?"

"Gun, we've got a situation here."

Gun gave him a grin.

"Yeah, I know. I just received the flash message. Lewis has engaged them. I take it the battle goes well?"

The General ignored his question and continued speaking.

"Gun, I need you to look at this."

The image shifted to show the same external feed the General and Admiral Lewis had been watching of the comet. Gun looked at it but could see nothing of note. It was the same orb of rock, water, and junk he'd seen on the newsfeeds.

"I don't understand. The comet is like any other."

General Daniels shook his head quickly.

"No, Gun, it isn't. In the last few hours, sections have split off and changed course. Look at this."

Now the image changed to that of the fleet of ships making its way from the comet. The imagery flickered continually, and the schematic layouts were rough due to the continuous jamming signals coming from the enemy ships. There were several different designs, but the largest looked very similar to a manta ray, the large cartilaginous fishes native to the oceans of Earth. They were short but with a wide wing shape. Additional surfaces ended from the tips, and it was followed by a short but heavily armored aft section.

"Those are heavy warships, and they are heading toward Eos. Admiral Lewis says they show substantial biosignatures. That means they are either filled with something, or the ship's themselves are semi-biological."

He moved a little closer to the camera.

"Gun, it's much worse than that. We counted thirty of these larger Bio ships, but there are over eighty smaller transports. Our scans show they are constructed for rapid atmospheric entry, and like the bigger ships, the readings are off the charts. These thing are big, Gun, really big."

"Planetary entry?" asked Gun in surprise, "You mean they are heading for us?"

"It is likely. Get your marines ready and in shelter. The arrival trajectories are being sent to your command posts across Eos."

Gun scratched at his head in confusion.

"I don't understand. What about the fleet? Can't you stop them?"

General Daniels tried his best to look confident, but he couldn't hide the concern showing on his face.

"I'm not going to lie to you, Gun. Their fleet outnumbers us substantially, and these are not Helion or

Khreenk ships. Look at the insignia on them."

The image blurred and then focused on a single one of the manta ray style ship. It showed the metallic serpent shape emblazoned on its flank. Hundreds of tiny craft hung like clouds around the ships, providing a protective cordon against attack.

"The Biomechs, so they have returned with their… Biomanta ships!"

Unlike anybody else that had seen the images of the enemy, Gun's expression was unique. Whereas General Daniels looked concerned and grave, Gun looked almost excited. If the General had seen Gun's response to the news, it might have scared him. Even as they finished their short briefing, Gun could barely conceal his excitement.

* * *

Every single one of the senior officers aboard ANS Conqueror waited at their posts. Even so, the ship felt eerily quiet as the crew went about their business as if it were any other day. Marine guards stood as silent sentinel at key locations everywhere from the hangars and gun control rooms to the CIC and engine rooms. She was a ship prepared for battle, the same as the other twenty ships in the entire fleet.

"Tactical, any change?" asked Admiral Lewis.

Lieutenant Vitelli shook his head.

"No change, Admiral. They are still coming, and they are refusing our hails."

Admiral Lewis was in a difficult, if not impossible situation. This was the first time an actual Biomech fleet had ever been seen before. This wasn't a group of lackeys or even allies. These ships were actual warships, and every one of them had set a course for the Helion moon of Eos.

"Admiral, what if they don't shoot?" asked Captain Marcus.

The Admiral moved his eyes to look at his XO.

"I know it's a problem. If we fire first, we could trigger open war."

Admiral Lewis shrugged at his XO's last words, looking less concerned than might have been expected.

"Yes, very true, but if we let them through, they could bombard or even invade Eos without any contest by us."

Admiral Lewis moved his attention to the main screen and then to the tactical board showing the position of every single ship and unit in the fleet. General Daniels was also there, along with Colonel Brünner and two of his Marine Corps officers.

"Admiral, I've been in touch with Colonel Gun and Koerner. Their forces have secured their military bases. They will be ready for whatever comes. They are awaiting further news from us."

How can they prepare for what they don't know? He thought.

"Good work, General. Your people have done their

job, but it is my intention to avoid a ground fight. Hell, they might not even want the planet. What if those craft are planning on bombarding the moon from orbit?"

He rubbed his chin and looked at the formation of ships on the display.

"Now it is time for us to do our job. If they get past us, your people on the ground will have one hell of a time. Either we stop them, or at the very least we will thin out their numbers."

He beckoned for the tactical officer. As he waited for him to approach, he nodded to the General.

"I promise you, not one of those ships will get past us without one hell of a fight. We have good ships, crew, and weapons."

"Admiral?"

"Are we in range yet?"

The man nodded.

"Affirmative, Admiral, the fleet awaits your orders."

He looked to his XO and then to General Daniels, both appeared as concerned as him. The Biomechs were not just the Alliance's enemy, they were perhaps the greatest enemy any living creature had ever known, and now they were heading for people he knew. Eos might be Helion territory, but they were now their allies, and thousands of Alliance marines and civilians were on that moon. He closed his eyes and breathed slowly. Finally, he nodded to his communications officer.

"Send out one final message. Tell them...they have thirty seconds to withdraw, or we will open fire. This is our sector, and we will defend it to the last ship and marine!"

He waited, the entire crew waited, and nothing happened. Five seconds ticked past, then ten. He looked at the large formation of Alliance ships and wondered what would happen if it came to battle. He had divided his force up into three divisions. The first was spread out over nearly a thousand kilometers and was made up of two Crusader class ships and half of the escort frigates under Commodore Hampel. Behind them were two more groups based around his Battlecruisers. ANS Royal Oak was protected by all the remaining escorts, while the other nine Crusader class heavy cruisers waited in a wide formation around his flagship, ANS Conqueror. Multiple fighter wings were spread out, half flying escort for the three divisions, and the remainder drawn up in five large assault wings to be used offensively in front of the fleet. He counted nearly ninety fighters in total, including Thunderbolts, Hammerheads, and even six Marine Corps Maulers that had been rushed out to provide additional fighter cover with their multiple point-defense turrets and large ordnance bays.

Admiral Lewis continued to countdown silently to himself. Twenty, twenty-five and then a crackled video feed appeared on the main screen. It showed a dull gray machine, flanked by two more that looked almost identical.

It seemed motionless, and for a brief moment, the feed looked as though it had frozen. Then came the sound.

"Surrender," was all it said.

Admiral Lewis moved his head back slightly as though confused at the word. He shook his head before answering.

"I am Admiral Lewis of the Alliance Navy. Eos is under my protection. Who are you, and why are you here?"

Again came the pause before the machine spoke again, in its dull, monotone voice.

"We bring your doom."

The CIC was silent. The men and women watched the machines with confused fascination. As to how they understand their own language was of little interest right now.

"Is that a threat?" asked General Daniels, his voice bitter and sarcastic.

A noise not too dissimilar to laughter came from the middle machine. It twisted slightly and took a single step closer. The front of the machine opened up to reveal the shattered remnants of some creature. The remains floated inside a translucent orb of green fluid. Some of the crew recoiled at the sight but not the Admiral. He looked at the thing and said nothing. The more he looked, the more he was convinced he could see the outline of a brain inside the green cloud of fluid and gas.

"We have returned to reap your harvest."

The video feed finally cut, leaving just the image of

the three horrific machines. They barely moved other than the central one whose frontal armor closed up around the ancient body that lay within. General Daniels turned to his friend.

"Well, it seems clear enough to me. These bastards are insane, completely, hopelessly insane. Does that make your decision any easier?"

For the first time that day Admiral Lewis seemed to smile.

"Indeed it does."

It wasn't entirely true. Until the enemy opened fire, there was a chance this was nothing but rhetoric. The ships were still moving toward them, yet his last briefing with Admiral Anderson and General Rivers had been clear. The Biomechs were the enemy, the greatest threat to humanity, and he had orders to strike at them wherever he found them. He then nodded to his tactical officer and lifted the intercom sitting in its cradle on the unit in front of him.

"This is Admiral Lewis; you may start your attack."

Scores of confirmations flashed about the display as individual ships and fighter squadrons acknowledged their orders. The entire fleet must have been waiting on tenterhooks because no more than five seconds later the bombardment began. Even General Daniels was impressed at the sheer amount of fire being leveled at the approaching fleet. He looked to his colleague and friend and tapped his shoulder.

"Admiral, it would appear the Battle for Eos has begun."

Admiral Lewis tried to look confident, but even as the first impacts were made, he felt a little queasy. It wasn't that they were engaged in battle, it was the small number of words from the Biomech commander. He had said they brought their doom. The only mention he was aware of, was the ancient prophecy spread from Helios and out to the worlds of the Alliance, T'Kari, and the others. He recalled it referred to the return of the Biomechs. There was something that worried him even more.

What do they hope to gain here, on this unimportant moon? What is their plan?

* * *

"Three minutes!" called out the co-pilot over the internal speakers.

The Hammerhead shook slightly, hitting a pocket of cooler air as they flew fast and low over the surface of Eos. Two more followed close behind and almost a kilometer away loitered a pair of Lightning fighters. They were not the only aircraft in the sky near Fort Macquarie, but they were the closest to the base.

"Private Morato, that was some good soldiering back there," said Lieutenant Elvidge.

"Thank you, Sir," Jack replied politely.

"Command has been trying to get their hands on insurgents to interrogate, and I think the guy you grabbed is something out of the ordinary."

Jack nodded but said nothing more. The Lieutenant looked at him carefully, trying to gauge the character of the young man.

"Son, you've been in action before, haven't you?"

Riku and Callahan both winced at his question. They were equally aware of the trouble Jack had with the combat on Helios during their last two operations. He might have emerged with physical scarring, but he was a different man now. The brutality of close quarter battle affected people different, yet for Jack it seemed to be more personal than for any of them.

"Yes, Sir, two operations on Helios plus...well...a few minor incidents elsewhere when we first came out there."

The Lieutenant could sense the marine didn't want to go any further and decided to stop where he was, instead looking at the small side window near him. They were barely larger than his hand but still provided a narrow view of Fort Macquarie. From just a few hundred meters up, the site looked incredibly flat, with not a single structure over two stories. The outer wall looked more like a minor barricade, and the towers placed at hundred meter intervals were barely visible. As they dropped down lower, it was clear the impression was based more on their height and the total surface area of the base because the

Fort was anything other than small.

"Home sweet home," said Callahan.

The place was always busy, but as they lowered down to the ground, something else was going on. Many of the aircraft waiting to be used were being hidden inside their enclosures, and the amount of marines in the open had almost vanished. Jack watched with a mindful eye, taking in all the details. The place looked completely different to when they had left for their operation.

Back home and yet another drill, he thought.

He looked at a dozen aircraft waiting on the landing pads in readiness for their next mission. Some were being loaded with supplies for other patrols, others waited as columns of marines ran from them and into the nearest buildings. Off to the right were the two main airstrips, each built to accommodate the fast-attack craft like the Lighting fighters. Though the craft were capable of vertical takeoff, they would be able to retain more fuel and take heavier combat loads using a conventional take off. One blasted off, leaving a trail of dust directly behind it on yet another mission.

"Jack, what the hell is that?" asked Callahan.

Both of them looked out through the door at the shape of a large transport craft waiting on one of the landing pads. It was easily twice the size of a Marine Mauler, and at least five ramps ran down from the lower levels. Lieutenant Elvidge leaned over and looked out at the vessel.

"Yeah, that's a Helion clipper. They use them to ferry people to industrial sites and moons. Since the treaty, they've been requisitioned for use by the New Helion Army."

The other marines looked at the vessel with disinterest, but Jack and Callahan seemed to have a morbid fascination with the craft.

"I've seen one before, on Helios," explained Jack.

"Yeah, what was it doing?"

Jack's lip quivered slightly at the question.

"It was one of the many ships I saw at the spaceport in the last hour of the revolution. I guess these things are pretty common then?"

Lieutenant Elvidge sat back down and checked his harness.

"Yeah, you could say that. Why do you think we suggested they used them? Have you seen the numbers of the NHA?"

Jack shook his head, and the Lieutenant took that as a signal to continue.

"The population of Helios itself is massive, nothing like any of our own worlds. Add that together to the colonies at their other four stars, and you have a formidable number of people."

Jack started to add them up in his head, but the Lieutenant didn't wait.

"According to them, they have a single habitable world

at each star, and at least a dozen orbital colonies or moon colonies at each of them."

Jack raised an eyebrow, not quite believing what he was hearing.

"So, five worlds and sixty colonies of different sizes. That must be about half of what we have in the Alliance."

"Almost," said the Lieutenant, except their worlds are denser and more heavily populated. Helios has over six hundred billion alone."

Callahan had between listening with interest, but the last part surprised him.

"Six hundred? How can that be? Isn't Terra Nova less than ten billion?"

They were now only fifty or so meters from the ground, and the downdraft from the Hammerhead caused vibration and shaking through the craft. There was a final blast from the engines, and then they were on the ground. With the door already open, they were able to step out onto the dusty surface. The other marines moved out of the craft, but the group of four stayed together.

"Callahan, don't forget the multiple-levels. Helios is a planet of cities; some call it one great city. They could manage trillions, assuming they can feed them."

Even Jack found it hard to believe the planet could have anything like that number. It did explain why the Alliance had been so keen to keep them on side though; billions of citizens would make the perfect cannon fodder if there ever were a renewed war with the Biomechs. They moved away from the dust cloud about the Hammerhead and found a squad of marines waiting for them, led by a short Lieutenant. Elvidge stopped, and they exchanged salutes.

"Colonel Gun wishes to see you and your prisoners immediately."

Elvidge shook his head.

"Lieutenant?"

"Lieutenant Martinez. As I said, Sir, the Colonel insisted. It is urgent."

He considered arguing, but it wasn't her fault, even if he had things he needed to sort out first. When your Colonel came calling, you had to do as ordered, especially when your commander was somebody like Gun.

"Very well. The prisoners are on the next Hammerhead; perhaps your security detail could bring them along."

She nodded in reply and with a final salute, the newly arrived marines left the perimeter of the landing pad. It was a short walk to the center of the base, less than five minutes. Jack, Callahan, Riku, and the Lieutenant moved at a brisk pace along the designated walkway. It was no more than a marked out area on the hard, dusty surface of Eos. More marines moved about as they maintained continuous patrols of the compound. Before they made it halfway, at least five more marine craft had landed, unloaded, and taken off again.

"This place, have you ever seen a base like it?" asked

Jack.

The Lieutenant shook his head as they moved. Jack found he had to quicken his pace to match the speed of the officer. Groups of marines carried heavy weapons between them as they made their way to the outer wall. Jack watched one team as they slipped and dropped the tripod unit to the ground. He moved to help, but the Lieutenant grabbed him.

"We have orders, Jack. The Colonel want to see us, and I'm guessing it's more important than helping grunts drag their own gear about."

He agreed reluctantly, and they proceeded on their previous path. It took nearly thirty seconds before anybody spoke.

"Sir, about the base?"

The Lieutenant looked confused for a moment before remembering Jack's question. He felt like an idiot for having such a one-tracked mind. Either that or he had the worst short-term memory in the battalion.

"Right, the Fort. No, I don't think so. This place is unique. The closest I've seen are some of the bases back on Prime, at the start of the Uprising but only on vids."

Jack recalled some of the stories he'd read about his father's operations back then. Bizarrely, he had spent little time with the man and heard more of his exploits from others rather than from him directly.

"My father, he was involved in the fighting back there."

Lieutenant Elvidge slowed just a little as he considered what Jack had said.

"Jack Morato...Your father is?"

He moved another three steps before replying.

"Spartan."

The name had its usual effect, and the officer stopped to look back at Jack.

"Spartan, the hero of the Uprising, the man that led the assault on Terra Nova and helped end the War? That Spartan?"

Jack tried to smile.

"Yeah, you've heard of him?"

Elvidge continued back on the path and said nothing for a moment. They made it past the last of the Hammerheads and then onto the path by the warehouses and storage bins for the aircraft. Dozens of simple sheds had been erected to protect fighters and shuttles from the elements, and a Marine guard waited outside every third shed to keep an eye on them.

"I'm surprised you didn't use the clout your father has to go directly into the Corps as an officer. Why start as a grunt? No offense."

Jack had been asked this question so many times in the past that it was starting to become old habit. His father was something of a celebrity in the civilian world, but for the military there were fewer men or women alive that had the recognition factor as his father. He had never come across a person in the Corps that didn't have something to say about him, and it wasn't always good.

"My father…he was good at fighting but not so good at making friends higher up. He was barred from promotion. That's why he started APS Corporation. It was a good company, well, before it collapsed it was."

They were now just moving around the corner to the command center. There were more guards outside the larger structure next door, but it was all part of the classic ruse to protect their commanders. Only those that needed to know had any idea what the larger building was for, but Jack had worked it out quickly from the trails nearby. The marks were similar to those near other automated construction sites he'd seen before. It was the original control hub for the drones that built the base.

"What happened?" asked Callahan.

"With what?"

"APS Corp."

"Uh…" Jack started, but they were now just a few meters away. "The private security market collapsed, and APS died with it. We had to find new work where we could."

The airlock hissed open, and all four walked inside the prefabricated building. Three steps led down into the basin the structure had been built over. From the outside it looked modest, but in reality, there was more below the surface than above it. They went through the second and final airlock section and emerged inside the main control room. A pair of Marine guards waited motionless at each side of the airlock.

Lieutenant Elvidge came through last, noticing that Jack walked with almost a swagger to his body. It reminded him about what he'd said about his family's company. APS Corp was a well-known entity in the Alliance and had been involved in dozens of high profile security operations, hostage rescues, and military support missions in the past. It left him with more questions about Jack than answers, especially as to how his family had managed to squander the obviously massive benefits to running such a profitable enterprise.

It doesn't make sense.

The sound of voices turned his attention to the interior where he could see a number of officers, as well as one giant and fully armored Jötnar. He had seen them before but not often, and like most citizens, found the sight of the creatures to be rather unsettling. The images of the Biomechs and their warriors in the Uprising were still commonplace on the worlds of the Alliance, and many of the public was still wary of such beasts being given free rein. He had no thoughts either way, but as the warrior turned, spotted the group, and then stared directly at him, he found his gut reaction was one of suspicion. Without thinking, he reached for the pistol on his belt at the sight of such a monstrous creature, but he was too slow, and he lurched toward them. He grabbed for his sidearm and took one step back.

"Jack!" he cried.

He might have been expecting trouble, but instead Jack barged toward the Jötnar. The two crashed together, and the Jötnar smashed his fist down onto the young man's shoulder while shouting out. Riku reached out and pushed down the pistol in the Lieutenant's hands.

"No," she said.

Elvidge looked at her and was shocked to see her laughing.

CHAPTER SIX

Like most Alliance planets, the world's defenses were based upon the fleet. There were no great stations or orbital platforms on this world, just a single docking platform that could handle the loading and departure of two or three ships at a time. The surface was another matter, and only a fool would ever consider attacking the place while occupied and protected by the fiercest citizens of the Alliance, the Jötnar.

The downfall of Hyperion

The battle for Eos began with a massive bombardment from every ship in the Alliance fleet. The particle beam emitters on the front of the newest ships fired invisibly through space, and massed volleys of railguns fired clouds of solid shells toward the approaching ships. Even ANS Royal Oak, the Alliance carrier and newest capital ship in the fleet, loosed of thirty torpedoes from her spacious ordnance mounts. Only the newest frigates and this carrier had been modified to carry these new weapons. Although slower than the primary weapons of the other ships, the torpedoes were able to change their course and could operate autonomously.

Approaching this veritable cloud of weaponry came the fleet of machines, known only by their nickname of Biomechs. The thirty large manta ray-like ships moved in a wide, loose formation; the smaller craft followed a short distance behind. Their course shifted slightly as they moved closer to Eos, but it wasn't enough of a change to allow them to bypass the waiting ships. The particle beams struck first, invisible blasts of energy that blew holes in the lead ships. One of the manta ray vessels lost half of its port wing section, yet not one of the vessels responded. Flashes of energy rippled through the fleet as one ship after another took damage from the invisible beams. As dust and debris began to scatter, the light from the weapons began to show up as a faint wisp on the particles.

Admiral Lewis watched the assault from within the CIC of ANS Conqueror, and the feeling of nausea was hard to ignore. The distance had already halved, and still the Biomechs came on. Every member of the crew was busy organizing the sections of the ship while the marines watched and waited.

"What is their status?" he asked his tactical officer, as a second volley of gunfire hurtled out toward the ships.

"I am showing good hits on the five lead Mantas. They are four minutes away from us."

Admiral Lewis allowed himself a quiet chortle at the name, even in the midst of such carnage. They had no idea of the capabilities of these ships, let alone what class they were or what the enemy called them. All they knew was the size and shape, hence the temporary name assigned to them by his own crew.

As for the closing speed, it was clear the Biomech fleet was planning on smashing its way through his forces and then on to the moon that lay behind them. That last thought had a sobering effect on him, so he turned his attention to the large mainscreen showing the view toward the enemy fleet. Most of the ships were too small to be seen, but the Mantas at the front appeared substantial. He could see the flicker of blue light along their structures, as the beams from the Alliance ships exploded sections the size of frigates from their hulls. Finally, one on the left side of the formation flashed once and broke apart. The officers in the CIC broke out in applause and excitement at the sight of the ship's destruction. The tactical officer seemed less excited.

"What is it?"

The man turned his head briefly.

"Admiral, they are powering up their systems. I think they're about to fire."

The words were expected, yet the memories of what

happened in these battles had never sat particularly comfortably with him. He connected to the fleet instantly via the battle communication network.

"All ships, prepare to receive fire."

His words must have arrived just seconds before one of the skirmish line of frigates vanished in a cloud of dust and fragments. The cheering aboard the ship stopped immediately, to be replaced by anger and fear.

"What just happened?"

The view on the mainscreen changed to show the shattered remnants of the frigate. Admiral Lewis had never seen anything like it. There was no sign of the ship, just pieces of metal no larger than a meter in length.

"Admiral, my sensors show a feedback loop on their ships and an energy signature similar to that of our own ships. They are using the same weapons as us, but according to my data, they are putting out almost twice the energy."

His heart felt dulled and heavy. He shouldn't have expected it to be any different. The particle weapons had only been perfected after making use of technology seized from the Echidna Union in the Uprising. Nobody had known where the rebels had obtained such advanced and formidable weaponry, and it had always been assumed they had been given the information from an unknown third party.

"Another energy surge, they're firing again."

The Admiral watched the mainscreen, looking for signs of which ship they were targeting.

"Keep firing; don't stop until every one of their ships has been destroyed."

The words might have made him feel better, but even as the guns of the fleet continued their bombardment, another of his frigates vanished in a blue blast of energy.

"I have their targeting plan, Admiral. It is essentially the same approach we found with the automated fleet."

Hardly surprising, is it?

"They are focusing their fire on a single ship at a time?"

"Yes, Admiral."

"I see. Well, it increases their chances, destroying one ship at a time, but it does give us the opportunity to strike at the rest of their fleet unmolested."

He thought about this for a moment. After the last engagement there had been many attempts at solving the problem of the tactic of selective targeting and focused fire. In the end, no perfect solution had been found, but there were a number of interesting proposals. He recalled the most important of them all, to reduce the effectiveness of the weapons as quickly as possible. As he considered his tactics, the Biomech fleet reached within sixty seconds of the remaining frigate skirmish line. It was, of course, a nonsense description for a small group of ships spaced so far apart. Even so, each of them was perfectly capable of tackling the expected waves of incoming missiles or projectiles, just not the focused use of particle beams. He hit a button and connected directly to the CIC of ANS Royal Oak.

"Captain Harper," came back the immediate reply from the ship's CAG.

"I have new targets and objectives for your squadrons."

"Understood, Admiral. They've just arrived."

He paused for a moment as he checked.

"You want the fighters to target the enemy weapon systems rather than attempt to cripple the ships?"

"That's right, Captain."

"Understood, Admiral."

He placed the intercom back on its cradle and noticed his XO looking at him.

"We remove their guns, and then let our capital ships finish them off?"

Admiral Lewis nodded in agreement.

"Exactly, particle beam emitters are fragile things. Remove them, and we can start taking their fleet apart."

* * *

The red nosed fighters accelerated to their maximum combat speed and set a direct course for the nearest of the Biomech warships. Super-hot flames roared silently from their twin engines in the coldness of space. Behind them waited the fleet and the dull orb that was the moon of Eos.

Here we go.

Captain Jim 'The Hammer' Evans checked his weapons load one last time. His Lightning fighter was the lead ship in a large ten-fighter formation that had moved into a flanking position to strike down hard on the enemy fleet. These were the fastest and most agile manned fighter in the Alliance arsenal. Behind then followed two groups of five Thunderbolt heavy fighters and a single Marine Corps Mauler. It was a formidable formation with a mixture of cannon, torpedoes, and missiles available and capable of damaging or destroying several major ships.

"Watch the flak!" he said automatically, without even thinking.

Though the primary guns on the Manta warships were invisible to all but the sensors on the craft themselves, the fighter defenses were nothing as advanced. Even at a range of three hundred kilometers, the ships started to unleash hundreds of kinetic rounds toward the fighters. Some were solid, but the major exploded nearby and sent fragments of shattered metal toward their targets. One piece struck his port wingtip and tore a chunk of metal away the size of his hand.

Close, and it's gonna get a lot worse!

He had already selected his initial target when the new orders came in. His helmet-mounted display showed the pre-selected threats, all of which were the newly designated

Manta class warships.

"So, they want the guns down first. We can do that."

He checked the tactical display to ensure all the other craft were still in formation. They were getting close, but he didn't want to fire their missiles too far away. Although deadly accurate, the guided munitions were easy to track and destroy with conventional guns. The closer they could make it, the better chance they would have at causing damage to their targets.

"Red One, we have bogies on your vector. Check your scanners."

Captain Evans acknowledged the message and checked his sensors. Nothing had been picked up so far on the radar, and the passive thermal sensors had found nothing either. He reverted to the ancient art of using his eyes to watch space around him and was instantly rewarded by the line of fighters.

"Red Wing, Green Wing, we have incoming. Check your targets...bring them down!"

The group of almost jet-black fighters approached at surprising speed. They were half the size of the Alliance fighters and shaped like small baths with large round engines fitted to the center that made up nearly half the total mass. A pair of light guns was built into the stubby wings, giving them similar firepower to the Lightning fighters. The radio comms filled with chatter as the two groups of fighters moved ever closer. Missiles streaked away from the fighters while the guns of the approaching black fighters opened up. The almost invisible kinetic slugs ripped through the fighter formation and claimed two Lightning fighters, tearing them apart in a terrible cloud of wrecked metal.

"Lightnings clear the fighters. Everybody else follow the set coordinates. The Admiral needs those particle weapons removed. Do your jobs, people!"

The battle turned into a mess as the fighters intermingled, and as had happened for centuries, a bloody dogfight ensued. The Alliance fighters were more heavily armored, yet the Biomech fighters were agile and equipped with a battery of rapid-fire guns. The battle raged while the two Thunderbolt squadrons smashed through the battle and rushed at two of the Manta warships. Streams of slugs ripped into them, but none were damaged sufficiently to force them back from what needed to be done. All ten released their missiles and then broke away to find their next target.

"Good work, people, now onto the next two," said Captain Evans.

Though he was busily engaged in a deadly dogfight, he was still able to maintain control of the space battle. Dozens of warships filled the view from his cockpit as the Manta ships and Alliance heavy cruisers closed to a distance of less than a hundred kilometers. Back on Earth this would have been long range for warships, but in space it was point blank range. Explosions and flashes occurred everywhere now as the ships pounded each other with every weapon they had available.

"Watch your flank, Red One," said his wingman before his fighter vanished in a fireball.

Captain Evans checked his visor overlay that showed targets in almost every direction. What concerned him most was that his wingman had been vaporized, and there were now two Biomech fighters on his tail.

"Time to spin the bottle," he laughed nervously.

With a deft tap, he activated one of his preset maneuvers. It was nothing particularly fancy and just a one hundred and eighty degree spin while maintaining acceleration, but using his forward facing braking thrusters as temporary primary engines. Now facing backward, he tagged the two fighters and then pulled the trigger. The nose-mounted cannon blasted the two enemy craft in seconds. Then a quick tap, and he continued on the same path but facing the forward direction.

Okay, how about the rest of them?

A quick check showed two more casualties, and from what he could see, the Biomech fleet had now slowed or changed course. The missiles from the first wave were rushing in to the selected target, but he didn't have time to watch them. Instead, he sent the waypoints to the rest of his fighters. He needed them to continue to the next pair of ships so they could finish their attack run. That was when he spotted the Marine Mauler in trouble.

"MM3, what's your status?" he asked.

The fighters had reformed; the surviving Lightnings taking up formation around the eight remaining Thunderbolts. The nearest craft showed black scorch marks where they had come dangerously close to weapons fire. The Mauler had moved on ahead and was halfway between them and the next two ships.

"Lost one engine, three dead, and we have wounded."

Captain Evans swallowed, his throat dry with the tension. The Mauler wasn't supposed to be used in this way. It was heavily armored and hard to destroy, but it was a lander, not a fighter. Even so, it was his job to attack the enemy ships. He could dwell on this in his own time.

"What about your weapons?"

There was a short pause before the Mauler's pilot replied. His voice was strained, and Captain Evans wondered if he'd also been wounded in the attack.

"One turret out of commission. Torpedoes intact, we're not out of the fight yet, Captain."

He allowed himself a short smile.

"Good work, Lieutenant. We'll watch you in from here."

The fighters moved in around the Mauler, the heavy Thunderbolt fighter-bombers behind, and the escort Lightning fighters in a loose cloud about it. As they moved in closer, he could see dozens of bullet holes on the thick armor plating of the craft. All four of the engines were intact, and the multiple gun turrets fired almost continually as a flight of Biomech fighters moved to intercept.

"All fighters, the release window is twenty seconds away. Hold your course."

"What about those fighters?" asked the leader of the Thunderbolts.

"Maintain course, slide but do not veer from this course."

The formation hurtled onwards while Biomech fighters attacked from all directions. They couldn't change direction during their attack run, but they could alter their heading for brief moments before returning on their course and firing their engines once more. Gunfire rippled about the formation, and the Mauler provided continuous gunfire from its multiple turrets. A dozen enemy fighters were downed for the loss of just one more Lightning, and then they were close enough.

"All wings, launch now!"

Each of the Thunderbolts launched their remaining missiles while the Mauler launched six heavy torpedoes, each the size of a fighter's engine unit. The weapons took only a few seconds to reach their targets, yet the Alliance fighters had already broken from their attack run. More Biomech fighters pursued them and even managed to bring down some of the missiles. It wasn't enough, and the volley of weapons struck two of the Manta warships, followed by a blinding light.

* * *

Lieutenant Vitelli watched the dotted lines as weapon trails from the fighter wings moved to the Biomech ships. Several of them flickered, vanishing as defensive weapons destroyed them. Each missed attack sent a shiver through his body. Finally, the surviving missiles and torpedoes struck their target, and he smiled with satisfaction as the data came in.

"Yes!" he stated, a little too excitedly. He looked over his shoulder to see Admiral Lewis looking back at him.

"We have good impacts, Admiral," said Lieutenant Vitelli.

Admiral Lewis watched with a brief glimmer of happiness on his face. The missiles and torpedoes from the fighter wings had removed the weapon emitters from five of the enemy capital ships, and two had been completely destroyed by the powerful blasts from torpedoes. The ships were now intermingled, and red indicators flashed across the tactical display showing where his ships were taking fire. He tried to avoid spending too long looking at them. He had a battle to fight and worrying about individual details would help nobody. What concerned him most was that the smaller Biomech ships were amongst his own vessels and showed no signs of stopping.

"What is our status?" he asked quickly.

"Four of our escorts are lost or out of the fight. One Crusader is abandoning ship, and two more will be joining her soon."

Seven ships from twenty-one. We can't keep going like this.

"And the enemy?"

Lieutenant Vitelli pointed to the shapes on the tactical display.

"Nine of the Biomantas have been destroyed, and half as many have lost their primary weapons. Seventeen remain, but they are bypassing us and continuing on to Eos with the remaining landers. There's another ship behind them as well. Our database says it's a Ravager class, some kind of heavy carrier. That must be where their fighters are launching from."

Damn it!

He had only two choices, and he liked neither of them.

"How many of the landers have they lost?"

"A quarter, Admiral."

The ship shuddered, and the schematic showing the complete ship on the right of the CIC showed multiple sections in red.

"What the hell is happening?" he growled.

Lieutenant Vitelli changed the mainscreen to the rear of the enemy fleet as it moved through the Alliance line and on to the moon. A large group of ships had stopped and were waiting like a line of sentries.

"The Biomantas, Admiral. All seventeen are standing their ground, and the Ravager has moved into the center of their formation."

The bastards, they are trying to stop me interfering with their attack.

"Crusader is taking fire. They are spreading their attacks against the entire fleet. Casualties reported on Serenity, Victory, Valor, and Sentry."

I have fourteen ships, all damaged, and they outnumber me. Do I stay, or do I signal the retreat?

* * *

"Jack!" he roared with a bellow.

"You know each other?" asked Lieutenant Elvidge.

When they had finished their rough embrace, Gun looked to the officer. He stared at his face and then gave the man a cursory glance from top to bottom.

"You could say that."

Gun took a few steps back and waited next to his tactical map of Eos.

"Jack and I, along with his family, have spilled more blood than I can imagine. How is Teresa?"

Jack let out a slow sigh, but he was clearly starting to relax.

"My mother is recovering well. She should be back with the 17th shortly."

"Good…How is the unit doing? You know you should be in my battalion."

Jack laughed at the suggestion.

"And be under the command of my own mother? Hell, no!"

An orderly brought them water, and all four snapped it up eagerly. Gun looked back at the tactical map for a moment. He was clearly happy talking with his old friends, yet there was something about him that surprised Jack. He couldn't put his finger on it.

What's wrong? Wait, is he excited about something?

"Gun?"

The towering warrior looked to him and raised the corner of his mouth slightly. He moved a little closer to the tactical table and tapped a button. It showed the entirety of the base, as well as all the land around it for five hundred kilometers.

"As you know, we're the main military base on this rock, but we have four smaller forward bases further south, with one quite close to your patrol earlier today. Do you know how many marines and soldiers that is?"

Jack had no idea, but Lieutenant Elvidge seemed to.

"Uh, about five thousand marines and at least five times that number of NHA."

Gun looked at the officer with an expressionless face.

"Not bad. Most of our marines are running patrols and training alongside their new recruits. They haven't been at this long though, and less than half have spent more than a year in the old Narau Army. I'm curious about them, are they as you expected?"

Jack placed the water down, and the orderly removed the canteens to refill them.

"No, they are not. About half are Animosh. You can tell from their skin tattoos and the gear they use. The others are a weird mix of refugees, outcasts or idealists from the other factions on Helios."

"It's true. Many of those in the minority groups on Helios are now losing money, favor, and influence since the Zathee were granted equal rights."

Gun shrugged at this.

"Tough luck, I say."

Lieutenant Elvidge stepped closer to him.

"Perhaps, but we end up having to clean up the mess. They need to be involved in the political system back on Helios, or we'll end up with the reverse situation, a place where the minority is well financed and assisted to turn against their own people and government. This could go on for many years."

The airlock hissed open, and in walked four marines from the second Hammerhead, along with a prisoner, the Helion Jack had fought with so hard back in their small battle.

"Remove his protection," said Gun with interest in his voice.

Callahan, Jack, Riku and Lieutenant Elvidge stepped back to the Colonel while the other marines removed the Helion's restraints and facemask. There was an audible gasp from Riku as the mask and its inbuilt respirator was removed.

"You're Khreenk!"

The alien looked at him with yellow eyes but said nothing. His cloak was pulled away by one of the guards to reveal the hidden shape beneath it. The alien refused to move, and it fell the floor around him. Underneath the cloak was a bizarre set of armor that looked as if it had been assembled from a dozen different sources. The breastplate was golden and well fitted while the waist was protected by thin bands that coiled about him. His legs were encased in a dull iron colored set of plate sections, and a black collar ran around his neck and down into a gorget that vanished behind the breastplate.

"We saw the guys on Helios. They're Khreenk mercenaries," said Jack.

Gun seemed to be in agreement and walked about the alien, as much interested in him as he was by the armor.

"Do you understand me?" he asked slowly.

The alien's yellow eyes seemed to twitch as he watched Gun move about him. Finally, Gun returned in front and stopped to face him.

"You and your people are responsible for the deaths of eleven marines so far. What do you have to say?"

One of the screens lit up with a flash message. It was secure, but Jack was all too familiar with how the system worked. Gun walked to the screen, looked at it for a few more seconds, and then returned his attention to the alien. Now he seemed only mildly interested, as if something else was holding his attention, and Jack could only assume it was the message. He wiped his mouth, and Jack could tell something bothered him.

"What is it?"

Gun looked at him and considered his words for a few seconds before speaking to his guards.

"Take this...alien to the holding cell. We will speak shortly."

He then waited, saying nothing until the airlock seals were closed and the place only occupied by Alliance personnel.

"I...we have a big problem. You've heard about the comet that is passing this moon?"

All four of the marines nodded in unison.

"It looks like our Biomech friends have been hiding either on it or inside its cloud of debris. Several hours ago, a formation of over a hundred ships broke free, and they are heading this way."

"What?" Lieutenant Elvidge asked before the others could speak.

He walked over to the tactical display and made to touch one of the buttons before stopping and looking at the Colonel.

"May I?"

Gun nodded and then looked to Jack.

"Admiral Lewis just sent out a flash communication to all Alliance units in the Eos Sector. It's not good news either."

Of course, it isn't! Jack thought impatiently.

"Well?" he asked, forgetting for a moment that he was speaking with the senior ground commander on the moon. Gun was far too preoccupied to waste any time on complaining or reprimanding him. Gun beckoned for them to come with him.

"They have already broken through the fleet. The battle is ongoing, but all we need to know is that there are more than fifty vessels and they are heading for us."

He moved to the table where the Lieutenant was busy looking at the shapes that represented combat units. Green and blue identified the many Helion and Alliance units over the moon. Gun pointed at the red markers along the top of the table.

"According to the Admiral, the first Biomech landers will enter orbit very soon."

He then moved the map slightly to show the areas controlled by the Alliance on the moon's surface. The airlock hissed open, and in walked a Major and a Captain; the niceties of saluting brief before the Major spoke.

"Colonel. All units are either dug in or have found areas

to relocate. We're ready for whatever is coming. I have your personal Hammerhead fuelled and ready to leave."

Gun did not look impressed.

"Leave? I don't think so, Major."

"But Colonel, it is standard…"

Gun lifted his hand to stop the discussion.

"That is enough. If this is to be our first standup fight with these things, then I will be here when it happens."

The Major looked as though he was about to speak again, but Gun's raised left eyebrow seemed to stop him. The man relaxed his shoulder a little and changed tack.

"I have already sent out alerts to all our bases. According to Intelligence, we can expect to lose communications at any moment, however."

Gun sighed.

"Yes, interesting how that always seems to happen just when they might be useful."

The younger Captain moved to the tactical display and indicated toward it with his hand.

"Sir?"

Gun nodded at the officer. He was in his late twenties and somewhat highly strung. Even so, the man was considered the best analyst in the unit. He changed the display to one of the moon's orbit.

"You can see here that half of these craft are on a direct heading for our Fort. The rest are going for our other bases in the south, as well as the major Helion compounds, cities, and industrial sites."

He looked back at the group who seemed unable to comprehend the enormity of what he was saying.

"They will be here soon."

Jack looked at his old friend and thought the concern about what was to come was obvious. He could also see the fire and excitement in his eyes. He doubted it was just the possibility of combat. Gun had a personal interest in a fight with the Biomechs, his tormentors and his creators.

The crazy bastard, he's looking forward to this.

"What do you want us to do?" asked the Major.

Gun then crashed his hands together, making them all jump.

"It is time, marines. Sound the alarm. I want them to feel pain before they even hit the ground."

More marines entered through the airlock. At the same time, the emergency sirens started up across the base. They started off as a low drone but quickly increased in volume until reaching a continually rising and falling tone.

"To your posts, marines. You have the plan; it is a simple one. We fight and defend our territories until relieved."

The dozen officers now in the command center moved to their posts where they could best manage the battle itself. Gun waited at the tactical display and watched, saying nothing for a moment. It showed every single unit down to individual fireteams. He could tap into any of them, access their details, and issue combat orders directly to their officers. He tapped his fingers on the metal frame and then looked to Lieutenant Elvidge and his unit. Jack knew it was coming now. He just didn't know what it would be. In some ways, he hoped they would have orders, but the idea of marching out into the open to die in the avalanche of Biomech gunfire was an ending Jack preferred to avoid.

"There is always a chance, even a tiny one, that these machines could do something out of the ordinary. Something so deadly that this base could fall."

Jack and the others looked positively offended at the suggestion. The Fort may be new, but the Alliance Engineers had worked wonders. Jack shook his head in surprise.

"Are you kidding? We have strong walls, towers, air defenses, and reinforced numbers and trench works throughout this base."

"Jack's not wrong," Lieutenant Elvidge continued.

"The base follows the standard practice of four defensible quarters with a compound in the center. They'll have to work through every layer of defense to succeed."

Jack nodded at this and walked to the schematic of the base on the wall.

"This is a standard template. That's why they built it so fast. It would take thousands of troops to even consider attacking this place. I doubt even three of four Marine battalions could do it on their own."

Jack continued speaking, but Gun lifted his hand to

stop them all.

"I know, and you are all correct…but as Colonel and commander of this sector, it comes down to me to prepare for any situation. I want all of you to stay close, just in case. If anything unexpected happens, I will need people I'm familiar with."

He looked at Jack in particular.

"What about your personal guard, Colonel?" asked Riku.

Gun smiled at this.

"Yes, I do have a unit of Jötnar and Vanguards waiting outside behind the defenses. Even so, Jack and I have been in a few scrapes before. I would like you to stay."

A red indicator flashed on the tactical display, and three of the monitors changed to show a view of the sky above them.

"Colonel, they are here."

They all looked at the screen, each wanted to see the shapes coming to the surface. It seemed like an age, but finally one dark shape came through, sheathed in flame and trailing smoke.

"Look at that thing. How big is it?" asked one officer.

Somebody answered, but Jack, Gun, and his comrades had already changed their look from the screen to the tactical display. The single red shape had multiplied it three, then five, and then after a few more seconds, hundreds flickered in a bright pattern over the map. Jack looked to his friend who gave him a contorted frown.

"Yes, I think the numbers might be on their side this time."

Jack shook his head and looked back at the video stream. The burning objects were now in their hundreds and heading for the surface at substantial speed.

When were they not?

Jack could now see the shapes of the craft and was surprised that they looked similar to a skate or stingray fish. They were quite flat and trailed by a long tail that gave them a smaller, more agile look compared to their larger brethren still in space.

How many warriors can they carry? Jack wondered with trepidation.

CHAPTER SEVEN

The return of Spartan to Sol was an event few considered a great importance. They would soon come to understand that the anger and wrath of this fearsome warrior was a sight to behold. His body was battered; many of his bones fractured or broken, his lower arm torn apart, and his mind savaged by the interrogation and torture of the Biomech machines. Was it surprising that when he was presented with a chance for vengeance, that he would take it, no matter the cost in lives on either side?

The Rise of Spartan

Spartan wiped his brow but said nothing. The man across the table looked almost as uncomfortable as he felt, not that Spartan would let the other man know this, even for an instant. He lifted himself to his feet and walked several meters away from Spartan and to a painting of a medieval city. It was an odd thing to have in such a room, and Spartan wondered if it were there to make the place seem less like a cell or interrogation room. He guessed he'd been there for about three hours now, and that was after he had been given a thorough medical examination and cleared before entry to the rest of the station. He'd been given access to several parts of it, but nothing that would allow him to come into contact with people or information. He sensed there was something serious going on, but they weren't giving up anything, not yet.

"Well?" asked the man once more.

Spartan looked at the man with the cool, harsh, and emotionless attitude he'd shown his torturers on the Biomech command ship. The room was more pleasant than expected, though as usual there were no windows and the walls were bare, other than for the four paintings showing different places on Earth.

"Spartan, as a former senior officer in the Marine Corps, I would expect a little common courtesy from a fellow Alliance operative."

This made Spartan smile slightly. He wore no bindings or shackles, yet he had not been given free access to this facility. He had been given a basic set of fatigues baring the symbol of the Earthsec. They were nothing fancy but were at least clean, and a refreshing change following his shower and haircut that had made him look almost human again.

"Is this the legendary hospitality we can all expect from the armpit of the Alliance?"

That seemed to offend the man far more than he expected. It was a cheap, hollow victory, but Spartan was getting angry.

"I've traveled to more worlds than you have hairs on your head, boy. I've killed machines and Biomechs by their hundreds, but even they had the decency to fight me up front, and with weapons raised."

He slammed his right fist onto the table.

"So why don't you tell me what the hell is going on here? Contact Admiral Anderson for verification of who I am. Or just contact my company. Actually, do anything but sit there like a sad bitch with nothing better to do!"

The man lowered his gaze and said something Spartan couldn't quite hear. It just made him even angrier.

"Are you in charge of this piss poor operation, or what?"

Spartan leaned back in his chair and laughed.

"No wonder we left Sol when we had the chance. This place always had the reputation as a backwater pit full of bureaucrats and dead worlds."

Again the man didn't respond so Spartan extended his battered left arm.

"What about this?" he growled.

The man looked surprised, but Spartan wasn't sure which particular bit had shocked him the most. He looked over his shoulder at one of the walls before turning back to Spartan. He may have been trying to be discreet, but Spartan knew a two-way mirror when he saw one.

There must be officials out there.

"We have sent requests to Terra Nova. Luckily, due to your long military service, you have your biological details on file. I suspect the engineering teams will be able to fabricate you something...eventually."

"Hmm," murmured Spartan in irritation.

"We will know more when we can restore access to the Spacebridge back to Prime."

Spartan remembered to his family, especially Teresa whom he hadn't seen for so long now. He thought of her face, and her long black hair before his thoughts rushed back to the present situation.

"Perhaps we can approach this from a different direction," asked the man.

Spartan nodded slowly, a half smile showing on his lip. "Yeah, you do that."

He had questions, but he'd be damned if he was going to give up whatever this obnoxious man wanted without getting something in return. Clearly he wanted information, yet there were no signs of drugs or inducement, so it couldn't be too serious. At least he hoped that were true. He was becoming a little bored with the torture routine.

"Let's take it in turns. I ask a question, you ask a question?" he suggested.

The man seemed positively enthralled at the idea and moved back to his chair and sat down.

"Very well, ask me."

Spartan knew he had him, though he took little pleasure in it.

"Where am I?"

"You are in the Alliance Holding Center, on board the primary transit station."

"For Earth?"

The man nodded in agreement.

"My turn," he started, "How did you and Khan get here?"

We escaped from a Biomech ship, stole a Confederate bomber from before the War, and then came through a temporary Rift…to here."

He gave the man the slyest of smiles that must have annoyed him terribly. The man seemed completely unfazed however.

"Why am I being held here?"

The man slid over his odd-looking datapad. The model had long been replaced by the secpad in most Alliance departments, and he could only assume that out here, on the outer edges of the Alliance, things were a little slower.

"What do you know about the Doomsday Comet?"

Spartan looked at the image and laughed.

"Is this the one the Helion prophecy is about?"

The man nodded.

"I know what everybody else does. It's some bullcrap story about the return of the Biomechs."

"Perhaps," said the man, "Even so, this comet appeared unexpectedly and arrived in Helios, and has already resulted in casualties."

He raised an eyebrow and tilted his head forward to gaze more closely at Spartan.

"Ever since it was spotted, a number of unusual events have occurred, including your arrival, as well as the wreckage that followed you."

Spartan rubbed his chin as he listened.

"First the Rift here opened, then you arrived. Shortly after that, reports of individual unidentified ships were flagged across the Alliance."

He smiled in a way that Spartan knew to be far from pleasant.

"Now, we may be the backwater of the Alliance, what do you expect after being abandoned by you Centauri centuries ago? Even so, we survived and run things out here as we want. This might technically be Alliance territory, but you will find no military units here. Sol maintains its own forces and command structure. So show a little respect, please."

Spartan sensed there was more, but the man was holding back. He stared at him and spotted the shifting of his eyes. It was as though the man was trying to look important, perhaps even just delaying him while something else happened.

He's afraid, of what, me?

"You think I am behind this?"

He lifted his left stump.

"A man with one arm and a broken body?"

He may be battered and broken in many ways, but he was still more muscular and better built than most. His broad chest was strong, and his arm and leg muscles bulged with potential. Even though the Biomechs had held him and Khan for a long time, neither had given up on their physical strength or fitness; on the off chance that one day they might be able to fight back. The man said nothing and asked another question.

"How were you captured by the Biomechs?"

Spartan's blood started to rush, and he immediately recognized the old rage rising in him. He wanted to grab the man, bash his head down onto the table, and wring the information out of him. He had to restrain himself. He closed his eyes and breathed in, reminding himself that this was human air, not the filth he'd been forced to endure on that ship.

"I was on an Alliance sanctioned operation with my company, APS Corp. We'd boarded a T'Kari Raider when a Rift opened up. The ship escaped with us on board. It gets complicated after that."

He rubbed his cheek with his left hand before remembering once more that it wasn't there. He cursed the missing part of his limb, and then the machines that had done the work. Looking back at the man, he wondered quite what they expected to get from him.

"Alliance sanctioned mission on board an alien vessel? We have heard of these T'Kari back here, but none have been seen. Why exactly were you involved with these non-humans?"

Spartan was getting the distinct impression from the man that this entire sector was riddled with racist, possibly xenophobic citizens with an interest in maintaining their own particular brand of society.

"My company was conducting a special ops mission with the support of the T'Kari. I assume you understand they are our friends, allies even?"

The man grinned.

"A lot has changed since you left us, Spartan. The T'Kari are part of this happy Alliance now, just like us. That doesn't make them the same as me, or perhaps even you."

He paused and considered his next question.

"Well, that doesn't quite answer my question though, does it? I want to understand how it was that you vanished from human controlled space and then returned, many months later with Biomechs in tow and entered our space through an unchartered Spacebridge. A bridge, I might add, that conveniently closed up after your arrival."

Spartan went to scratch his left hand as happened so

often. The fact he couldn't scratch was sometimes more annoying than having lost the hand to start with. Finally, he stood up and glared at the man.

"How long is this crap going to take? I have things to do, and that includes contacting my wife and family."

The man stayed in his seat and beckoned for Spartan to return to his previous position.

"Please? This won't take much longer, and then you will be free to go."

I doubt that very much, but if there's a way to speed this up, I'll take it.

He sat down slowly, never taking his eyes from the man's face.

"The rest is messy, but the important bit is that eventually we were taken by the machines, and they did this, among other things."

He raised his shattered arm.

"That's when you were tortured and questioned?"

Spartan nodded.

"Of course."

He said no more; the memories of his imprisonment were as fresh as the first time the machines had questioned him. As he sat there, he recalled the cell where he and Khan plus the other silent prisoners were kept. He also remembered the machine that had removed his arm, and it filled him with rage.

"And how are you now? Are you managing without it?"

"Yes," he said through clenched teeth.

"My family, where are they?"

The man tapped the datapad, and it changed to show the faces of Teresa and Jack. Spartan lifted the device closer with his right hand. There was little that could soften him, but the sight of his two closest family members could do just that. Both of the images showed them in uniform, and it took a moment before he noticed the insignia on Teresa's tunic.

"Uh, are you sure about this? Teresa hasn't worked in the Corps for some time. Neither have I."

The man was about to speak when a knock came from outside. He stood up and walked to the door. It opened and in came two men in suits. One looked at Spartan while the other spoke in hushed tones to his interrogator. Finally, they left and the man returned to his seat.

"Everything okay?" he asked.

The man looked a little flushed but moved back to the previous line of enquiry.

"Your wife, Ms Teresa Morato was reassigned during our last recruitment drive. As you know, all military personnel, whether retired or discharged are eligible for duty.

"She joined up, why?"

"Your company, APS has gone. It was broken up, along with most of the PMC sector just after your disappearance. Your wife and son have, well, they have seen considerable action. Major Morato is now second-in-command of the 17th Marine Battalion, under the command of Colonel Gun, a friend of yours, I believe."

A hundred thoughts raced about in his head. His wife had reached a level he never had, and his old friend now commanded what must be over a thousand marines. He had so many things to ask, but before he could open his mouth, the man returned to his own line of questioning.

"You came back with a group of T'Kari, as well as this Khan. How do they fit in with your narrative? With contact to Terra Nova and Prime lost, we are temporarily unable to verify any of your claims or the identity of the…non-humans you returned with."

Those last words shook him, more so when he realized that this man was referring just as much to Khan as he was to the group of T'Kari. With all that had gone on, he hadn't given the loss of contact any great thought.

"Wait, you have lost contact? Did you manage to reach my wife?"

The man nodded.

"Of course, we sent a full report to High Command within an hour of your vessel's capture. Once the technical issues with the Rift have been dealt with, you will be able to speak with her."

Spartan wanted to know more about both his wife and Jack, but the news of the Rift sat heavy with him.

"Tell me about the Rift, what happened?"

The man looked confused.

"I don't understand. We lost communications access to the Mars transfer station that controls the Rift. An engineering team will be there within the hour to re-establish contact, why?"

Spartan stood up and shook his head angrily.

"Because if you fools understood anything, you would know that all transfer stations have triple layer communications protocols with override protection. The only way to lose contact with the station itself is because they do not want to answer."

"Or?"

Spartan was already at the door when he turned back to the man.

"Or they are unwilling to answer. You already said that this prophecy is about the end of the world, or whatever it is, has been identified with this comet. What if isolating the Rifts is the first phase?"

The man looked even more confused, not that it seemed possible.

"First phase of what?"

"An attack, by the Biomechs, of course."

Spartan ripped open the door, and one of the men in a black suit stumbled in where he had been leaning on the panel.

"Stop him!" called out the man from inside the room.

The second man in his charcoal grey suit reached for

Spartan, only to find himself face down on the ground with Spartan's knee placed in the middle of his back. A loud emergency klaxon started to wail; yet none of the three could have triggered it. Spartan released the pressure and stood up straight. The two men approached at wary distance but waited for their comrade inside to emerge and stand next to Spartan.

"I didn't trigger the alert. Something is happening."

Spartan laughed at them all.

"You are fools, all of you."

The corridor running from outside the room was wide and lit from a double pair of strip lights that ran the full length of the shaft. The floor ran up at a very slight incline. It was an easy giveaway that the station used the primitive system of artificial gravity based on rotating sections. The klaxon finally stopped, to be replaced by the drone of one of the station's officials.

"Alert…alert, we have intruders aboard. All personnel are to move to secure quarters until this facility is returned to Alliance control."

"How do we look outside?" Spartan asked.

The three men said nothing at first, but when Spartan moved closer, the shortest one spoke up.

"At the end of the passageway is the recreation area. There is an observation deck off to one side providing views of Earth."

"And Khan? Where is he?"

The man that had been questioning him in the room shook his head.

"No, he and the others non-humans are being held securely…it is for their own…"

He didn't see the punch coming, and it connected harder than even Spartan expected. The man's nose seemed to explode in a flash of blood, and then he was on his back on the ground. Spartan turned to face the other two men but neither came at him, both seemed especially concerned to avoid him as he waited in an odd looking fighting stance. Most people would adopt a classic boxing position, but not him. Instead, his arms were low down, and his body weight shifted onto his back leg.

"I won't ask you again!" he said.

The men looked at each other and then pointed at the third door down on the left. Spartan moved off immediately while the two men helped their bloody friend to his feet. Spartan was at the door in seconds and slammed the palm of his hand on the release button. The door hissed open, and he moved inside. It was exactly the same as the room he'd been in, except that Khan lay prone on a bed; his limbs bound firmly to its surface. A man sat in the corner looking at a datapad. Spartan's rage continued to rise, and he stormed toward Khan who spotted his friend from his half open left eye.

"Spartan! What's happening?"

The klaxon had lowered in volume but continued

bleating in the background. The seated man was now on his feet and had whipped out a stun baton from a thigh holster. It seemed to amuse Khan greatly, and a low-pitched chortle came from his mouth.

"That's a big mistake, my friend."

He swung for Spartan in a way that suggested he expected no attempt to struggle from his haggard new arrival. Spartan avoided the attack without even moving his feet, and just a beautifully orchestrated tilt of his body. As the man overbalanced, Spartan brought his stump of a left arm down on the square of the man's back. He went down hard to the ground, in time for the men in suits to enter.

"Spartan, stop this madness," said the one with the bloodied nose.

Spartan had the restraints off Khan in seconds before he gave them even a glance. When he did, the fire in his eyes surprised even Khan. He pointed at his friend.

"Khan is a hero of the Alliance, one of the many Jötnar that has bled for us in war and combat. Now you treat him like a common animal, like some kind of…"

"Biomech," said the injured man.

Spartan took a step closer, but Khan grabbed his arm. Spartan looked up at him and lowered his head slightly. Khan then moved to the man and turned his head slightly, looking at the man's face intently with a bloodshot left eye.

"What are your defenses and who is attacking this

station?"

The man seemed surprised at the question.

"Answer me, you fool!" he roared.

The man was unable to respond, either from fear or from an inability to absorb what was happening, both in the room, and on the rest of the station. Khan looked to Spartan and snorted in derision at the men.

"Are these the Earthmen you told me about?"

Spartan bared his teeth with amusement.

"Yeah, something like that."

Khan went for the door, and this time none of the officials tried to stop them. Spartan followed, and the three men maintained a safe distance behind them. The klaxon continued as before, much to Spartan's annoyance.

"I think we know something is going on. Can't you turn that thing off?"

The nearest of the three shook his head.

"Figures," Khan muttered.

They continued along the passageway until reaching the recreation deck. It was surprisingly large and expanded out into a large domed area that included the normal gravity section plus a semi-dome low gravity area. Spartan was actually quite impressed by what he saw, and for the smallest moment wondered what it might be like to train there. The sight of a dozen civilians running toward him brought him back to reality. Three women and a child moved to his right, and he grabbed the taller of the two women.

"What's happening?"

She struggled, and when Spartan tried to reassure her, she spotted the stump and screamed. Khan put his hand to his forehead in frustration and then blocked her path.

"We're with the Alliance, here to help. Now answer the man, what is happening?"

She looked up at the monstrous shape of Khan and looked a little faint.

"Well?"

"The dock is under attack by something from the alien ship."

She then pushed past them and led her group back into the passageway. Spartan turned on the spot and pointed to the man with the bloodied nose.

"What is this alien ship?"

The man nodded bitterly.

"Yes, the ship you arrived in, the T'Kari vessel. What did you bring with you?"

Khan stepped between them and glared at the man.

"You brought us here, little man. If you had half a brain of common sense, you would have put the craft in quarantine away from inhabited vessels."

"He's right," Spartan added, his hand resting on his friend's forearm.

"You had no problem doing that with us. What about the T'Kari that were with us?"

The taller of the men in suits took a half step to Khan and then thought better of it.

"They are still on the ship. We've been using it as a temporary shelter until their story could be verified. They claim to have been prisoners of the machines."

Spartan was immediately suspicious of this, especially the simple fact of this apparent conversation when he knew too well that the T'Kari on the ship had not met humans before, let alone learned English or any other human language.

"Where is the ship?" he asked suspiciously.

The first of the men looked to his companion, but Spartan cut him off.

"I didn't ask him. I asked you!"

He pointed with his right hand accusingly.

"I...uh...we put the ship out on the largest docking arm. You can see it through the observation window over there."

He pointed off to the right, but they were interrupted by what sounded like an explosion. The lights in the recreation area flickered but stayed on, much to Spartan and Khan's surprise. Then came a graunching sound, and the ground shook and shuddered. A handful of people that had been lurking in the shadows cried out and ran past as fast as they could manage. More people came out from the recreation room, and two of them dragged a wounded man between then. Spartan moved closer and beckoned for them to head in the direction the others were taking.

"What happened to him?"

The two men in engineers' overalls looked at him nervously.

"There's a machine or something down there tearing the place up. You should get out of here."

That was when he spotted Khan and stopped to gaze at the beast.

"You...you're a Jötnar. You came here, to Earth?"

Khan looked at him for a moment and then bared his teeth in amusement.

"Yeah?"

The man stepped forward and slammed his hand into Khan's paw.

"My family were on Euryale, trapped underground and held by Echidna. Now you are here to help us again!"

Khan's attention was elsewhere, and only the man's adamant pulling on his arm could turn his head to face him. Finally Khan relented and almost snapped before the man continued to speak.

"Your Jötnar broke in on Euryale when nobody else would. How can I help you?"

This part did interest him. Neither Khan nor Spartan knew a thing about the station they were on, but this man wore the overalls and insignia of a member of Earthsec; the composite commercial and state body that had evolved to manage the decay of the old worlds of Sol. If anybody knew this station, it would be a man like him.

"Do you have weapons here?"

The man shook his head.

"No way, man. This is a transit station, not a military outpost."

"What about security, police? You must have something here?" asked Spartan.

The man paused briefly as he looked at Khan.

"There is a customs center, but it's on the other ring, too far away."

He looked at Spartan as if he was having trouble placing him.

"Wait, did you say you are Spartan?"

Khan chortled at his question. Spartan appeared less than amused.

"Yeah, why?"

The man called to a team of engineers that were running past. He spoke with them in rushed tones, but Spartan and Khan were beginning to lose their patience.

"We need weapons; do you have a workshop or tool room near?"

More screaming came from the other side of the recreation area. Dozens of people, including engineers, customs officials, and more random citizens streamed through the structure.

"They must be coming from the docking arm," Spartan

said, rushing over to the right. The others followed more slowly, each looking about nervously for signs of the terrible enemy machines. He finally reached the ramp that led up to the vast window with its thick metal panes.

"Look," he said.

He stood there completely motionless, with his hand pointing out from the observation deck. It was a raised area the size of a small room and outfitted with reinforced glass on one side, much like a goldfish bowl. The view was completely static, rather than the rotation Spartan expected. He tapped it, and Khan grabbed his hand.

"Glass, you fool, want to see us in the void without suits?"

Spartan laughed.

"Khan, you're the fool. That isn't glass. Look at the ship."

The two of them, plus the small group of engineers and the three black suited men watched the shape of the captured T'Kari warship. It was definitely the heavily damaged vessel they had escape in from the Biomech facility. Spartan almost felt a pang for the place that had been their home for such a short time. It was Spartan that spotted the shapes first.

"Look, on the underside."

Khan tilted his head as he watched the shapes moving along the hull.

"No…how the hell?"

He looked back at Spartan, shaking his head angrily.

"Biomech war machines. What are they doing here?"

Spartan grimaced.

"Yeah, looks like combat drones, the same as those on Hyperion. They must have come on the T'Kari ship."

He looked back to the suited official with the bloodied nose.

"You didn't scan the exterior before bringing it here?"

The man said nothing, and Spartan could do little to hide his anger. Looking back at the window, it was clear a large number of the machines were making their way from the ship. He counted them one by one before rubbing his forehead with his right arm.

"Okay, I count over twenty of them, plus however many got here in the last few minutes."

"More than twenty? Just one can take on a marine squad," Khan said incredulously.

"Yeah, in that case we need to get busy," Spartan replied, "Against green citizens and local security units, these machines will tear them apart. I reckon one of them could take this place."

He wiped his brow, considering his best approach to the problem.

"They'll secure the docks first, then move to take the station."

"And then?" asked the senior man in the black suit.

"They are Biomech machines; they'll do what they

always do. Entrench, expand, and then exterminate. They have to be stopped and fast!"

Spartan grabbed the engineer by the shoulder.

"We need to break contact with the docking arm. Can you do that?"

The man thought for a second before answering. At the same time the grinding sound of metal on metal sent screams through the station. The telltale thuds far away were the only indication that compartments had been breached and exposed to the vacuum of space.

"Yes, but not from here. It has to be done manually from the control station."

Spartan sighed deeply, resigned to what was coming.

Am I surprised? Like it would be easy.

"And where is that?"

The man pointed in the direction of the sound where the screaming was coming from. Khan laughed, the roar surprisingly all but Spartan, who moved back to the three men in suits. They seemed to be equally stunned about the situation.

"This station is screwed. Get everybody away from this deck and to the habitation deck. It's right above us, right?"

The closest man nodded quickly, now finally taking the situation as seriously as Spartan and Khan were.

"Yes, the next level up is habitation and retail."

Khan laughed loudly at the mention of shopping. It was one of those areas that had always amused him. Right now, in this awful scenario, the idea of people buying goods appealed to him in a twisted way.

"Good," he said, pulling the man close to him. "You need to get the order out to everybody on this station to clear this level. Seal every door, passage, and shaft in the next ninety seconds. Understood?"

The man nodded, but Spartan doubted the man truly understood his plan. He had seen these machines in battle before. They didn't cover ground particularly fast, but they were resilient, scheming, and even worse; they were deadly in a fight.

"What will you do?" he asked nervously.

Spartan glanced to Khan who simply nodded back to him. The two must have been in so many scrapes since their escape from the Biomech ship that even something like this was insignificant. A man shouted, and the glint of flashing steel beckoned off in the distance. Everybody in sight was moving away from it as quickly as they could manage. Only Spartan moved toward the sight with just the engineer and Khan following. He made it halfway before looking back over his shoulder.

"Whatever we can!"

Khan grabbed a fallen metal chair in one hand and smashed his fist into the frame to leave several fractured pieces of metal. It was barely a club but better than nothing. He lifted it to his shoulder and called back to them as well.

"Just do you job. Get these people out of here!"

The men in suits were still standing in the same place as the three vanished into the blackness and toward the screams. The shortest looked to the one still holding his bloodied nose.

"Well, what now?"

The man spat blood onto the ground. As the spittle hit the metal floor, the station shook again. He struggled to stay upright while the station settled.

"We do what the savage suggested...for now."

CHAPTER EIGHT

Ganymede and Titan were amongst the few remaining prosperous colonies in Sol. Though many still lived on the Earth and Martian colonies, they were the minority. The largest populations were those of Earth's single moon and on the moons of Saturn and Mars. The moons had avoided the decay of the planets and maintained a more powerful role in relation to trade and space travel. The construction of the Rift station in close orbit of Ganymede would see its fortunes rise as well, as its significance in the unfolding drama that had begun in Helios with the Prophecy of Fire.

The Lost World

The hull shuddered as ANS Conqueror took a final round of fire from the Biomech fleet. Even though they were hundreds of thousands of kilometers away, the energy from the Biomanta warships could strike the Alliance vessels in less than two seconds. Only the Conqueror Battlecruisers were equipped with after particle beam emitters, and every ten seconds they returned fire, doing equal harm to the opposing force. A young lieutenant struck his head on one of the bulkheads as yet another impact tore a chunk of plating from the rear port side of the ship.

"Almost there, Admiral," said the helmsman calmly.

Admiral Lewis did his best to hide the distress on his face as he watched the mainscreen. Although the fleet was accelerating away from the scene of the carnage, the multiple external cameras still showed the crippled ships they had abandoned. They had moved into a new lower orbit, placing them almost on the opposite side of the moon and out of direct line of sight with the Biomech fleet. It was a temporary respite, and if the Biomechs gave chase or split up, they would be exposed once more. The fleet was now returning to its original orbit distance from Eos, so as to not end up looping around to face the enemy fleet. Captain Marcus could see his friend and superior officer was hurting badly, but there was little he could do or say in comfort. He instead returned to the tactical assessment of the enemy ships.

"Our status?" asked the Admiral, almost dreading to check.

The XO had been in the middle of a discussion with Lieutenant Vitelli. He looked to the Admiral and pointed at the tactical display where it showed the green outlines of fourteen ships.

"Admiral, all surviving ships are still operational. We have damage and casualties on all vessels, as well as significant fighter losses. The last volley damaged the aft emitter array as well as venting four more compartments."

He paused for nearly two seconds before adding.

"Firing time and accuracy has been affected throughout the ship. Damage to power systems, infrastructure, and substantial crew losses are hurting us badly, Admiral."

"And them?" he said, pointing at the main screen.

Both looked to the scattered wreckage of the sixteen ships that had been lost between the two fleets so far.

"Our scans show no survivors, Admiral."

He could feel a sickness welling up inside his body at this news. The feelings of betrayal burned through his chest, and he found it hard to look at the screen. The battle had been shorter than he'd expected. Instead of the careful maneuvering and skirmishing, they had simply smashed through his lines and ignored the damage he'd inflicted. He closed his eyes for a second before the XO continued speaking.

"The Biomech fighters are finishing off what the Biomantas started. It is a slaughter out there."

Every part of him wanted to slow the fleet and turn it around, but with a third of his forces gone, he knew it was suicidal. He had just fourteen ships remaining while the enemy still had seventeen of their deadly vessels in action. The near destruction of a single ship had been a great blow to him, but this was something else.

What will force them back? They must have suffered as greatly as we did?

"What about damage? The reports from the fighter wings must be in by now. How did they do?"

Lieutenant Vitelli moved his hands in front of the tactical display to bring up a series of schematics that showed both the ships of the Alliance fleet as well as those in the enemy fleet. Columns of data ran underneath each one showing size, mass, specification, and damage.

"All but one of their ships sustained damage, and according to the reports from Captain Evans, they were able to destroy at least three of the emitters on the remaining ships."

Interesting, thought Admiral Lewis. *Is that enough?*

"What is your assessment, Lieutenant?"

The man rubbed the back of his hand on his chin twice before answering.

"If these reports are accurate, then they will have a fleet of roughly comparable size to our own and with similar capabilities. Even their fighter numbers are not so far off ours."

Admiral Lewis didn't like what he had to say, but it was as expected.

"So if we return to battle, we can expect what?"

He knew the answer but asked anyway.

"Well, our newer ships are undoubtedly able to match them, ship to ship. The older Crusader class is having trouble causing enough damage before being hit by their weapons. We have found no command ships of any kind though. The fleet operates like a single living organism that reacts and improvises instantly."

Admiral Lewis shrugged.

"That is something for us to consider for the future. All we can do right now is engage them with whatever weapons we have at our disposal. Why are they taking so long to destroy? Every time we damage them, they should lose a degree of effectiveness, just as we do."

He gazed at the previous images of the enemy ships. The shapes were almost beautiful to look at. The metal hulls were sleek, and the wide wings gave the impression they could glide through space like fish in the deep ocean. The human ships of the Alliance were the exact opposite. Their outer hulls had more in common with the brick shapes of twentieth century warships, with their thick armored belts, layered sections, and complex superstructures. The different in quality and technology was becoming more apparent, at least to him. He pointed at the Biomanta.

"Do you know why this isn't happening?"

Vitelli rested his chin in his hand and nodded.

"I have an idea, and it's our scans of their armor that

concerns me the most."

"How so?"

Lieutenant Vitelli tapped the nearest Biomanta, and it enlarged to fill half of the tactical display. The name was certainly apt, as it looked surprisingly similar to the ancient Earth fish. He pointed at the central structure.

"We are not detecting any form of individual life reading in this structure."

Admiral Lewis looked confused for a moment.

"I don't understand. You said our sensors detected life aboard them?"

Vitelli nodded furiously.

"Yes, but that was not entirely accurate. If you look at the data, it is clear these ships are nothing like we've seen before. I very much doubt they are conventional ships with AI Cores controlling them. It is something else."

He paused as if expecting the others to need a moment.

"These ships, they are partially or entirely organic. The living tissue is built directly into the spacecraft itself, with mechanical components fused over the surface."

Admiral Lewis lifted both of his hands in protest.

"Wait...no, wait a minute. You're saying these ships are alive?"

"Yes, Admiral."

The rest of the officers continued moving about their business, but Admiral Lewis stood in silence as he digested the information.

"Very well, let's assume these ships are biological. How does this help or hinder us?"

The tactical officer did his best to hide the look of pleasure on his face.

"Well, if their ships are biological, then their strengths and weaknesses are based on this."

"Well?"

He spun the model of the Biomanta about.

"These ships have hollow sections in their wings. We suspect these are for launching fighters and possibly for the storage of ground forces. The central section looks primarily mechanical, with biological elements like a spine running through the center."

"I still don't see how this helps us."

Admiral Lewis looked to his XO, but Captain Marcus seemed equally uncertain.

"Admiral, they have two potential weakness. The first is against weapons designed to kill or confuse biological matter. The second is they have no biological crew."

"Neutron missiles," said the XO under his breath, "they've been abandoned since before the Great War. Would they even work? Our ships have been fully shielded against all levels of harmful radiation. The reinforced and shielded interior bulkheads of our ships stop them from penetrating even a few sections."

None of them seemed to understand quite what the tactical officer was getting at, all of them except General

Daniels who had been listening intently. He nodded in agreement as Lieutenant Vitelli continued.

"If we can get neutron weapons aboard, we could detonate them inside their shielding and damage or kill the biological components of their ships."

Admiral Lewis finally smiled at this news.

"Wait, are you saying we could make use of our Enhanced Radiation ground strike missiles? What if they use layered armor, like on our ships?"

"It's true," the XO answered. "The reason we don't bother using them in combat anymore is because of the layered armor and shielded compartments. Even multiple impacts can only kill off parts of the crew in small areas. It's usually better to make use of micro-atomic warheads to vaporize sections."

Admiral Lewis had already thought on it, and his creative solution surprised even him.

"So, if we can open up hole in the hull of these Biomanta ships and insert neutron weapons, you think they could cause more damage than conventional weapons?"

The tactical officer smiled as he nodded.

"Exactly, Admiral, but it won't be easy. After the second fighter attack, they pulled back their fighters to defend against missile and torpedo strikes."

He brought up the battle schematic that showed the fighter attacks. Just as he'd explained, the follow-up waves had experienced substantial fighter defenses before finally falling back to the fleet. He pointed back at the center section of the warship.

"According to my data, however, their behavior and ability to repair damage, suggests a mixture of mechanical and biological to a level we have never seen. By severing the link between the component parts, we could weaken or possibly destroy them."

Captain Marcus pointed at the main display that showed the ever-shrinking site of the previous battle.

"Admiral, are you planning on returning to the fray?"

He shook his head.

"No, not unless we have to. Even so, we have marines down on the surface, and they may need our help. We're safe for now, providing nothing in their fleet changes."

General Daniels seemed to appreciate this comment as he waited there patiently. The mention of the fleet being safe allowed him to focus on the efforts of his marines on the surface, as opposed to those still in the fleet aboard the capital ships.

"General? What about your people, is there any news?"

He shook his head and stepped closer to the tactical display. With a brief hand gesture, he changed it to show the moon rather than the ships. The tactical officer almost protested, but the Admiral moved his head, indicating him to move out of the General's way.

"The first wave of spacecraft are already on their way down. We expect them to make landfall in the next ten minutes."

"I see," said Admiral Lewis.

He looked to the other officers waiting around them, including the small cadre of senior officers from the marines, as well as those responsible for the management of his Battlecruiser.

"We may have failed in the space battle to keep the Biomechs away from Eos, but the fight is far from over. In a matter of minutes, they will land on the surface of this very moon, and for the first time will face the wrath of the Alliance Marine Corps."

General Daniels smiled at these words, but it was a grim smile, not one that seemed to share the Admiral's optimism. Instead, he looked back at the display and at the three bases on the moon. Around them were the blue and green lines that indicated interception vectors for drones and fighters. Intermixed with them were scores, perhaps hundreds of ships, and they were all heading toward the ground at great speed. A number of red icons flashed about the display to mark the opening shot of the battle as Alliance fighters swarmed about the landers. He looked to the Admiral with a nervous but determined look to his face.

"Admiral, the Battle for Eos has begun."

* * *

"They are through the fighters, impact in thirty seconds!" shouted out one of the many officers in the command post.

Gun waited in front of the large tactical display table and watched as scores of shapes moved in around their position. The majority fell in a wide pattern while a small number came down directly on the base itself. Gun tapped a button on the unit.

"This is Gun. The enemy is upon us. Stand your ground. There is nowhere to hide on this rock. Fight well...and die well!"

Jack looked at him whimsically as he said the last words. They were typically excessive, and he wondered quite how many of the Alliance personnel would appreciate his attitude toward the coming fight.

"Listen to your unit commanders...and good hunting!"

He removed his finger and tapped the button on his JAS unit to seal the visor around his helmet before looking to the marines around him.

"My friends, this is going to get rough. Get ready!"

Jack and the others did the same and sealed their visors and then grabbed their weapons. Everybody inside the command center did the same. Even the computer operators who would have little to do in the actual ground combat once it got underway. The first impact knocked them all off their feet, but it was the second that collapsed the roof and left wall. Chunks of masonry dropped down and would have crushed Gun if it hadn't been for his toughened armor. Clouds of dust from the surface of the moon washed about them, scouring the paint and electronics of the command center in seconds.

"Take cover!" growled Gun in a low voice.

Already the dust was clearing to reveal the dark shape of one of the burning hot landers. It had crashed through the top of the building and then continued on another fifty meters before halting in the side on one of the many hangars. Five Vanguards moved into a loose skirmish line just outside the damaged structure, while a trio of black armored Jötnar smashed their way through the shattered wall to reach Gun. One nearly cast Jack aside to reach him, showing little interest in anybody else inside.

"Colonel, are you unhurt?" asked the first of them.

It was the first time Jack had seen this special Jötnar unit in their black colored armor. He was intrigued to see they bore the symbol of a burning sun on their chests, a symbol that was surprisingly similar to the insignia of the Helions.

Hyperion, he said to himself.

The nearest heard him and turned to look at his face. It took a brief moment before the warrior recognized his face, though it was impossible to see inside the thickened armor of the Jötnar.

"Jack...Jack Morato?" he said in an odd, slightly low-pitched voice.

A series of dull explosions shook the ground, stopping any further discussion. Gun stepped up to the ruined inner wall and looked out at the landers as a dozen managed to make it inside the Fort.

"This is it," he said calmly to himself.

The sky filled with hundreds of smoke trails as many more came down outside the base or were attacked by the Alliance fighter squadrons circling overhead. More landers crashed into the ground while the marines streamed out from their hardened barrack buildings and into their prepared positions around the base.

"Follow me!" growled Gun.

He stomped through the debris of the collapsed wall and moved to the unit of Vanguards while his personal guard unit followed right beside him in their black armor. All five Vanguards were blasting away with their armor mounted L48 rifles. Jack climbed past several large chunks of masonry and nearly halted at the sight in front of him. Thick columns of smoke rose from where the landers had crashed in the middle of the group of landing pads. One came in too steeply and vanished in a bright fireball, instantly destroying a second lander that had already made it to the surface. More came down and landed or crashed in the open ground opposite the hangars and barracks used by the marines. Jack could see them sliding and running as they rushed to their defenses.

This is insane.

Jack looked down at his carbine, checking once more that it was loaded and ready for combat. He sensed he would need it soon. Each of the craft appeared to be almost double the size of an Alliance Mauler, and all had embedded their forward structures directly into the ground. Middle sections of the nearest of the landers opened like the petals of a flower in just a few seconds. Jack couldn't see inside, but he had no problem identifying the shapes storming out from the craft itself. Sparks flashed about its metal frame as dozens of warriors leapt from the openings and down to the surface.

Biomechs!

He took aim at the nearest and pulled the trigger. The power of the triple charge burst through the chest armor of the closest of the creatures and dropped it to the ground. It looked similar but not identical to the images of the creatures back in the Uprising. This one move upright like a man, yet it seemed larger, at least two meters tall, thickly muscled, and protected by a metal skin of armor that appeared fused to the body. The heads were hidden inside dull iron helms that looked black in this particular light. They moved with an odd gait that marked them out as some butchered creation, a monster bred for death and war. They carried no weapons, save for the sickening blades built into their arms that extended out half a meter.

The small unit of marines took cover amongst the rubble near the Vanguards while the Jötnar grouped around Gun. As usual, the senior commander was at the front, and they almost had to hold him back to stop him rushing into the fray. Riku took careful aim and removed the head from another, yet dozens more came out.

There must be fifty or sixty in each of those things, Jack thought.

He did the math quickly in his head, and the numbers instantly sent a chill through his body.

Over seven hundred! And that's just the ones that made it inside the compound!

The enemy had fanned out now, with most heading for the hangars and parked fighters. A group of perhaps twenty moved toward Gun and the ruins of the command bunker. Out in the distance, legions more of the enemy surged into the Fort, fighting at close range with the defending marines and their Helion comrades.

"Put them in the ground!" Gun ordered.

The combined fire of the Jötnar, Marines, and Vanguards was impressive, and half of the Biomech creatures were cut to pieces before they could reach them. Even so, those still standing, crashed toward them with no care for their own lives. The Vanguards stood their ground, but Gun and his bodyguards lurched ahead and into the face of the enemy. Alliance metal clashed with Biomech blades in something that resembled a medieval battle. Though outnumbered two to one, the Jötnar were substantially stronger and heavier built. They crashed their armored bodies and scythe-like blades into the things. In seconds they had maimed or killed every single one of them. Gun finally turned around to look at the marines.

"That's one lot dealt with, now for the rest!"

He turned back and moved toward the hangars where scattered groups of marines held off the waves of creatures with careful volley fire. It took less than thirty seconds to cover the ground. Gun was at the rear of the Biomech horde before they even realized he was there. Then his bodyguards joined in, quickly followed by the Vanguards. Lieutenant Elvidge slid down next to a wrecked Lightning fighter and slammed in another clip. Jack, Callahan, and Riku stayed close beside him.

"Your friend, he's something else," he laughed.

Jack could only nod in agreement. They added their own fire to that of the other marines, but it was the great bulk of the Jötnar and Vanguards that stood out most. They looked like Titans, battling some kind of demonic horde around them. The marines were dug in around four hangars, each of which was protected by low meter-tall barricades. There was an under strength platoon protecting the site from their prepared positions. Most were lined up in front of the two central hangars while the others were grouped on the roofs of the structures where they had the perfect view of the battlefield. In front of them moved the rest from the lander that had attacked Jack's group, plus the warriors from another of the craft.

"Look!" said Riku.

She pointed off to their right where the petal door of another lander had opened. This time, instead of the living monsters, a trio of large metallic war machines climbed out. They were six limbed and the size of tanks. They scuttled like bugs and moved right into the battle, cutting down marine or Biomech if they blocked their paths.

"What the hell are those things?" asked Callahan.

"Large versions of the warriors they used on Hyperion. Aim for the center mass!" said Jack in a calm and reassuring voice.

The three marines took aim with their carbines while Riku pulled her L48 rifle into her shoulder. With each pull of the trigger, they sent precise shots at the nearest machine. The explosive rounds of the L48 blew chunks of its torso armor, but it was the high-power shots from the carbines that did the real damage.

"Riku, put explosive rounds on the smaller ones. We'll deal with the big one."

She turned a few degrees to the left and continued shooting. Her projectiles were substantially larger than those used by the carbines, and on this occasion used the inbuilt proximity sensor to explode them as they came close to the targets. Even with this weight of fire, the Biomech warriors were now at the low wall and fighting the marines in a deadly close range fight. Gun and his comrades cut their way into the flank of the force and toward the massive machines that were still further at the back of the horde.

"Come on, bring one down!" said Lieutenant Elvidge desperately.

Between them they put a dozen high power rounds into the thing's torso, achieving little more than annoying it. Two plowed onward with one heading for the hangars, another off to the right where it vanished behind plumes of smoke. The third stopped and looked at its tormentors and then trampled down half a dozen of its own side as it rushed toward Jack and his comrades.

"Great, I think it heard you!" he said bitterly.

Another squad of a dozen marines arrived and deployed around their position while a Ram moved right behind. It dropped down next to them, lowered itself to the ground, and deployed its turret mount system. A dozen more carbines added their fire to the small group led by Lieutenant Elvidge. Jack tracked to the right, looking for a weak spot on the machine. The center torso was the size of a Bulldog vehicle, but its limbs were much longer. Something extended from the side and short multiple barrels pushed out. One flashed and then another.

"Incoming!" cried out one of the corporals.

Jack was already in cover, but the newly arrived marines were not as well dug in. The withering barrage of gunfire that came in from the machine's sponsons hit two full on, and then it was on them.

"Fall back!" cried Jack, but most of the marines chose

to ignore him. He took three steps back and found Riku and Callahan doing the same. The machine halted three meters from where they had been hidden and struck at the ground with four articulated arms. The mass and power crushed anything it is path. In seconds, the marines had scattered. A dozen of the bipedal creatures rushed out through and chased after them, each hacking and stabbing at them as they came.

"LT!" cried Jack, spotting his officer being chased by two of them.

Jack lifted his carbine and fired a shot that missed by a narrow margin. Then they were on him and hacking away with the cruel blade. One struck the Lieutenant in the shoulder, and the second connected with the armored gorget section around his throat. He dropped to one knee, now just seconds from the end. Jack's heart pounded as he watched from the relative safety of a broken wall. Riku leaned against the rubble and took aim with her L48. The round exploded over a meter away from the Lieutenant and sent shards of hot metal into the two creatures as well as their officer. All three fell to the ground, and Jack had his chance.

Do it, do it now!

He burst from cover and ran directly into one of the creatures. He didn't hesitate though and pushed passed, leaving his life in the hands of Riku. It turned to give chase, only to receive an L48 round in the back of the head.

Jack slid down next to the wounded officer and grabbed him under the armpits. They made it two meters before Callahan arrived and helped him drag the wounded officer back to where Riku had made her stand. A dozen more of the creatures fell around them by the time they made it back. Callahan helped him rest the man on the ground, checking he was safe before lifting their own weapons back to their shoulders.

"What's happening?" asked the Lieutenant with a catch in his throat.

A handful of the marines from the squad that had arrived to help dropped down into cover around them and boosted their number to nine, but at least two showed signs of damage to their armor.

"The frontline at the bunkers has been overrun. The machine is moving through the base. The right has held, and the machine that hit us is on its way to the vehicle pool."

"Dammit, is there anything that can stop them?"

Riku looked off to her right and thumbed in the direction of the machine.

"I see the machine and about sixty of those things heading for the pool. Everybody else is moving to the outer walls. The rest of the Biomechs will be here soon. Look at your drone overview."

Jack already had and was doing his best to avoid looking at the red arrows marking the advance of the enemy.

According to the dozens of drones circling overhead, there were now over twenty of the massive machines, and most less than a kilometer away from the walls.

"Riku, look, it's Gun!" he explained upon seeing his friend.

She twisted to the right and spotted Gun, along with his retinue of bloodied Jötnar and Vanguards. They'd been joined by two platoons of marines and were formed up in ranks behind the storage tanks and machine parts of the vehicle pool. There must have been crew inside the waiting Bulldogs as well because four of them turned their turrets toward the advancing enemy and opened fire. The weight of fire was terrifying to behold. The large machine lost a leg and an arm in seconds; two-dozen of the creatures fell under the avalanche of gunfire.

"Jack!" Callahan shouted.

There seemed to be trouble in every direction, but the marine was now pointing off to their left. He moved his eyes and spotted the shape. There was a large group of the Biomech creatures creeping through the ruins of the barracks and moving in on the flank of Gun and his defenders.

"I see them."

He looked back at his commander who had now lifted himself up and leaned against the rubble with his carbine in his hands.

"Private Riku, you stay here with me. We'll watch your

backs. You need to take these marines and help Gun before he gets himself killed. I'll let him know you're coming."

He then beckoned to the other marines.

"Private Morato is your temporary sergeant. Now stop those things!"

Jack looked at Elvidge and then to Riku. She looked pained, presumably because she was being forced to stay behind. Jack could understand, but he did feel a lot happier at having her expert marksmanship watching them from a distance. He looked at the other six marines, including Callahan that he now commanded.

"Okay, they don't know we're here. Follow me, and keep your heads down!"

He moved off with Callahan right on his flank. The other five followed in a staggered line and with their carbines at their shoulders ready. Once out from the cover, they moved along the side of the collapsed barracks and toward the open ground near the vehicle pool. Their line of sight was partially obstructed, but already they could see the group of Biomech warriors moving in on Gun's position. Further in the distance, the vast shape of the metal war machine clambered on; its great arms smashing into parked vehicles and its weapon sponsons pouring fire into any marine that dared show his face. Jack's nerves were on edge, but the adrenalin pumping through his body gave him that feeling of recklessness, even immortality that he only felt in these situations.

"Fix bayonets," he said quietly.

Two had already done so, and it took only a moment for the rest to do the same. The blade on the end of the weapon only marginally increased their effectiveness as a weapon at close range, but Jack knew too well the psychological edge it gave a warrior when carrying such a device. He looked at them and was thankful it was so hard to see their expressions through their smoked visors. The last thing he needed to see was doubt or fear. He had enough of that himself. Jack turned back toward the enemy, took a single deep breath, and then cried out.

"Attack!"

He leapt from cover and ran as fast as he could to the rear of the group. The others charged alongside him, all with their carbines held low and the razor sharp blades extending outwards. None fired until they were on the back of the enemy unit. Jack stuck his blade between the shoulder blades of the nearest creature, and the others piled in behind him. Callahan opened fire first, and then all hell broke loose.

CHAPTER NINE

The Black Rift was an often-confused title for the region of space controlled by the Narau control facility. Apparently, the term was created by the Helions, as an insult to their Great Enemy during their banishment from the Council of the Great Powers. Only the massive starbase originally constructed by the Biomechs in the distant past could create and manage the Spacebridge to their homeworld. Now under control of the Narau, it could be shut down permanently or even worse, used to despoil the area of space around it so that no Rift could stabilize. It was the ultimate deterrent to the Biomechs ever attempting a return from their remote home.

Accounts of the Prophecy of Fire

The shuttle moved to its final docking phase at it approached the gleaming shape of ANS Dreadnought, the latest warship to move into position around the capital world of the Alliance. As one of the Conqueror Class Battlecruisers, her design was incredibly flexible, and it had been boasted by the Naval engineers that the universal design ships could be refitted in less than two months from a battleship to a carrier, or even as a dedicated marine transport. This particular model was new to Teresa though. Her mind was elsewhere, but she tried her best to show some degree of interest in her temporary home.

Another ship and more people I've never met before.

She tried to swallow, but her throat was dry, almost making her cough. Teresa noticed a few changes from the last ship of this type she'd seen, and for a moment was able to concentrate on it. Now it was becoming more obvious that Dreadnought had been fitted out differently to the popular carrier variants being built throughout the Alliance. She pulled out her secpad and selected the schematic for the ship. It listed the weapons and configuration, as well as the current commander and her command staff. Although structurally the same, she was one of only a few that had found her mission modules reduced in size to accommodate the large flank weapon modules. With a pair on each side of the ship, she would have forward facing railguns, as well as the standard fitment of particle beam emitters. Teresa looked up from the display and back out of the small window from the shuttle. The warship filled most of her view, but she could also see the twinkling light reflecting off scores, perhaps hundreds of other vessels.

So, the fleet is getting ready for war…again.

She gazed at the glinting shapes; none of them proved particularly reassuring. They might be ships, but she knew the disposition of the Alliance Navy well enough to know that almost every vessel out there was a civilian craft. Most would be large transports, haulers, and refinery ships while a smaller number would ferry people to the moons or to larger ships. Thoughts of ships brought her right back to her family and their scattering through the stars. Spartan was stuck in Sol somewhere, Jack fighting on Eos, and her other two children, Matius and Ingo had been split up to serve on different ships in the fleet.

What is normal with our family?

She tried to remember the last time they'd been together. The best she could manage was when she'd first arrived at the medical station on Terra Nova. Spartan had been gone for so long she'd forgotten he wasn't even there, and that sent shivers through her body. Teresa was still in shock at the news from Earth.

"Major, we have docked," said the young crewman nearby.

Teresa looked at him before realizing they had entered the aft hangar bay and already linked up to the docking clamp inside the landing bay. She looked out of the window. Instead of the blackness of space, there was the gray interior of another ship.

Ah, well, let's get this sorted.

She lifted herself from her seat and walked to the door. She was the only passenger, with the bulk of the space being used to transport fresh food and materials for the voyage. She moved out of the small doorway and ducked slightly to avoid striking her head on the bulkhead. She wore her Marine Corps uniform with the long coat that was cut in a similar fashion to that of the Navy. Her long black hair was technically well past the regulation length, but so far nobody had been brave enough to bring it up with her. She'd tied it back to keep it out of the way. Just a few more steps and her feet touched the reassuringly firm metal floor of the massive warship. A man's voice called out, and a group of officers stood smartly to attention. Teresa had been so busy looking about the expanse of the hangar she'd failed to realize they were waiting for her.

Great, the welcoming committee!

She stepped away from the shuttle and moved to the line of officers. A tall blonde woman smiled as she stopped in front of her.

"Major, it is good to see you. Welcome to ANS Dreadnought, the most powerful ship in the fleet. I am Captain Vetlaya Nikova, commander of this task force. I'm afraid I don't have much time for formalities. We leave orbit in thirty minutes."

"Captain," replied Teresa, "we are not staying here with the 2nd Heavy Strike Group?"

Captain Nikova smiled, but Teresa could see it was a front.

"No, the 2nd is fully formed and already en route to the Proxima Rift. They are establishing a blockade force on both sides to keep Terra Nova safe. We have to maintain the link between Proxima and here."

"I see."

"We have a different job, to operate as a reserve for forces assembling out on the border. We will be linking up with a small T'Kari contingent and reinforcing the Admiral Jarvis Naval Station. If trouble kicks off at Helios, we'll be just hours from the Rift."

"My transfer orders say I should be rejoining my unit upon their return from operations in Helios. In the meantime, I am to assist in the command of the 39th?"

"That is correct. The 39th is a temporary field unit made up of units we've been able to scrape together."

She looked a little embarrassed.

"I'm afraid I have duties to attend to, Major. We will be joining the 3^{rd,} and time is critical."

She paused and reached down to take out a small pouch. With no attempt at ceremony, she reached out to Teresa with the small object in her hand.

"I'm sorry about the lack of, well, you know. Due to your new command, you have been given a temporary promotion to Lieutenant Colonel."

She placed the pouch in the palm of her right hand.

"We're spread out thin, Colonel. I need your unit ready for combat and fast. Major Terson will bring you up to speed with regards to your posting."

That was it, and as Teresa stood still and looked at the small metal objects in the pouch, the ship's Captain walked away. With these niceties over, the Captain and her small cadre of Navy officers vanished from the hangar, leaving just Teresa, Major Terson, and three captains. Teresa watched her go with more than a little annoyance showing on her face.

"Don't blame her, Colonel. You see we are not technically a Strike Group. We shouldn't even be leaving this sector, not for at least six months. Instead, we're operating as a reserve for the 3rd, and Captain Nikova is not happy."

"Yes, I can see that. Things are a little more strained than I expected. Is it normally like that here?"

The younger Major smiled and nodded to her officers.

"No, we were all rushed here, along with most of the other marine units and ships for this. We are seriously under strength, just three complete companies made up of a bizarre assortment of platoons. These are our three company commanders."

Teresa looked up from her new insignia at the marines.

"I don't understand. My orders were that my transfer was a temporary one to the 39th. What's going on?"

Major Terson nodded in agreement.

"That was correct, maybe an hour ago. Since then, reports are coming in of major reversal in Helios. Reserve units are being called up, including half of this ad-hoc battalion. I hate to break it to you, Colonel, but your posting to the 39th will be for the duration."

"Duration?" she asked, still not entirely comprehending what the Major was saying.

"Have you not seen the news? The Alliance has announced formal declarations of war against the Biomech invasion of Helios."

Were we ever at peace with them?

"I see, and I am in command of this unit until this so-called war is over?"

Major Terson nodded once more.

"Yes, Sir."

Teresa sighed to herself but let none of her frustrations show. Although she wanted to be back with her unit, it was clear that rejoining marine units engaged in hostile action in Helios was now impossible. The journey to the fleet would take her multiple trips to the relevant Rifts, including travelling to Proxima, Prometheus, T'Karan and then the final Rift to Helios.

"Then you had better introduce me to your officers."

Major Terson twisted to her side and pointed to the small group of male officers. All three were older than her, with one showing pronounced gray hair and another was completely bald. She stopped at the gray haired man first.

"This is Captain Nathaniel Rivers. He has command of 1st Company."

Teresa looked at him carefully, trying to gauge the man's character with just a few careful observations. The name Rivers was rather uncommon, but it could easily have been a coincidence.

"Captain, are you related to the General?"

The man looked at her with a stone cold face, showing even less emotion than she would have expected from Spartan. He said nothing for a moment, and then something must have jarred as he spoke with a start.

"Sir, Yes, Sir. My father is the Chairman of the Joint Chiefs."

Teresa lifted her lip slightly at the mention of the man's position. She was still surprised he had taken the post, being such an old and uncompromising warhorse.

"The Corps is my family, Sir."

Teresa looked at him for a moment longer before speaking.

"Yes. I wonder how his leg is doing?"

It was a rhetorical question, but she enjoyed the look of surprise on his face at the mention of something so personal. Few knew of his leg trouble, certainly only those close to him.

"You know him?" he asked almost in a whisper.

"Know him? Captain, your father and I spilled blood

together on a hundred battlefields. Both our blood and the enemies."

The man had nothing further to say, so she moved on to the next one. Teresa knew exactly what he meant, and she wasn't impressed. She had seen it often enough with the children of well-to-do families. Their children either resented the power of their parents and rebelled early, or took advantage of their privileged position to coast through their chosen career. This Rivers looked like he was every inch the career soldier. She spotted the campaigns markings on his tunic; all showed he had spent some time in the Corps, yet none were what she would consider frontline work.

"Captain Thomas Thompson," said the Major.

Teresa walked on to the next of the group. This man was the tallest of the group, thin, bald, and with a narrow black mustache. His expression was a little softer than Captain Rivers, and she recognized a calm confidence in his face, something that reminded her of General Daniels. His uniform was no more decorated than his comrade, but she did spot the markings of the Jaeger, a relatively new mark of distinction for marines that had taken part in the great Jötnar hunts on Hyperion against the hordes of marauding Biomech creatures.

"You're a hunter?" she asked.

The marine looked surprised she recognized the small marking.

"Yes, Sir. My platoon took part in the annual hunt. It was…interesting, Colonel."

Teresa thought back to her time on Hyperion. Though she'd visited after the fighting with the Biomechs and their legions, she had never really warmed to the place.

"How did you find the climate?"

The man's torso relaxed a little as he answered.

"Warm, and the air is something else. You've visited Hyperion, Sir?"

Teresa nodded slowly.

"Quite. I fought with Gun and General Rivers back at the end of the Uprising."

The Captain raised an eyebrow at this.

"Colonel, you fought in the Battle of Hyperion? The last battle of the War…where the Biomechs tried to come through the Rift?"

Teresa nodded.

"Yes, I was there, along with my husband, Spartan."

The mention of the famed warrior sent a chill through the small group.

"Hyperion was the last stand-up fight we fought in. Trust me, you don't want a repeat of that event."

She then moved to the third and final of the group. The short and squat man looked unlike most of the marine officers she'd met. Even so, in Teresa's experience, she could be surprised by even the most unassuming of marines.

MICHAEL G. THOMAS

"Captain John Tycho, a Lieutenant recently returned to service after the casualties taken during our original foray into Helios territory."

Teresa took the man's salute and looked him over, starting with his head and moving down. She could see the scars that had been carefully sewn on his neck and face. It was his limbs that seemed the strangest though.

"Your injuries, you sustained them in a boarding action?"

"Yes, Sir, my platoon attempted to sabotage a Biomech cruiser. They rigged the entrances with improvised explosives and killed half my people."

"That's when you lost your legs?"

He shook his head.

"No, Sir, one of the Biomech creatures took them from me as we took the control room."

He pulled up his left sleeve to show a fully mechanical arm. It was well built and fitted inside a sleek ceramic-looking housing to emulate the shape of the arm. The fist was more mechanical looking and fully articulated. He moved the fingers in sequence and looked back at her.

"They patched me up, and I'm back on active duty."

"You're combat effective?" she asked in a concerned tone.

Captain John Tycho turned his hand and extended it in front of him.

"Colonel. I had to pass the physical training tests the

same as I did nine years ago. I came third out of thirty."

"Impressive, well, good to have you here, Captain. We need marines with skills and experience if this struggle is going the way I think it will."

Her mind drifted back to Spartan and the cuts and markings she had seen on his body. The report from Earth had been minimal in scope, yet she feared for what he had been through. They'd suffered enough with the loss of APS Corp, something she suspected Spartan would know nothing about. They'd both worked hard to build it from nothing, only to have it taken away by the cancellation of contracts. Teresa shook her head to rid herself of the thoughts and looked to the Major.

"Major, what do we have then? I'd like to see our unit."

"If you come with us, we'll show you our facilities."

"Thank you."

The small group walked away from the hangar, making for the hexagonal doors that led into the vast internal structure of the ship. Teresa had been aboard a number of similar ships, but she could already see how the hangar and mission part of the ship were so small compared to the similar sections on the other Battlecruisers. They passed through the first of several bulkhead doors, passing small pairs of Marine guards.

"As I'm sure you're aware, this particular ship is using one of the trial combat units for use as a heavy Battlecruiser. Because of this, we're lacking in space for marine units."

"Yes, I know," replied Teresa, "Even the Crusader class have space for half a battalion on board. From the specs, it looks like we'll be hard pressed to do that?"

Major Terson nodded.

"That's true, Sir. I've had our people use every bit of space they can find. Even so, we have all the 39th here under one roof. Just over three hundred marines plus officers and specialists."

"So few? Can we expect any more?"

The Major shook her head.

"No, Sir. The 39th are just under of the expected number. I've arranged for platoons to merge to create something useable. We have some experienced marines and half came from either the new cadet intake on Terra Nova or from the reserve units. We have enough marines to make up three complete heavy companies plus a single Jötnar platoon on transfer from Hyperion."

"Hyperion? Who is their commander?"

Major Terson looked lost as she tried to find the relevant page on her secpad.

"I…uh…they have not yet transferred through. Their ship is meeting up at Prometheus, along with the remainder of our ships. We have to stop there to collect our equipment."

"Wait," said Teresa, "we're stopping at Prometheus?"

They had now reached a large open passageway with four hatches leading to barrack rooms and a mess area. A small group of marines in training clothes spotted them and moved away, speaking quietly.

"Yes, Sir, the foundries on Prometheus have our stores and armor. All we have at the moment are personnel, provisions, and uniforms. We don't even have a training ground. Have you ever been there?"

Teresa tried not to bark out a laugh at the question. She'd spent some uncomfortable weeks on that burning hot world. It had been where she and Anderson had spearheaded a rescue operation for General Rivers and Spartan. It was also where they'd met Gun and his comrades for the first time.

"Yes, I've been there, and I'm not excited at the prospect of going back."

Major Terson suspected there was more to this and made a mental note to check on it later. She pointed toward a door.

"We have converted one of the larger munitions bays into a temporary fitness area and sparring room. It isn't big, only enough for a dozen marines at a time."

Teresa walked in while the Major continued to speak. Inside was a small group of marines, each of them stripped down to just their training clothes and working on a series of weights. Off to one side was a trio of marines taking it in turns to spar with a muscled black fighter. All wore straps on their hands and padded helmets to protect their jaws and forehead.

Nothing changes, Teresa thought.

* * *

How the three of them reached the control station was beyond Spartan. They'd covered nearly two hundred meters through the station and moved past a dozen wounded people trying to make their way out from the transport dock part of the station. This was as far as they could get without exposing themselves to the glare of the invaders. All three kept down low along the side of the small passageway and looked to the end point that ran into a tall crossroads.

"The control station is in the room to the right of the crossroads. It's positioned on the outer wall of the station."

Spartan looked to Khan who waited patiently with the smashed piece of metal still in his arms.

"What about the machines?" he asked his friend.

Khan shrugged.

"Without armor and weapons it isn't gonna be easy."

As they waited, the sound of clanking metal feet became louder. Spartan stopped talking, and all three waited and watched. The body of one of the metallic beasts appeared at the crossroads and stopped for a moment. Spartan paused and readied himself, even though there was almost nothing he would be able to do against such a thing. He lifted his hand to warn them to make no noise. The machine finally moved on, and the sounds of its feet faded into the distance. Spartan looked to the other two.

"Ready?"

Khan nodded, and they rushed to the crossroads. None of them paused upon reaching the middle section, and they moved through to the door of the control station. The engineer tapped the control pad, and they were inside. Khan pulled the door shut behind them, and they breathed a sigh of relief. Spartan nodded in appreciation to the man who had moved to a row of computer screens. The control room was smaller than Spartan had expected. It was rectangular in shape with a low ceiling and plain walls. The computers were arrayed in a unit in the center of the room and seating for six staff around the screens. One wall was different to the rest. He could follow the shape of pistons and bars in the corners.

"Does this open?"

The man looked up from the display and nodded.

"Yeah, that's the monitoring window. Want to see?"

Without waiting for a reply, he tapped something on the console. With a soft whirl, the panel slid in four directions, revealing a wide pane of quadruple reinforced glass. There were protective bars running through the structure, but it still provided a perfect view of the docking arm and the T'Kari ship.

"Look," said Khan in a hushed tone.

Both he and Spartan watched as the arachnid-looking machines moved along the hull of the ship from their hiding places in units fitted beneath the vessel. A large group of them had stayed behind and were moving around on the outer hull of the ship.

"Damn, so they must have fitted that to the ship before we left. Some kind of protective measure?"

Khan shrugged, but the engineer interrupted both of them.

"Maybe they knew you would try and get away and made sure these machines came with you."

Spartan looked at him and back to the machines.

"But why? What can they do?"

As if in direct answer to his question, the station shook again, and the lights flickered.

"They are Biomech war machines. They do only one thing, destroy," said Khan.

"If that were true, why leave so many on the ship? Look at them."

Both of them watched for what seemed an eternity before it became clear to Spartan.

"Wait, they're building something, right on the outside of the hull. Look, near the cargo hatch."

Khan followed his gaze and then spotted the thick metal coils.

"Cables, big ones, and they're taking them right to the station. Why?"

They looked to the engineer who noticed they'd both fallen silent.

"What?"

Spartan pointed out through the window and at the machines working away on the ruined T'Kari ship. Five of them moved along its length and continued to move and alter the thick array of cables running along the ship and to the docking arm.

"That."

The engineer stared at it for far less than the other two before shaking his head and returning to his screen.

"Well?" continued Khan.

The man moved through screen after screen until reaching a page that showed the internal layout of the docking area of the station. He stopped and looked at it for a moment and then pointed at a series of discs.

"This station is a standard design. We have them around all the moons and planets here. I think the basic design is even used on some of the Alliance worlds in Alpha Centauri, well, some of the older colonies maybe."

Khan bent down and looked at the screen.

"Cut to it, what are they doing?"

The man wiped his brow.

"The docking arm has a direct feed to the fusion reactor plant on this station. The connection is used to provide external power to waiting ships, or to recharge systems."

"So they need to recharge their machines?" asked Khan.

The engineer looked up at the scarred warrior and lifted the side of his lip slightly.

"No...they have already bypassed the filters and have connected whatever they are building directly to the station itself."

He moved the screen to one side and brought up another that showed the T'Kari ship.

"There's something else as well. The ship is showing a power build-up cycle like nothing I've ever seen on a ship before."

Spartan and Khan looked at each other.

"They are going to blow the ship and the station," said Khan.

Spartan sighed. He had another completely different idea.

"No, that's not their plan. I've seen this signature before, out on the new colonies at Epsilon Eridani. Back when the first engineer ships had finished their work."

The engineer nodded, immediately understanding what Spartan was referring to. He moved several overlays to the ship and placed them together.

"Yeah, it's a match," he said, and then stood up and moved to the glass to watch the busy machines.

"Uh...is somebody going to tell me what's going on?" Khan asked irritably.

Spartan's shoulder lowered a little in resignation though not in surprise.

"These machines have the components on or in that ship to operate a Spacebridge, and they're using the station as a massive power source."

"No," Khan said slowly, "these machines are building a Rift, right above Earth?"

The other two answered in perfect unison.

"Yes."

Spartan looked at the thick power cables and couplings joining the ship and the station together. He'd wondered all along if their escape had perhaps been a little too easy but hadn't wanted to believe it. They were at least a day away from any military ships coming to help them, and that was probably enough for the machines to do what they wanted.

"Either they planned this, or it is a default programming mode for them. They arrive, seize a major power source, and then assemble a Rift generator to bring in reinforcements."

"I don't understand. I thought the Biomechs were hundreds or thousands of light years away?" asked the engineer.

"Yeah," replied Khan unhelpfully.

"It's more complicated than that," started Spartan, "They can only create bridges of up to about four light years but some places can go further."

The engineer's face lit up, remembering something he'd seen.

"The Nexus? Like at Prometheus and in the Orion Nebula?"

"Exactly," said Spartan, "The Biomechs had a Rift station and a fleet the other side of the Spacebridge we came through. These machines must be trying to create a Rift, using the equipment on this side to manage it."

The engineer looked as though he didn't understand.

"Why not just build the generator on the other side and send ships here?"

Spartan smiled.

"Their station is gone. It exploded as we came through."

Spartan looked at the screen and then to the man.

"What's your name?"

"Simon...Simon Ford."

"Okay, then, Simon. This isn't going to be easy."

He threw a quick glance at Khan before returning to the man.

"I'm Spartan, and this is Khan. Between us we've spent a lot of time fighting these things. Out of everybody in the Alliance, we are probably the best two people you could find that know how these things work."

The engineer said nothing, but his face showed a mixture of confusion, and more significantly, fear. Spartan pointed to the window.

"There are dozens of Biomechs ships out in space using a network of Rifts we know nothing about. I suspect they are about to reveal themselves, and this might be one of their first targets before they try and open the Black Rift."

"We need to stop them, Spartan," Khan said.

Spartan looked over his shoulder to his friend.

"Thanks for that, Khan. I mean to do more than stop them coming here."

He looked back to the engineer.

"I mean to see every one of their ships destroyed and their homeworld burned to ash."

The man looked nervously at him, perhaps sensing the rage within the battered looking warrior. Though Spartan had been through tough times, there was no way to hide the muscles and strength. He glanced to Khan, but the expression on the Jötnar looked almost identical.

"Yeah, I think it's time," he said stoically.

Spartan moved back to the screen.

"How much longer?"

The man worked frantically, and a trickle of sweat had already started to run down his forehead.

"Another minute, maybe two. The more you talk, the slower it will be."

Spartan wanted to say something, but he was all too familiar with what it was like when somebody sat peering over your shoulder. Khan moved to the door and bent down low to get a look. He pushed it open a fraction. Spartan moved to the other side, looking about for a weapon. All he could find was a medium hammer that was part of a small escape kit near the door. It was only designed for smashing glass but was better than nothing. The engineer spotted them both and started to speak, but Spartan cut him off with a raised fist. Khan whispered as quietly as he could manage.

"One of them is coming this way."

Spartan felt his heart skip a beat and altered his stance so that he could drive forward to the doorway when necessary. Khan had already pulled back the door as quietly as he could and lifted the metal bar to his shoulder ready. He looked to Spartan and nodded very slowly. The sound increased in volume and separated as each of the metallic feet clattered in the metallic floor. It moved closer and closer until reaching a meter from the doorframe. Khan took in a long, deep breath and tensed himself for the fight.

This is it, Spartan thought.

The engineer pressed one more button on his computer display and then turned in his chair to face the window in the same direction as the other two. He gave them the thumbs up but said nothing, much to Spartan's relief. The sound returned outside the door and increased in volume, finally fading away. Spartan pushed it open and gave a quick look.

Nobody there.

He looked back at the engineer who grinned.

"Okay, the clamps are disconnected. That's all that can be done from here."

"It's gone," whispered Khan.

Both Spartan and Khan waited at the door for almost a minute in case the thing came back, before moving to the window. Spartan watched for a few seconds and twisted about.

"Why is the docking arm still attached? Has that machine out there found a way to counter your work?"

The engineer said nothing; he merely nodded at the window with raised eyebrows. Nothing seemed to happen, then slowly the section of the docking arm near the station tugged, pulled, and finally detached. Arcs of blue energy rippled between the arm, and the station before one final blast separated them. The light flickered and came back but at half the brightness of before. For a second, Spartan felt as if he was falling, but it was just the motion of the rotating section starting to slow prior to the backup power units kicked in. He grabbed the nearest computer unit and slammed his right hand down onto Simon's shoulder.

"Great work there. You may have just saved this station."

Shouting from outside, and the clanking sound of metal feet spoilt his words.

"Not quite yet," Khan said grimly.

He pushed the door open wide and stepped out. The sound of shouting and the occasional scream returned where in the last minute it had been silent.

We need to secure the station," said Spartan.

Khan looked in agreement as he moved back toward the crossroads.

"What about the ship and the broken docking arm?" asked the engineer.

Spartan watched it drifting away from the station as the dozen or so machines moved about impotently

"Leave them. It won't stay up here long. Give it a few hours, and Earth's gravity will pull them down. It's all they deserve."

CHAPTER TEN

When news arrived of the initial attacks in Helios, many
citizens clamored for the Rifts to the Orion Nebula to be
closed. In theory, it could have fixed the possibility that the
enemy could attack the Alliance, but the reality was far from
the truth. Biomechs had already been seen on Hyperion, and
minor incursions in Sol announced once and for all that at
least a small number of Biomechs remained throughout the
galaxy, and not just those trapped tens of thousands of light
years away from Helios. Most quickly realized that turning
from Helios would simply cut off the Alliance from a source
of allies and resources. The battle against the machines would
be decided in every part of occupied space, whether the citizens
of Terra Nova or Earth liked it or not.

Orion – The future?

Jack and his five surviving comrades worked their way
back through the rubble to find Lieutenant Elvidge

being lifted onto a stretcher. An automated Ram lowered itself into position just four meters away and deployed its turret weapon system to provide covering fire. Private Riku waited alongside the shattered barracks wall with her heavy L48 rifle pointing toward the northern wall. Small groups of marines ran to the defenses with extra weapons and ammunition. Jack slid on the rubble, stopping next to the stretcher.

"Lieutenant?" he asked, but there was no immediate response. He twisted around to face Riku.

"How is he?"

A triple thud from a nearby mortar battery shook the ground, but Jack barely even felt the impact as he moved to the right-hand side of Lieutenant Elvidge. Riku grabbed for another clip before she answered.

"The armor's diagnostics say there are three penetrations, but he'll live. That's what the medic said anyway."

Callahan dropped down next to them as another burst tore into their position. A single projectile struck his shoulder and glanced off, embedding itself in one of the nearby walls.

"Keep your head down, you fool!" laughed Riku.

It was an attempt at humor, but the nervousness in her voice was easy to see. She turned to Jack and opened her mouth to speak when she spotted a squad of Helion soldiers rush out from cover. At first she thought they were attacking something, but then she saw the pair of

Biomech creatures chasing them. The soldiers easily had the firepower to deal with them, but they were green and barely trained. She took aim, but a Helion was torn clean in half before a Vanguard marine arrived and intervened. The massive armored form blocked her path, and she was unable to help as the marine hacked the creatures apart before sending the terrified Helions back to the inner defenses. Riku turned back to Jack and shook her head.

"The rest of our unit is here, but we're scattered over half the base."

She pointed at the running Helions.

"I thought these soldiers were supposed to be improving?"

Jack didn't quite understood and had to lean out from cover to look at the shapes of the Helion soldiers. Though thinner and faster than the human soldiers, the donated armor from Alliance stocks had at least bulked them out to something a little more impressive. The armor was mainly of the older PDS type used for the last two generations but some seemed to be using variants of the gear used by the Narau military. Every one of them carried the standard Alliance carbine, however, the trusted L52. Riku slammed her fist onto the top of his helm to get his attention.

"The Sarge has vanished, along with half of our heavy weapons. Lieutenant Elvidge said you were to take command of the platoon until Corporal Frewyn gets here."

Jack looked at her suspiciously.

"He said that, when?"

She spotted something and twisted to the right before firing a single shot from her L48. Jack couldn't see the target but the smile showing on her face showed him she'd been successful. This time Riku kept her eye on the sight while speaking.

Private Jenkell appeared with another dozen marines from their platoon. Two were struck by flying debris, but they all reached the cover of the shattered walls without injury.

"Good to see you all," she said with a chuckle.

Jack shook his head, but before he could say anything, the screaming sound of two Biomech landers flew overhead with a trio of Hammerhead fighters strafing them as they fell. One disappeared over the outer wall, but the second crashed into one of the surface-to-air missile arrays. A series of violent explosions rippled through the base, yet somehow the lander remained intact. The petal like door hissed open, and more Biomech warriors streamed out.

"Get down!" shouted Callahan.

Jack threw himself to the floor as a stream of metal slugs smashed the masonry to powder behind him. He kept his head low and crawled to the right where he could just see the flank of the nearest lander. Callahan followed close behind as more rounds slammed into position above them.

"Reports are coming in from our other two bases. It's the same everywhere."

Jack looked at his friend's face and could see the fear in his eyes. He might be taller, stronger, and scarred from whatever had happened to him in his past, but Jack suspected he never expected to be in a situation like this one. An image appeared showing the face of Gun to the side of his visor.

"Jack, this isn't going well. Grab as many as you can, and meet me at the eastern wall."

There were plenty of other marines Gun could have asked, but he spoke directly to him in a crisis. Jack looked to Riku and Callahan, but it was hard to tell who had faced the worst so far. Their armor was covered in dust and splatters of blood. He banged his fist down on the shoulder of Callahan where the projectile had bounced off.

"APS Corp designed the modified chest piece for that armor you know."

Callahan had no idea why Jack brought it up, or quite why he might care about a defunct private military contractor. He crawled over to him, always keeping down low enough to avoid being seen by any remaining Biomech warriors. More explosions rocked the base, and he looked about in disbelief at what was happening.

"This is insane!" muttered Private Jenkell.

The skies of Eos were full of hundreds of different smoke trails from the falling landers, destroyed fighters, and the hundreds of aircraft that continued to duel for supremacy. No more of the larger Biomech ships made for the Marine compound anymore. Instead, they crashed down into positions up to ten kilometers away. This put them out of range of the marines' firearms but still in easy range of artillery and fighters cover. Outside of the fortified zone, the Biomechs massed in large numbers for their next assault on the base around the crashed landers that provided cover from the defensive fire of the fortress.

Fort Macquarie had withstood the initial assault of the machines, but at a very heavy cost. Most of the prefabricated barracks had been shattered, and the large field hospital was now a hollow black husk after one of the massive machines had exploded, tearing the structure apart. One of the landing strips was strewn with wreckage, and a dozen fighters burned out in the open. The only fighter cover now available was that remaining in the air. All the Alliance facilities on Eos were under attack in the same fashion as Fort Macquarie.

Jack looked at the group of battered marines and knew he needed to take charge. His visor overlay was still functioning and showed the outer defenses were holding, and small groups of marines were dealing with the isolated pockets of Biomech warriors that remained in the base itself. Quick moving shapes were the fighters from both sides, as Alliance fighters fought against the Biomech drones that had now deployed from the landers.

"Lieutenant Elvidge has put me in temporary command of our platoon."

"Platoon?" muttered one of the men.

Jack threw the man a grim look and then pointed to the eastern wall.

"The enemy has landed almost a thousand troops outside the base and are moving in under heavy fighter cover. We need to get out there and stop them."

He moved to stand, but Callahan grabbed him.

"Are you insane? This place is going to fall. We need to get our people out of here."

Jack looked at him and then to the faces of his weary marines.

"There are two full battalions here. We'll hold."

It was a mixture of bravado and faith, but it seemed to do the job. He was correct, of course, there were two full battalions, but not all of them were actually in the base. Most of the manpower was actually there as logistical support to manage the base, the aircraft, and to assist in the training and preparation of the Helion military. He glanced at the fortified compound's layout and made his plans. It was based around a four-quadrant square, with a fallback bastion made from four low structures surrounded by walls. The two nearest the landing strips had been hit hardest.

That's where we'll go.

He'd made up him mind, but as he opened his mouth, an urgent flash message arrived from Gun.

"Biomechs are approaching the east wall. To the defenses!" roared Gun over the Marine Corps open frequency. It was unnecessarily loud, but Jack knew only too well how loud the grizzled warrior could get when he was fired up. Jack thought for just a second.

The Biomechs must number just a few dozen inside the perimeter now.

"Follow me!" he cried and then leapt over the broken wall and toward the eastern wall. The rest of the depleted platoon followed with Callahan, Riku, and Jenkell flanking him. They burst out into the open and found scores of warriors, including large numbers of Helions emerging from their hiding places and moving to the outer defenses. In seconds, the platoon vanished among the throng of defenders, and Jack found it hard to tell them apart. He checked his overlay and spotted the red shapes.

"Keep moving!"

Jack was fast and quickly moved ahead of the marines. He reached the inner ditch that ran a meter down and then up the other side, to see Gun with his escort of Jötnar and Vanguards moving like a force of medieval Huscarls. Platoons of marines moved to the inner walls that were raised up nearly five meters tall and topped with metal crenellations, as well as sloped roofing to protect them for falling shot and debris. Marines ran from a hundred positions as they made for the outer walls on the four sides of Fort Macquarie. Jack and his small group made for Gun when the fortified entrance to his right vanished in a red fireball. A dozen of the defenders nearest the gate were vaporized in the explosion, and body parts and pieces of armor scattered like dry leaves in the blast. Jack stumbled and almost fell but was lifted to his feet by Callahan and Riku.

"Thanks."

Gun's voice roared over the communications channel, letting everybody in the base know his intentions with perfect clarity.

"Protect the walls, all heavies to the breach!"

Dozens of those nearby clambered up the ramps to the walls, and the amount of gunfire increased tenfold. In the sky above, more black streaks marked the arrival of many more landers as they came down outside the base. Streaks of flame rushed up from the base to reach them as the anti-aircraft guns and missile systems did their work.

"You heard him, the breach!"

He led the marines to take cover behind any bodies, masonry, and equipment that lay a short distance from where Gun had stopped. The Jötnar and Vanguards formed up in a thin line two deep and as wide of the shattered entrance. The Vanguards aimed their powerful batteries of L48 rifles into the smoke while the Jötnar waited in fighting stances. All but one of the Jötnar was armed with bladed weapons, and Jack watched in amazement as they waited patiently. He'd never seen such calm from a group of them before. It reminded him of his friend Wictred he'd not seen in weeks. For a second he recalled Hunn, but quickly moved the thoughts away.

Come on, Jack, concentrate!

The overlay showed all the information coming into the base from the units on the wall as well as the fighters and drones overhead, and it sent a shiver through Jack's body. Normally, fighters and artillery would have kept the base clear, but the amount of Biomech aircraft was now triple that which the Alliance could conjure up, and they were being shot down one at a time. With nothing to stop the buildup, the surge of creatures and war machines had increased to thousands of warriors and scores of the large machines. They must have been close because the amount of fire unleashed from the walls sent flashing arcs of light throughout the base. Jack looked over his shoulder at Riku, Callahan, and the others. All stayed down low and waited for what was to come.

"Attack!" roared Gun. He vanished in the cloud of smoke and dust as hundreds of the creatures swarmed in the through the breached entrance. Half of the Vanguards were pulled to the ground, yet they continued to fight even as armored plates were torn from their suits.

"Fire!" shouted Jack.

The marines added their own disciplined fire to the horde, but nothing seemed to stop them. The Jötnar ripped a dozen to pieces, but more ran past the giants and into the base. Jack stood up and fired from the hip. The others did what they could.

"Jack, I don't like this!" muttered Riku.

The line of marines gave ground and retreated to the wrecks of two bulldogs laying a short distance back. A squad of NHA soldiers waited in a neat line and with their carbines raised. When one of the massive articulated mechanical monsters crashed through the breach, they turned and fled, with no one firing a shot.

"Take cover and hold them back!" said Jack.

Few of the marines were paying much attention now, and the disciplined firing line had broken down into small groups of warriors trying to defend the tiny areas they had retreated to. More explosions ripped through the outer wall, and a heavy round struck Callahan, leaving a fist-sized dent in his chest. He staggered down and was dragged into cover by Riku. She checked his damage that was merely superficial and then looked to Jack.

"What are we going to do? Fort Macquarie has fallen."

Jack emptied his magazine at the horde and then took a step back. The breach was shattered and now filled with hundreds of creatures, as well as three of the massive mechanical war machines. Gunfire from the surviving Bulldogs plus several other squads of Vanguards blasted them. They succeeded in bringing one of them down with a crash. It was a minor victory as small groups of the creatures managed to climb parts of the wall. In just a few minutes, there were bitter hand-to-hand fights at every point. Streams of non-combatant and Helion soldiers ran about, but there was nowhere to hide.

What the hell are you going to do? Jack thought, watching the disaster unfold before his very eyes, even as he continued to shoot one creature after another.

He glanced in the direction of the breach, looking for any sign of Gun, but all he could see were hundreds of bodies; including the creatures, marines, and shattered armored hulks of the Vanguards. Then he saw the streaks of fire coming from the vehicle pool.

Bulldogs! We need to get out of here!

* * *

The journey through the Rift to the Proxima side of the Centauri triple star system had been uneventful. Even the subsequent trip to Prometheus through the newly installed local Rift connection had gone by without Captain Vetlaya noticing the subtle bump as they moved through to a different part of space. The formation of ships was long and widely spaced apart; the massive shape of ANS Dreadnought taking up the vanguard. Small groups of tugs and escort vessels had circled the Rift, but as they moved through the fold in space, none of them followed, just the long column of Alliance warships made their slow and steady journey to the other side. The Battlecruiser nearly made it completely through when a number of flash alert warnings flooded into the ship. One indicated a local threat, but then they were through, and the Rift collapsed behind them suddenly.

"Captain, something's not right," said the helmsman.

The view from the CIC should have been one of the fiery red world of Prometheus, but the external feeds showed an inky blackness with massive arcs of power jumping about. The great Battlecruiser shuddered as a great arc of blue light stuck the nose and sent sparks along the hull.

"Battle stations!" called out the XO in a calm, yet assertive voice.

As per usual the lights dimmed, and the warning siren sounded for a few seconds.

"What the hell happened?" demanded Captain Vetlaya.

They should have been near the arrival station in high orbit around Prometheus, but instead they were right on the edge of the most violent storm Captain Vetlaya had ever seen. Prometheus was infamous for its unrelenting series of dangerous storms that filled the area and made it perilous to even the mightiest warships. From her position in the CIC, she had the perfect view of the storm, and even to her experienced eyes it was truly terrifying. Clouds of energy surrounding the small fleet, and great arcs rippled around them and lashed at their hulls.

"What happened?" she asked from her position again, "Why the hell aren't we at Prometheus?"

A triple flash of energy ripped into the port side of the Battlecruiser, and the entire ship shuddered as though a full broadside of gunfire had just hit her. A few officers were forced to grab onto the myriad of grab rails fitted throughout the ship for such an eventuality. Finally, the helmsman established where they were and whirled about to face his Captain.

"Sir, we're approximately three days from Prometheus. Something happened with the Rift when we came through."

"What exactly?"

"I think I might have an idea," called out Lieutenant Dan, the ships tactical officer.

"Well?" said Vetlaya with a raised left eyebrow.

"Sir."

He brought up a video feed of the Rift behind them as they'd arrived. He paused it just before it collapsed.

"At this point, we received a corrupted and heavily scrambled message from the control station. I don't have much, Sir, but at the same time our sensors detected high levels of radiation, levels that match the expulsion of significant quantities of gamma radiation."

"Gamma? What caused that?"

The man rubbed his chin as he explained.

"I've run six reference checks, and it matches a fission explosion, less than a kilometer from the Rift entrance. Either the station suffered a catastrophic explosion, or somebody triggered a weapon as we went through."

The helmsman nodded in agreement at this analysis.

"If we'd entered the Rift two seconds earlier, we'd have been destroyed in the collapse."

That thought sent shivers through the Captain's body. It wasn't just the danger to her and her ship; it was the rest of the fleet. She turned about and looked to the tactical display, but it showed little more than their ship and the storms around them.

"The task force?"

There was silence in the room as the officers checked their logs and scanners. Finally, the XO spoke up.

"Well, where are they?"

Lieutenant Dan looked to them both nervously.

"We were the first through the Rift. I'm getting no IFF signatures from them."

"That cannot be," muttered the XO.

He wandered over to the computer displays around Lieutenant Dan to see for himself. Even so, every single display throughout the CIC showed nothing more than the data coming from their own ship and the storm outside. Finally, the XO turned around and placed his head in his hands.

"It's just us then."

Captain Vetlaya leaned back in her seat and sighed uncontrollably. The task force was small, but every ship contained hundreds and hundreds of Alliance crewmembers. Even the loss of a single ship would be hard felt. The loss of all but one ship was unimaginable.

"This cannot be. They must have been scattered, or stuck in the Rift behind us."

It was at that moment the science station officer finished her analysis. She checked her data one last time before closing her eyes at the terrible news. Then she looked up at the Captain and tried to think of a way, any way that she could explain the news without crushing her. There was nothing though in the end, just the cold hard truth of what had just happened.

"Captain, I've finished analyzing the radiation and debris behind us. The computer gives an eighty-seven percent likelihood that the blast signature matches a cruiser size ship. It is my opinion that one of our Crusader class ships was caught in the collapse, and their powerplant went critical."

The possible loss of the ship was devastating enough to Captain Vetlaya, but what truly worried her was that if the explosion had come from the ship, then what had forced the Rift to collapse around them? Her attention was brought back to the present as yet more lightning surges whipped along the ship. The doors hissed open, and in walked a confused looking Colonel Morato. She marched in, flanked by two of her Marine guards.

"Captain. What's going on? I've just lost contact with my Marine detachments aboard ANS Falcon."

Teresa could see the screen around the Captain, and the flashes of light from the storms. She'd seem them before during her adventures in the Great Uprising, but it was the look on the face of Captain Vetlaya that startled her the most.

"Colonel, we have lost contact with them all."

The ship shook again, and this time one of the screens flickered black and then came back to show an external feed of the right of the ship. Great black marks ran down the length of the vessel, and two patterns the size of an entire fighter had burned right through the hull.

"This is insanity. We will never navigate through this storm," said Captain Vetlaya.

There was a hint of hysteria to her voice that panicked the crew, and Teresa could tell they were all on the edge. She was easily the oldest of the crew there, and she suspected none of them had ever been through a storm like this one. Teresa looked at the mainscreen and remembered the dangerous routes they'd needed to follow when travelling to Prometheus on the top-secret ship known as Tamarisk. It was something she didn't really think about much these days, but today was different.

"Helm, we need to get away from the epicenter. Plot a

new course on this heading."

Teresa listened to the words of the Captain. None of them made any sense. These storms were almost impossible to chart and required a degree of knowledge and instinct to move through.

"Captain, I don't think I can get us through this," said the helmsman.

Captain Vetlaya walked to his position and looked at the display herself.

"Nonsense, just follow my directions, and get us the hell out of here!"

Another arc of blue light flashed along the ship, but this time there was no obvious damage. The Captain spotted Teresa watching her and indicated for her to leave.

"Colonel, there is nothing for you to do here. I suggest you check on your marines."

Teresa shook her head in disagreement.

"No, Captain, I think I'm the only chance you have."

The Captain turned about, her face a panoply of misery and worry.

"Really? You've navigated through the storms of Prometheus in a starship before, have you?"

Teresa smiled calmly.

"Actually, I have...more than once."

The XO, helmsman, and even the tactical officer stopped what they were doing and watched the Marine officer with look ranging from suspicion to astonishment.

The XO spoke first.

"You're serious, Colonel? You've honestly been through these storms?"

Teresa walked closer to the main screen and examined the storms carefully.

"More than that. I've been involved in ship boarding actions and space combat in this very region. Now, if I may?"

The XO looked to Captain Vetlaya who nodded quickly. The look of disbelief on her face would have been amusing on any other day. He looked back to Teresa.

"Very well, how should we proceed?"

Teresa moved her hand in front of the display and brought up the region of space around them. There were few navigable features as was common in space, yet they were still only a few days away from Prometheus. There were a sizable number of debris fields that circled the star, much like the asteroid belt of Sol.

"Back in the Uprising, we lay down a series of public and secret beacons to be used for emergency deployment in this area," she said to nobody in particular.

"Of course, back then we had no ability to reach the planet, except by taking the long route of nearly a year to avoid the storms. Using our secret routes, the journey could be done in weeks."

Captain Vetlaya couldn't believe her ears.

"Are you telling me these navigation beacons are still

out here?"

Teresa moved to the science console and took over its operation, leaving the young officer looked confused. Teresa accessed the communication arrays and sent out a series of pulse-coded transmissions on a wide band. Nothing happened.

"Well, what now?" asked the XO.

Teresa said nothing and simply waited, watching the screen for signs of the illusive beacons. To the shock of every single person in the CIC, a small green flashing symbol appeared on the tactical overlay. It was a long way off, perhaps half a million kilometers. One of the officers started to speak, but another light and then another appeared. In less than a minute, there were a dozen on the display, and more continued to appear.

"Colonel, I was told to not underestimate you by Admiral Anderson. I can see why."

Teresa grinned politely.

"Anderson is the man I came through these storms with. Now, I will help your navigator with the route. It won't be easy, but I think I can get us to Prometheus in a few days, and without taking too much damage."

"Whatever you need is yours, Colonel. What can we do?"

"Right now the most important thing is the magnetic shielding. Deactivate the weapons and any non-essential equipment, and put all you have into the shielding."

Captain Vetlaya nodded and looked to her XO to start the arrangements. Teresa, on the other hand, turned her eyes back to the display and the flickering lights that showed her the secretive beacons.

Now all I need to do is remember how to get through all of this.

* * *

General Daniels and his small entourage looked on at the live stream of the battle on the surface of Eos with horror. They'd just finished assessing the situation at the two smaller bases and had moved to the much more serious attack at Fort Macquarie. As the primary Alliance base on Eos, it housed the bulk of the marines as well as all the New Helion Army units.

"This cannot be true," said Colonel Brünner.

He pointed at the casualty reports and then to the flagged enemy units.

"According to the last report from Colonel Koerner, the smaller bases are holding, but they can't stand for much longer."

"I know," replied General Daniels, "What really concerns me though is Fort Macquarie."

He enlarged the map, bringing up the Fort and an area fifty square kilometers around it. The amount of red units surrounding the base still shocked him.

"We estimate heavy casualties from the Fort. The

last messages were fragmented but said the Biomechs had breached the eastern wall and were at defenses. The estimate on their numbers is insane."

Colonel Brünner nodded in agreement.

"Yes, the lowest estimate is now twenty thousand, with half as many scattered up to fifty kilometers away. Can they hold?"

He looked to the General, waiting for something on his face that would fill him with confidence. Instead, he saw the look of a man that knew it was only going to get worse. The NHA had broken under pressure, and their air cover was gone. He just needed to hear it from the General himself.

"Not a chance. The best estimate is losses of at least fifty percent from the initial bombardment and the first assault. At some point today, they will overwhelm the wall. My best guess is that once they breach the wall, it will be over in less than an hour."

Colonel Brünner looked as unimpressed with this news as was his General, but there was little either could do other than monitor the battle from here. They paused for what seemed like an age, and then General Daniels moved from their small combat center and toward Admiral Lewis and his cadre of officers.

"General, what's the plan?"

Daniels turned his head as he walked, and Colonel Brünner instantly recognized the decisive look on the

General's face. Any decision was preferable to inaction.

"I want our boys out of there."

"We're going to send in the reserve?" asked the Colonel.

General Daniels stopped, lowered his head for a moment, and then spoke.

"No, this isn't a battle we can win. This has become a rescue operation. Get your marines ready, Colonel. I need to speak with the Admiral."

CHAPTER ELEVEN

The small iron silicate world of Luthien would provide a powerful base of operations for both the T'Kari and Jötnar citizens of the Alliance. Rich in resources and strategically placed, it provided a pool of hardened warriors and advanced technology; the equal of which even the worlds of Prometheus and Hyperion couldn't match.

The New Colonies

Khan slammed his heavy foot into the corner of the locker, and it split in three places. Into the widest gap, he jammed the broke piece of metal and tugged once, twice, and then the door tore off and fell to the ground.

"Good work," said Spartan. He reached inside and pulled out a thermal shotgun. He recognized the design as being the kind of gear used on civilian ships for probably the last fifty years, perhaps even longer.

Not like they get to see much in the way of new tech out here, is it?

There were five shotguns plus the same number of bandoliers, each filled with a dozen boxes to reload the weapon. Spartan tossed a set of gear to the engineer and a shotgun and two bandoliers to Khan. He placed them both over his shoulder as if he was carrying a small bag. The shotgun looked tiny in his large hands, but there was a problem.

"Uh…I don't think they made this in my size," he said with an odd grin.

Spartan extended his stunted arm, and Khan threw it back. Just a few seconds after being cradled under Spartan's arm, he pulled on three levers. With a single twist, the trigger assembly fell off, leaving an exposed trigger.

"There! Modified and upgraded for your enjoyment, my friend."

Khan laughed and pulled out a box to slam into the base of the weapon. It hummed slightly as the capacitors charged up and the shells loaded into the weapon. Only after they were all armed and ready did Spartan turn his attention back to Simon, the station's senior engineer.

"Glad you remembered about this place."

The man nodded with an almost expressionless face.

"We don't carry weapons as a general rule, but I should have thought about the customs tugs a little sooner. There are two more on the station."

Spartan shook his head.

"No, we don't have time. Where are they now?"

Simon pulled out the tired-looking datapad from the pouch on his left leg and tapped it twice, turning it to show them.

"The two machines that made it on board are making their way here, the headquarters and command center of the station."

Khan leaned down to look.

"Why, what do they want?"

Spartan put his right hand on his friend's arm.

"Does it matter, old friend? They will do what they always do, control and destroy. It's time for us to do what we do best."

Khan seemed to like that and walked back to the doorway. He looked back at the other two.

"Well, what are you waiting for? We have machines to kill!"

He vanished, leaving the two of them waiting in silence. Spartan moved for the door first, his thermal shotgun held down low at his waist and resting on his shattered left arm.

"How will we stop them?" asked Simon.

"Easy," laughed Spartan, "We find them, then we kill them."

The poor man chased after them and could hear nothing but laughter from them both. He looked down at the shotgun and struggled to find the safety. He'd never used a weapon in anger before, and now he was chasing after two warriors who seemed to enjoy nothing more than the hunt.

What the hell are you doing? You crazy old fool!

It wasn't enough to stop him from following them.

* * *

The battle for the walls of Fort Macquarie was over, and the casualties among the Marines and New Helion Army soldiers were substantial. Two of the walls had been smashed in a hundred places where the war machines of the Biomechs had literally pounded them with metal arms until they broke. For every marine that had fallen, there were five dead or horribly maimed Biomech creatures on the ground. Resistance continued inside, as the marines withdrew to the two remaining internal quadrants and their defenses. The quadrant containing the vehicle pool was the most heavily defended, and over a thousand marines had dug in to the wall, trenches, and system of six bunkers. Jack and his small group waited in the trenches on the right-hand side of the quadrant, directly opposite the vehicle pool. Three-dozen Bulldogs waited while another ten mobile gun variants had been moved to provide fire support for the defense of the Fort. Flickers of gunfire ran around the two quadrants, as they halted and then beat back what was now the seventh full frontal assault on their position.

"Do they have any plan or is it just to keep attacking, no matter what happens?" asked Riku bitterly.

It was a short moment of respite even though the long arced trajectories of weapons fired from the crashed landers announced the arrival of yet another bombardment.

"Incoming!" shouted a sergeant from the middle of the quadrant.

Explosions rippled through the base as indiscriminate fire landed on marines, buildings, and the dozens of already damaged fighters. The handful of remaining air defense systems did what they could, but there was little a few weapon batteries could do against such an overwhelming bombardment. One blast shredded a Ram as it moved crates of ammunition to one of the bunkers. It vanished in a bright fireball that sent pieces of the machine in every direction. Streaks of lights lifted up into the skies as the ammunition exploded. The shockwave sent yet another layer of dirt and dust over the marines.

"What's the plan, Jack?" asked Riku.

It was hard to tell any of them apart now. Each was covered in dirt and their armor cut and scratched in a hundred places. The entire Fort was full of dust clouds, but it was the thick black smoke coming from a hundred burning vehicles, machines, and buildings that reduced visibility the most. Jack kept down low and rested his carbine on the emergency parapets the Rams had been assembling even in the middle of the battle.

"We need to get everybody out of here in those Bulldogs, and fast."

She looked at the armored vehicles lined up neatly in rows. Three burned in the corner because of stray fire rather than any direct involvement in the battle. More shells landed nearby, and Riku shuddered at the sight of three marines vanishing in the middle of a terrifying explosion.

"What about the Lieutenant?" asked Callahan.

Riku was still shaking her head as she looked at the two of them.

"If we try and leave this place, they'll catch us. We're trapped!"

Jack looked at the Bulldogs once more before turning his attention back to his comrades. He could see the look of desperation on their faces, and the sound of Riku's voice was of a marine on the edge of a complete breakdown.

"We need to get them all out of here," Jack said sternly. "They've not landed any vehicles that we know of, and our fighters and drones are still keeping them busy."

Callahan looked up as though he doubted Jack's very words. As promised, the trails from scores of fighters and spacecraft continued to fill the sky. The overlay on the visor marked out those identified as friendly, and he was happy to see there were still aircraft up there fighting for them.

"We can escape, but only so long as we have air cover to keep them off our backs. We have to do it now, and fast, or we'll lose everyone!"

Callahan considered the idea for a moment and then shook his head angrily.

"Jack, are you insane? We might get a squad in each of them. That's just over three hundred. We have triple that number plus wounded. Don't forget about Gun and his unit. Where is he?"

Jack had already done the math, and even if the marines clambered on top of the vehicles, it would leave at least half of them behind. There didn't seem to be any great answers though.

"Gun can look after himself. He's done it before. We have to save all that we can."

The armored form of Lieutenant Thom Jason stopped their conversation. The man was burly-looking and with the markings of his elite Drop Unit, one of the experimental aerial insertion units being trialed in some of the battalions. He stepped out from the forward trench so his marines could see him.

"Marines, they're coming through again! Get ready!"

Every marine had already fixed bayonets to their rifle or carbine. Even the few remaining platoons of the NHA had done the same, but it was unlikely they would stand in a hand-to-hand fight with such deadly and brutal warriors. Shadows appeared throughout the base as the creatures moved closer. With them controlling two of the walls, they were now able to enter the perimeter relatively unmolested and could make use of the two quadrants near the landing strips to assemble.

"Fire!" cried out Lieutenant Jason.

He wasn't the most senior marine on the base, but he was the only officer remaining at this particular section of the defenses. As the first volley of gunfire erupted, he remained out at the front and on top of the closest trench to the creatures. His height seemed to draw them to him, and in just a few seconds, scores of the creatures moved directly at him.

"Lieutenant!" Jack called out, as he grabbed the officer and yanked him back to the shallow trench. As they hit the dirt, a group of the things tried to jump in amongst them. Gunfire from the marines further behind them shredded the things, killing every one of them that tried to reach the Lieutenant.

"Sir, are you hurt?"

Lieutenant Jason shook his head.

"No, I'm fine. Get back on the line, son. We have blade work to do here."

"Sir!"

The orders were short and curt, but it was exactly what the marines needed. The gunfire coming from the defenses around the two quadrants was now overwhelming. The L52 carbines did most of the work, but every squad was equipped with L48 rifles for support fire, and between them they killed hundreds of the creatures. Jack began to wonder if staying might be more advisable when he spotted the burning shape of a falling object above the base. At first he thought it was a missile, but then he realized it was another type of lander. This one seemed smaller than the others. It trailed smoke and seemed to change course as it fell.

"Uh…Jack, I don't like this," said Riku.

The overlay on their visors had already calculated course, trajectory, and velocity. The data suggested a direct impact right on their position.

"I see it," said Jack numbly.

He stepped back from the trench and moved off to the left, following the angled corner to join the second set of trenches. Riku, Callahan, and the others did the same. Private Jenkell and Lieutenant Jason remained at their posts with carbines at their shoulders. Jack dropped to one knee and waved at them to follow.

"Come on, we've got trouble!" he shouted out.

Private Jenkell heard him over the comms channel and finally jumped away from her position, but the Lieutenant stood his ground. He turned to look at Jack.

"We can't fall back, Private. Hold your position!"

Jack was dumbfounded until he spotted the damage to the man's armor. The right arm was cracked and scorched, but it was the equipment on his helmet and back that had taken the brunt of the impact. The man dropped to his knee, his carbine falling uselessly to the ground.

"Lieutenant!"

The man groaned and then reached down for his pistol. Jack turned back, but Riku and Callahan grabbed his arms and dragged him back from their previous position. He was still protesting when the craft came crashing down ten meters from where they had been fighting. Before the thing even slowed to a halt, the hatches and door blew open; and out streamed more warriors. Five landed in front of the Lieutenant. He emptied his magazine at the first before the five shot him down. Small bloody marks indicated where the projectiles had entered his body, and still he refused to acknowledge the injuries.

"No!" cried out Jack.

He took aim and released a high-power shot at the closest of the group. The three rounds cut through the frontal armor neck, instantly decapitating the thing. It dropped to its knees and tipped over. Gunfire from the other marines slammed into them, but only the high-power shots from the carbines or the explosive rounds from the L48s had the power to stop them.

"Get back, come on!" Riku shouted.

She tugged at Jack, but he shook her off and continued to blaze away at the group as even more of them leapt from the lander. Another of the craft crashed down fifty meters away, and dozens more of the armored warriors joined the fray. Jack finally moved back, and by the time he and the others had moved to the next and final trench line, the battle had reached its climax. More and more creatures swarmed from outside the base and into the fallen quadrants while the new armored warriors spearheaded a vicious firefight around the marines at the car pool. More shapes appeared out in the distance, and two marines fired at them before realizing they were a group of four surviving Vanguards. These mighty armored warriors moved at a quick jog until reaching the open ground near the Bulldogs. One opened fire, and then all four put a powerful burst of fire into the flank of the enemy force.

"Yeah! One marine shouted; the others quickly joined in with the excitement. Caught out in the open, the enemy warriors took a number of casualties before they split up and sent a party directly at the Vanguards.

What the hell are they? Jack thought.

He took aim and shot off one of their arms, but it failed to put them out of the fight. As best as he could tell, these new warriors were another variant of the seemingly infinite variety of artificial warriors created by the Biomechs. Like those already engaged in battle, they were bipedal and the same size and stature as the Helions. Their skin was itself armor, a thin metallic substance that looked like aged iron. Their faces were blank and protected by a plain helm that hid every part of their faces from view other than glowing red eyes. These warriors hunched as though forced to by a cruel trick of genetics or perhaps it was due to their muscular arrangement. It was the weapons that surprised Jack most. He'd never seen anything like it. Rather than carrying a single projectile weapon or edge weapon, they carried a shorter weapon, similar in size to the L52 but strapped to both forearms.

* * *

Admiral Lewis and General Daniels looked at the formation of Biomanta warships in orbit over Eos for what must have been the tenth time. Around them waited the senior Naval and Marine officers of the rest of the fleet. Half were represented by virtual presences. Admiral Lewis had made up his mind after he'd seen the reports coming from the surface of Eos. It had been a little harder to persuade the other ships' captains though. He looked at the assembled group standing in a circle around the projected model of the moon and the ships around it. General Daniels' command room was eminently more suitable for the briefing with its newly fitted mapping and communication equipment.

"Well, that is the situation, Gentlemen. This will be a risky operation, but I cannot stand by and leave our marines to this fate."

He nodded to General Daniels.

"The most recent data coming in shows both of our

small bases were overrun in less than forty minutes, with no survivors. This is unlike any assault we have ever seen."

They all knew the fighting had been fierce, but the news of such horrendous casualties shocked them. The last report from the General had suggested they could hold for weeks, perhaps months until a relief force could be mobilized. Now it seemed they had just hours before complete extermination. He moved his eyes to look at each of them as he continued.

"Fort Macquarie's defenses have been breached, and they are broadcasting a general distress call. Either we help now, or we lose them all; that's eight thousand people, including the bulk of the 17th and 8th Marine Battalions."

He left them with those figures while Admiral Lewis showed them the fleet's dispositions. It was something of a surprise, but more than one officer recognized the basic strategy.

"The enemy force of approximately seventeen ships is in high orbit and strung out in a wide formation to act as a buffer. According to the battle statistics, we are more than capable of matching them ship to ship, but they still have three more vessels than us. We have to rescue the marines and come out of this alive."

The ship shuddered slightly as the massive engines made a slight course adjustment. Even as the officers spoke, the fleet continued on its path toward the enemy. Only those in command of the ships understood they were slowing down and losing height around the moon. Bizarrely, this meant they were actually traveling in the same orbital direction as the Biomechs and at a higher speed.

"In just over an hour, we will adjust our final position and move directly between the Biomech fleet and the moon. If the plan is successful, we will smash through their defenses and continue down to low orbit. General Daniels will conduct the rescue operation of Fort Macquarie and rendezvous with the fleet upon our return above the objective seventy-one minutes later."

Again he waited to let that information sink in. The plan he'd made meant they would sail beneath and past the Biomech fleet at such a speed, the engagement would last just seven minutes before they would be out of visual range. As they skimmed the thin atmosphere of Eos, the effectiveness of direct-energy weapons would be dissipated slightly. Timing was going to be critical, and any ships unable to escape would be left behind.

Captain Perry, the commander of ANS Royal Oak pointed at the image of the fleet.

"How long will we need to complete the rescue operation?"

General Daniels took a long, slow breath before answering his question.

"I'll need at least an hour to get craft on the ground, clear landing zones, and then grab the survivors. I have the timings...and it's going to be very close."

Admiral Lewis looked at the model showing their dispositions, trying to imagine how the battle would unfold. He'd tried to use the basic principle of the Battle of the Nile, but in space there were some things he simply couldn't ignore. The long range and almost instant speed of the particle-beam weapons were deadly, but that was just the beginning. It was fighting the battle in orbit that caused the greatest problem. The two fleets couldn't maneuver around each other. They would simply pass by each other with a narrow window to use their weapons. On the second and final pass, he would need to extract the marines' rescue craft and then use the slingshot effect of the moon plus his engines to blast off into space.

Could this work? he wondered.

He looked back at the officers and the model of the moon. The aerial images and video streams from the remaining drones reminded him he had to do something. If there was any chance of the marines holding out, he might have felt differently; but they were looking at the complete annihilation of two battalions plus their New Helion Army allies and hundreds of support personnel.

If we don't succeed, this could be the biggest disaster since the capture of the Titan Naval Station in the Uprising.

* * *

Spartan and Khan moved slowly into position around the

control room of the station. Streaks of blood on the floor and walls showed where the two machines had worked their way inside. Spartan placed his finger over his lips and leaned out to take a look. He could see three metallic limbs near the entrance, and there was a great deal of noise coming from inside the station itself. The legs shifted and vanished inside.

Just like old times.

He moved back and waved at them both. Khan moved up behind him. Simon waited patiently behind them, beads of sweat running down the poor man's face.

"Forget the legs, aim at the body. They are like spiders. The loss of a leg does nothing to them. We kill the one at the door first."

Khan smiled that great wide beam he never showed, except when he was about to commit copious amounts of violence or engage in some form of physical contest with his brethren. He held up his modified shotgun and aimed it at the doorway. The engineer watched them both, doing his best to look confident, but his shaking hands and white face betrayed his true feelings.

"Now!" said Spartan.

The two moved for the doorway. Spartan took the right, and Khan moved to the left. Spartan took two steps and then cleared the door. Khan didn't wait and followed right behind, but it was harder for him to move with the stealth that Spartan could manage. The command room was on two levels; the raised section further away and flanked by computer displays. One of the machines waited in the middle and turned to face them.

"Where's the other one?" asked Simon, stepping in behind them.

The two experienced warriors took quick aim at the machine and opened fire. Unlike conventional shotguns, these weapons released scattered pellets of superheated metal and ripped chunks out of the metal armor covering the machine. Spartan fired more slowly and took careful aim. Khan emptied the box magazine in less than three seconds. The engineer didn't even have time to shoot before two of the machine's legs had been blown off and its body shattered from a dozen impacts. It still twisted about and stumbled toward them, with two of the legs extended.

"Shoot it!" shouted Spartan.

Khan was reloading, and Spartan had just fired his last shot as it moved even closer to them. At this range, the shape was much clearer to see. The body was easily the size of a man's, and the arms were like some metallic appendage torn from an octopus and fitted with pistons and curved blades. It hacked and stabbed at Khan, who instead of reloading used his shotgun like a club. He parried the first attack, but the second arm managed to embed in his upper right leg.

"Damned machine!" he snapped in mock amusement.

Spartan took a step to the side and finished fitting the box magazine when the engineer opened fire. His shots were wild, yet three managed to strike near the middle of the target. Each impact ripped a chunk the size of a man's fist from the housing until finally a blue flash announced its death. Ripples of energy ran about its frame. It slid to the floor on lifeless, weakened legs. Spartan took aim, but it was over. The machine was now unable to continue the fight.

"Great work, Simon..." Spartan said, a sly grin forming on his face.

He turned to look at the man, and his face transformed as though some great magnet had pulled his features down to the floor. Right behind Simon was the shape of the second and last of the Biomech machines. There was no clear face, but its torso was upright and shielded by the form of the engineer. Three red shapes appeared, one in his chest, one in his stomach, and one in his throat. It took a second for Spartan to realize they were the razor edged tips of three of the machine's legs.

"Spartan, watch out!" roared Khan.

He grabbed Spartan, yanking him to his left just as the machine withdrew its blades and stepped over the body of the fallen engineer. Spartan staggered and almost fell before crashing into one of the computer displays, sending glass flying.

"Die!" roared his friend, throwing himself at the

machine.

Khan was nearly two and a half meters tall, slightly shorter than the larger of his people, but a veritable giant compared to a normal man. His thick, bulging muscles flexed as he grabbed the nearest limbs and tried to hurl the machine into the wall. They must have been equally matched in size, weight, and strength though. He was unable to move it. Spartan looked to his left, then right before spotting his fallen shotgun. He leapt for it, reaching out with his left hand; once again forgetting it was now nothing but a stump. Cursing, he used his right, checked the box and took aim.

"Out of the way, you fool!" he called out.

Khan tried to move, but he was locked in mortal combat with the machine and from the way it had twisted its metal limbs around him, he was unable to move. Spartan shook his head angrily and then ran back with the shotgun held up high.

"Hold on, I'm coming!"

He ran to the right of Khan, stabbed down with the shotgun's muzzle pressed firmly at its body, and pulled the trigger. The recoil was substantial, especially when held in just one hand. At this range, the hole it burned went halfway through the thing's body.

"It's still moving!" said Khan, crying out in pain.

Spartan could see a red line running along his friend's flank.

It's going to open him up, come on!

He pulled the trigger over and over until the machine released two of the arms on Khan and flailed out at him. Spartan flew backward and landed hard on his back, the impact almost knocking him out cold. It was enough though and freed up Khan's arms. He reached inside the hole, ignoring the smell of burning flesh as the superheated metal on the scarred housing burned into his fingers and wrist. He could feel tubes and cables and pulled and tore at whatever he could find. The machine seemed to shriek, and then it fell motionless, like some twisted metallic spider. With a few pulls and tugs, he dragged himself away from the machine and staggered over to Spartan. Blood dripped from a dozen deep wounds on his body. Something gave way in his leg, and he dropped down next to his friend.

"You crazy fool," said Spartan.

Khan was in great pain, but the sight of the two smashed machines put a smile back on his face, a smile Spartan couldn't remember seeing for many months. He lifted himself from the floor and looked for the sign of a medical kit. Luckily, there were small red signs in every room and passageway of the station. There was one near the door, and in just a few short seconds, he had the unit and ripped out a sealant package to help staunch the blood flow and block up the wound. As he applied the gooey material, Khan looked to him.

"We did it, Spartan, two more machines down."

Spartan nodded and looked back at the case for a dressing.

"How many more do we need to kill though?"

As he fitted the dressing, Khan groaned a little. It wasn't much, but if Khan made any noise, Spartan knew it must be hurting his friend a great deal. It seemed to take an age to patch him up, but finally his work was done, and the two just sat there, both of them physically and emotionally exhausted. Khan twisted his head, the pain returning as he moved.

"It doesn't matter how many are left, Spartan. We'll find everyone of them and do the same to them."

Spartan looked back at the wrecked machines and blood all around them. He started to smile, then noticing the lifeless corpse of their newest friend, Simon, the engineer who had risked everything to help them. His smile to turned to a frown, and his forehead tightened as the rage returned once more.

"You're right, Khan. We need to finish this once and for all."

CHAPTER TWELVE

Alliance holdings at the start of the Biomech incursions into Helios were impressive, especially when considering humanity had only spread to two star systems a mere generation earlier. The eight planets of Sol were the old worlds of the Alliance, recently brought back under central control. Then came the thirteen rich worlds of Alpha Centauri and the equally successful eleven worlds of Proxima Centauri, all of these had formed the core of the loose Confederacy. In the last generation, the Alliance had grown to include fledgling colonies at the stars of Epsilon Eridani, Gliese 876, Procyon, and finally T'Karan in the Orion Nebula. Only through the use of the Interstellar Network was any of this possible, and it would prove to be the single greatest strength and weakness of the Alliance.

A Concise Guide to Interstellar Travel

A rocket whistled out from the defenders and slammed

into a group of Biomech warriors. Two vanished in the flash, and a third struggled on with just one leg and a shattered left arm before succumbing to the gunfire of a shoulder-mounted rocket launcher. Two more moved out from the cover to take its place and put down a hail of fire into the marines' position.

These newly identified fighters were known by their temporary disparaging nickname of 'Tin Cans', or 'Canners' for short, and had secured most of the base. Scores of them had dug in closer to the marines and now engaged in a bloody series of firefights that wore down both sides in a slow attritional battle.

"Get down!" Jack cried out.

His comrades had withdrawn to the safety of the shattered bunker that held almost a dozen marines. Two crew-served heavy weapon emplacements saturated the open ground that had turned to a deadly killing ground for both sides. The left wall of the bunker was now partially collapsed but still provided the most substantial cover around them.

"What about the Bulldogs? I thought we were getting out of here?" asked Riku.

Jack fired a single shot, doing his best to conserve his ammunition and then looked to his right. He could see the lines of vehicles, as well as the black columns of smoke rising from the nearest six that had been destroyed in the last ten minutes.

"Yeah, that was the plan. We need to create an opening, so we can try and get out of this place."

He looked back at the killing ground and the hundreds of flickering lights signifying the enemy that had dug in and were moving forward centimeter by centimeter. Arcs of fire crossed from both sides, but neither seemed to have much of an advantage.

"How do we do that?" asked Callahan.

The marine had taken one of the larger L56 Mark III heavy guns from a shattered gimbal mount on the bunker. It was heavy, but the slightly lower gravity on Eos made it easier to use, and the amount of fire the twin box fed, multi-barreled weapon was the equal of an entire marine squad.

"Canners!" shouted Riku with her hand extended into the distance.

Callahan tracked her hand and found the group. He pulled the trigger, and the five barrels fired one after the other, each sending a hypersonic round into the dirt, masonry, and armored bodies of the enemy. Three were cut to pieces before the other took cover. In answer to the gunfire, the warriors returned fire that slammed around the bunker.

"Something needs to give. We could try a push," suggested Jack.

Riku and Callahan both shook their heads.

"No way," said Riku firmly, "You've seen how many of

them are out there. There's no chance in hell."

Private Jenkell lowered herself down from the damaged wall of the bunker and turned to Jack.

"She's right, Jack. If we go out there, it will be just like with the Lieutenant. It's a no-man's land now."

In answer to her point, a group of marines ran out from cover to grab one of the abandoned L56 weapons from a shattered Ram. They had started to move the thing into position when two of the warriors dropped into their trench.

"Dammit!" said Jack as if he had been caught napping, "Canner, in the reserve trench!"

He tried to get a shot, but the angle of depression made it impossible from where he was positioned. He was forced to watch as the combined firepower of the guns on their arms tore into the marines. Two were killed outright, with a third falling to the ground; five holes in his chest armor.

"Medic!" An unidentified Naval crewman called out as he tried to drag the wounded marine to safety. One of the enemy warriors struck the man in the neck and then blasted him as he lay there screaming on the ground. Another pair appeared behind the trench and clambered over the top, finally giving Jack a target he could see. He tapped the firing mode selector and took careful aim. Just one squeeze, and the high-power shot put a hole the size of his fist in the creature's head. It dropped backward lifelessly.

"Fall back!" shouted one of the survivors, and they scrambled back, leaving the weapon in the pile of rubble and bodies. Three more frontal assaults had ended in the same manner as the dozens before them, and nothing looked as though it would change. Jack was desperate to make a move on the vehicle pool, but every time he plucked up the nerve to try, another group of the enemy moved into position and pinned him down.

If we stay much longer, we're dead.

He lifted his head a tiny fraction to look at the group of enemy troops moving in to block them off from their only chance of escape. They dropped down into a sink in the ground that allowed them to move around their flank while staying hidden from gunfire.

"We've got a problem."

"Really?" replied a familiar voice.

Jack checked the IFF system on his helmet overlay, confirming what he already knew.

"Gun?"

"I think you'll find that's Colonel," replied the grizzled warrior.

Jack checked for his position and spotted the green shape, but it was right in the center of the enemy position.

That can't be right.

He popped his head up a little and winced as arcs of fire flashed from both sides. Nearly a hundred meters away walked one of the large metal machines. It moved slowly as it led the massive wave of troops for a final big push. Its gun sponsons fired heavy projectiles that shredded man and building alike. Around its legs swarmed scores of different warriors, every one of them the foot soldiers of the Biomechs. An explosion shook one of the massive machines' legs, and then he saw him.

Gun?

The machine dwarfed the great bulk of the Jötnar, yet he and two of his surviving bodyguards were right in the middle of the enemy unit. Where they had come from Jack couldn't tell, but they hacked and slashed at their foes until they reached the machine. Gunfire rattled away from their shoulder-mounted weapons, and then the impossible happened. Gun had clambered onto one of the legs and was working his way up the torso. The machine was as big as a Hammerhead gunship, but Gun treated it as though he was fighting a wild boar. One of his comrades tore off one of its legs, and it stumbled. Gun must have found an opportunity because he rolled off the machine, landed on the ground, and jumped up just as a blue flash tore off the armored head of the war machine. It dropped onto its haunches and just sat there, completely stationary.

He's for it now.

The warriors around Gun and his guard completely surrounded them, yet as each of the creatures moved in to attack them, they were hacked down. Jack couldn't believe what he was seeing in front of him. The three were like armored gods standing back-to-back in a triangle of flesh and metal.

"Help them!" he shouted.

Paying no attention to the approaching gunfire, he lifted up to the parapet and emptied what was left in his carbine magazine. The other marines did the same, trying to ease the pressure on their commander. Even so, scattered groups of the so-called Canners reached their lines, and bloody hand-to-hand combat filled the final two quadrants.

"Jack, this is it. We can't hold for much longer," Callahan said bitterly.

Riku and Private Jenkell covered the left of the bunker. Jack and Callahan had taken over the center when the Sergeant had taken a round to the face. Four Helions of the NHA protected the right even though they were clearly terrified of what was happening.

"Jack, what the hell is that?" asked Riku.

Jack refused to turn his head but could just about make out her arm from the corner of his eye. She was pointing out to the left, near where the old command bunker had been. A burning lander covered its partially collapsed roof. Out in the distance behind it was one of the shattered walls that had been breached early in the battle. There was no fighting in that part of the base, although a small number of the Canners were moving methodically through the ruins to look for survivors to finish off.

"The prisoner!" she added in irritation.

He followed the highlighted shape on his visor and saw the dark form. At first he thought it was a marine, but the long robe took him right back to the violent struggle with the Helion prisoner that had turned out to be a Khreenk. The warrior looked back in the direction of Jack before a group of five of the Biomech warriors leapt in to attack him. Three fell down from a weapon the Khreenk was carrying, and then he dodged to one side before finishing off the other two with some kind of blade.

He could have killed me if he'd wanted, Jack realized as he watched the speed and ferocity of the fighter. For a brief moment, he could see the cold bands of his armor before the dust of battle obscured them. Just as quickly as it had started, the five warriors were dead, and the Khreenk warrior stood alone on the smashed wall.

"What's he doing?" asked Riku.

"Who knows? Probably trying to work out a way to kill us before he leaves us to rot," suggested Callahan.

Jack looked back to the middle of the field and the large numbers of enemy that had moved closer to the marines. It was clear to him this wasn't just another assault. They had positioned larger numbers than before, and they were massing at both the front and on the flanks. Even as Gun and his bodyguard continued to fight out in the middle, they were preparing for something big.

"This is going to be their major assault."

He looked to Riku who shook her head.

"We're screwed then. I'm out, and half of the marines left are wounded. One rush and they'll roll us up."

Jack shook his head angrily, grabbing a fallen carbine to check for ammunition. It contained a single half loaded magazine but was of an older type, with just two narrow barrels joined together over a single magazine. It wasn't much but was better than no weapon. He flicked the lever to extend the spike bayonet. Riku seemed unimpressed.

"Check your wide area overlay. Have you seen what's out there?"

Jack used his retina to select a different distance mode and almost choked at the aerial view from the drones. Markers identified the small number of remaining fighters, but there were still landers coming down all around the northern and eastern approaches to the base.

"We've had it," he agreed bitterly.

* * *

The formation of fourteen capital ships left a great streak behind them as they skimmed the surface of Eos' thin atmosphere. The two Battlecruisers took the lead, with the rest strung out in a short column directly behind them. All of the massive ships used their primary engines and maneuvering thrusters to keep from being pulled down to the moon, without providing too much thrust so that they might rise in height and effectively slow down. There were no fighters anywhere near the ships, and only the tiny group of surviving escort ships dared to go any closer to the abrasive atmosphere of the moon.

Genera Daniels waited patiently as one of his subordinates double-checked the strapping inside the Mauler. There were only three other marines inside the cavernous interior of the craft, and all four of them wore the new APS Alpha Armor. It was the first time the General had worn the gear, and he was pleasantly surprised at its ease of movement. He nearly forgot why he was there, but only for the briefest of moments. The craft shuddered a little, but the clamps held it firmly in place.

"Four minutes until emergency drop," said a monotone computerized voice.

"General, is it wise going to the surface? Emergency drops are incredibly dangerous," asked the young Lieutenant.

The General said nothing and instead checked his secpad for what must have been the hundredth time. It showed the disposition of the fleet as it hurtled around Eos in such a low orbit that three of the cruisers had sustained heavy structural damage from the atmospheric friction. He looked up to the officer with an expressionless face.

"Son, I will not leave my people behind. Just make sure

this is ready to go."

* * *

Admiral Lewis waited patiently as the formation of ships moved around the moon. His eyes were on the visual feed from the bow of his ship as he looked for the first sign of the enemy. Because of their height, and the line of sight problems of orbiting Eos, the enemy had been unable to target them. He looked to the right where a counter ticked down. When it reached zero, they would be in sight and therefore in range of the Biomanta particle beam weapons. He found himself counting down as it reached the final thirty seconds.

What have I done? Will this mean the end for the fleet and for our people on the ground?

"Target!" called out Lieutenant Vitelli.

The Admiral nodded, but still his eyes remained on the visual feed. A red diamond appeared over the shape of the first ships, then one by one the others appeared to mark out the rest of the fleet.

"Admiral, they appear to be transferring cargo or something between their ships and the smaller landers."

The tactical officer turned in his chair with a look of sheer joy on his face.

"Admiral, we've caught them with their pants down!"

"Excellent!" replied the XO.

Just those few simple words instantly transformed the bridge crew from the misery and despair of certain death to one of hope and possibilities. Admiral Lewis could see that, and he gave his XO the smallest of smiles before giving his orders.

"Prepare for the combat drops."

The XO moved a short distance to the right where he could assist with the deployment to the surface. Admiral Lewis, in the meantime, grabbed the intercom and connected to the captains of every ship remaining in the fleet.

"We will have clear, uninterrupted targets in thirty seconds. Remember the plan. Follow the Nile pattern and keep moving. No course changes and no staying behind. This is a hit and run operation!"

* * *

The officer looked to his General and then extended his hand to the man. It was far from procedure, but General Daniels knew only too well how risky the mission was that they had undertaken. Never in his entire life had he been involved in such a massive emergency drop, and never at this height. The computer simulations hadn't been particularly positive, but he refused to back down. He remembered the discussion with the ships' officers just minutes before as they had moved closer to their drop-point. Two of the captains had almost mutinied at the requirement to pass so close to the Biomech warships, but General Daniels and Admiral Lewis had been adamant. Eos might fall, but the Alliance would never leave their people behind to die.

"Good luck, General."

He shook the man's hand and then glanced to his right, checking where the spare weapons were fitted as well as the escape hatch, just in case, before looking back at the man.

"Thank you, Lieutenant. We'll be back on board in less than two hours. Make sure all marine units are ready. There are going to be a lot of casualties on the return leg of this trip."

The man saluted and stepped back to let the double airlock system lock down safely. The mounts holding the craft in place groaned and then moved it into position over the exit hatch that was barely larger than the Mauler.

"Twenty seconds," said the computerized voice.

General Daniels could see the doors in the hangar close shut, blocking off his view of the other crew and marines. He felt oddly lonely as he and the other three marines waited inside the Mauler for the start of the operation. The craft began to shake, and the small side windows flashed yellow, white, and red.

Here goes nothing!

There was no sound as the clamps detached, just the

massive force as the deployment jets blasted the Mauler from the bay and into its vertical descent to the surface of Eos. From inside the craft, General Daniels could see nothing but flames as they plummeted down through the atmosphere at incredible speeds. If this had been Terra Nova or Hyperion, the Mauler would have instantly disintegrated. Luckily, the thinner atmosphere reduced its impact on the hull, but it was still a very close run thing.

* * *

The Biomech warriors had smashed the defenses in seconds, and now every part of the quadrant was being overrun. The dulled iron warriors pitted their weapons against the bayonets and carbines of the marines, and as each minute past, their victory became clearer.

"Back to the vehicles!" shouted out Callahan.

He was already moving by the time Jack and the others chased after him. The vehicle pool might have less cover, but it was also the part of the base containing fewer of the enemy warriors. Instead of fighting as a single bloc, the marines had been split up into dozens of small groups, each fighting a miniature battle until casualties and lack of ammunition forced their defeat. Jack made it to the nearest Bulldog in time to see a rocket rush overhead from one of the Biomech war machines and strike the crew section. The impact rolled the Bulldog to its side and sent him plus three others flying through the air. For the briefest of moments, he thought he might never come back to the ground, but he did, and the impact almost knocked him unconscious as he crashed down onto his back. Incredibly, the reinforced spinal ribbing absorbed the crash and spread the impact away from the fragile parts of the body.

"Look! They're sending in more warriors," called out a marine, two seconds before a pair of Canners put a dozen rounds into her chest and waist. The poor woman fell down screaming from the oozing wounds until a third stepped in and took her head clean off with a cut of its scythed arms. Jack pulled out his pistol and rolled to his right to get a clean shot before spotting the two warriors pinning Riku to the floor. He almost panicked, but his training kicked in. The drills they'd practiced time after time saved her life as he put two rounds into each of their skulls before checking for signs of more.

"Riku! Are you hurt?"

He lifted himself to one knee, but Jenkell had already beaten him to her. She grabbed the fallen marine's arm and dragged her back to the side of the smashed Bulldog. Small groups of marines moved about nearby as they looked for anywhere to make their last stand. Jack lifted his pistol and took aim, but the sight of the sea of Biomech warriors disheartened him. He could see them everywhere, and black plumes of smoke had now completely blotted out the background.

This is how it all ends, then.

For a second, he contemplated using the pistol to shoot himself rather than suffer the assault of the creatures. He just couldn't bring himself to lift the pistol though, and instead emptied it at the nearest two enemies. As soon as the last round fired, he flipped the catch so that the magazine slipped out and slammed in one of his last few clips. A bright yellow flash erupted to the left where the Khreenk warrior had vanished and quickly spread along the entire length of the broken wall.

"Keep down!" he shouted.

The explosion continued to spread and then smaller flashes rippled closer inside. Black shapes emerged through the darkness and then moved into the compound.

Great, like they need more to finish us off.

There was something wrong though. He took aim at the new arrivals and almost fired when he spotted the hooded shapes.

Just like the Khreenk.

His finger was half pulled on the trigger when the nearest group opened fire with thermal carbines and rifles. The blasts tore holes into the bodies of the Biomech warriors and quickly shattered their flank. Jack was sure he could see nearly thirty of these warriors, but they moved quickly and rather than hold back, they rushed into the fray, hacking at the warriors with curved blades. They fired their carbines from the hip and then just as quickly as they had arrived, the entire lot were hacking, stabbing and shooting. Without thinking, Jack sent an open-channel flash message to all the nearby units.

"Khreenk troops have broken through the wall. Do not fire upon them!"

He raised his pistol and fired, but dozens more of the warriors continued forward, many being spurred on to attack so that they might avoid the flanking attack coming from the Khreenk. One of the warriors lifted up and flew overhead, revealing Gun and his bodyguard. They barged through the enemy and directly toward Jack and his comrades like a charging herd of rhino. Any that blocked their path was shot down and smashed with edged weapons.

This is our chance. It has to be!

Jack grabbed Riku and pointed at the remaining Bulldogs.

"We need to get out of here, come on!"

Gun slid next to the wrecked Bulldog and spun around to unleash a burst of fire from the weapon mount on his shoulder. His guards pulled up alongside him and did the same. Gun cut down two more before barking out his orders over the communication network.

"General Daniels is bringing a relief force down. Everybody fall back to the vehicle pool."

Jack assumed that meant they were all to use the armored vehicles, but as he stepped to the open door of the nearest working vehicle, a hand grabbed him. He looked around to see the shape of Lieutenant Elvidge with the robed Khreenk warrior helping him to cover.

"Private, a little unexpected don't you think?" said the officer.

Jack sensed the man was a little light-headed, and he could only think it must be the drugs. The Khreenk warrior made almost no sound as he moved, and a group of his comrades, each similarly dressed, moved in behind them. Biomech warriors tried to pursue, but the combined fire of the final remaining marines plus the dozen or so Khreenk mercenaries halted the attack, even for just a few seconds. The Lieutenant threw his carbine to Jack who caught it with one hand. He automatically looked down at the ammunition marker.

Full, about damned time!

Gun lifted himself atop of the damaged Bulldog, exposing himself to gunfire but also allowing all the surviving Alliance personnel to see him.

"Whatever ammunition you have left, use it. Help is coming!"

He pointed up to the sky, and on cue a dozen objects appeared, each wreathed in flame and smoke. They looked little different to those of the Biomech landers, but Jack had faith in Gun. He checked that Callahan, Jenkell, and Riku were safe behind the shattered Bulldog and then turned his attention to the rest of the ruined base. His best guess was that there must be close to a thousand of the enemy inside the walls. On top of that, there were three of the massive war machines at the northern wall. He didn't even want to think about the large numbers outside the base. To his left, multiple platoons of marines fell back to the top of the vehicle pool. Some lay down in the open to present the smallest target while others crouched behind damaged vehicles.

This is going to be close.

He looked to his right where the shattered wrecks of at least a dozen Bulldogs marked their flank. A similar number of marines had dug, in along with at least two Vanguards plus Gun's personal guard unit.

"Jack, in front of you!" shouted Riku.

He twisted a few centimeters and took aim with his carbine. In front of them, a small group of nine of the warriors with the blades for arms clambered toward them. Their gait looked even more alien, due to the slightly lower gravity than normal. He aimed at the center of the formation and squeezed the trigger. One fell down howling, and another dropped down on one knee.

"Kill them all!" ordered Gun.

The mighty warrior simply pointed his arms at the enemy while his shoulder-mounted gun tore chunks out of the group. More rockets whooshed overhead and landed around the marines. The shots were wildly inaccurate, but at least two marines succumbed to the blasts.

"Here they come!" said somebody to the right.

But there was no time to look, as six large Marine Corps Maulers swept down over the overrun base. The multiple turrets on the craft sent a torrent of fire to the ground, instantly shredding any Biomechs that came too close. One took three rockets to the flank and rather than landing, it continued overhead and crashed a kilometer outside the base in a bright orange fireball. The other five came down hard around the vehicle pool, one even lowering itself down onto one of the damaged barrack buildings, using its engines to stay upright. Its doors flew open, and small groups of marines stepped out to add their own gunfire to the battle. One man in particular stood out amongst them all in his tiger striped armor.

"General!" howled Gun, delighted at the sight of his friend and rescuer.

"Which General?" asked Callahan.

Jack grabbed him by the shoulder.

"Are you kidding? Let's get out of here."

They leapt from their position even as projectiles crashed about them. Riku was fastest. As they moved closer, they ran into dozens more fireteams emerging from scores of hiding places throughout the base. More Maulers and Hammerhead gunships whooshed down; some landing to extract the survivors, the rest providing support. A flight of Hammerheads loosed a missile barrage that vaporized one of the war machines, and their turrets shredded any

Biomechs in sight.

Move it, faster!

Jack ran as fast as his legs could carry him. The low gravity made it awkward, and he stumbled twice before finally reaching the ramp leading up into the Mauler. The General waited at the bottom of the ramp, waving the marines in. Unlike the Hammerheads and shuttles used in the past, the Mauler was massive. Jack had heard tales of the craft being used to deliver entire combat companies into action, along with support units. He was a little dubious about that, but on this occasion, not one of them worried about numbers. One by one, they streamed inside, and as he ran up the ramp and past the General, he tapped him on the shoulder.

"Thank you, Sir!"

Inside were scores of marines busily pulling down the clamps and harnesses to secure them inside the craft. It was now two thirds full when Gun and his guard move through the entrance. The General followed close behind and then two Vanguards, their armor punctured and torn in a hundred places. General Daniels slammed his fist into a red pulsing button, and the hatches slammed shut.

"We're clear. Go, go, go!"

The pilots were evidently waiting for his order because the craft shook by the time the General had shouted go for a third time. Jack could just about make out the fires and smoke through the tiny windows as they lifted up and away from the Fort. His tactical overlay on his visor showed dozens more craft circling around the base, but it was the great masses of red around the fortress that astounded him.

General Daniels had fitted the clamp around his body and was busy watching two large screens on the wall nearest the pilots. They showed both an aerial view of the battlefield and a collage of camera feeds from those still on the ground. Craft were everywhere, and Jack could only imagine how many they would be forced to leave behind.

The Khreenk!

He tried to stand, up but the clamps held him firm.

"General!"

The man turned to glance at him.

"Son, I'm a little busy."

"The Khreenk, Sir. They helped with that last attack."

The General nodded, turning back to his screen.

"Private, don't worry about it. They are in a holding area on the third Mauler. We have bigger things to concern ourselves with."

Jack looked to his right where Gun stood up, clamped into position like the Vanguards along the sides of the craft. With his armor, he could never fit into the seating clamps used by the regular marines. He flipped open his armored visor to grin. Jack could see blood running down from a wound to his head, not that Gun seemed to care.

"The General means what's happening up there."

He pointed to the ceiling.

"What do you mean?" asked Riku from her seat next to Jack.

Lieutenant Elvidge groaned from across the craft and then muttered something.

"What did he say?" asked Jack.

The marine next to the officer called out louder than he intended.

"He said there's nobody waiting for us in orbit, just the Biomech fleet."

Jack looked to Riku, Callahan, Jenkell, and then to Gun. He found it impossible to speak as his throat dried up and seemed to clamp tightly, almost stopping any air entering his body. Gun laughed at his expression.

"Calm down, Jack. Admiral Lewis will be there when we arrive."

"Yeah," snarled Callahan, "and what if he isn't?"

Gun showed that ridiculous smile that unnerved Jack even more than he expected.

"Then we'll have to find other ships to land on!"

CHAPTER THIRTEEN

The fighting through the Helios System brought back the horrific specter of combat with Biomechs. As in the Uprising, they unleashed unholy creations made from the corpses of their defeated enemies. There were differences too though, and some Alliance scientists suspected the biology and technology of each group of warriors was based heavily upon the source material used. The ground combat on Eos, however, introduced the spectacle of Biomech frontline warriors for the first time. In space, the Biomanta class of warships showed what a fusion between technology and biology could produce. On the surface, a whole new breed of enemy was found, warriors that had been built as purely synthetic fighting machines with armor and weapons built directly into their flesh. The twisted creations fought in the Uprising were a mere taste of what was to come.

Evolution of the Biomechs

Admiral Lewis looked at the schematic of his ship, shaking

his head in astonishment. They had managed to get past the Biomanta blockade with nothing but minor casualties and a damaged bank of defense turrets. The attack had been so quick; they'd slipped past the enemy ships and destroyed three before they were even detected. The remaining eleven ships had targeted each Alliance ship one at a time as they passed; as opposed to the Alliance ships, they concentrated their fire on a single ship as they moved underneath them at incredible speeds. The XO looked at the damage reports and nodded his head happily.

"Admiral, I don't know quite how that worked, but we pulled it off."

Admiral Lewis gave a forced smile.

"Yes, three destroyed evens up the odds in our favor. I just hope when we come back around, they've not done anything to surprise us."

"True, still, we are in pretty good shape. The escorts even made it through, incredibly."

The communications officer turned and called out over the noise of the CIC.

"Admiral, an urgent message is coming in from the General."

"Good, put it on the main screen."

With no more than a nod, the officer transferred the feed directly to the main screen. The other video streams from the ship moved to smaller frames on the left and right of the image of the General.

"I've grabbed as many as I could. We are heading back for the rendezvous."

A cheer rang out through CIC, but the XO barked at them for silence.

"Great work, General."

He meant to continue, but the marine commander shook his head angrily.

"We've got a problem, Admiral. Some of my birds were hit on the way back up, and it's taken longer to get into position. We're going to be eleven minutes behind schedule."

It didn't sound much, but eleven minutes would mean the fleet would have passed the rendezvous point and continued on in their orbit about the moon.

"Damn it!" sighed Admiral Lewis. He looked at his tactical map and then the list of craft heading up from the surface. There were hundreds, perhaps thousands of survivors on their way to low orbit. If he weren't there when they arrived, the fourteen remaining Biomantas would massacre them.

"Okay, General, meet us at the following coordinates."

There was a short pause while the General checked the information. He looked back into the camera, a confused look on his face.

"Admiral, that is high orbit, and on the same level as the enemy blockade. Are you sure?"

Admiral Lewis did his best to look confident.

"Either we will punch a hole for you, or there'll be no Alliance fleet left."

The General nodded before cutting the feed.

* * *

Spartan and Khan waited at the secondary deck where so many of the station's refugees had arrived. Now that the fighting was over, the number of people had increased. Many returned to where they had been before, but others just sat down crying or running about to look for missing loved ones. Three medical staff helped move the body of the engineer that had helped them in the final stages of the fight.

"He did well, in the end," was the best Khan could manage.

Spartan touched the stretcher as it moved past the two of them.

"Better if he'd lived."

Multiple groups of officials emerged from the passageways, more than either of them would have expected.

"Here come the bureaucrats," muttered Khan.

A small group of Earthsec security arrived, none carried anything more than a stun baton. Their uniforms were the usual dark tunics and black trousers used by security guards throughout the Alliance. On their heads were grey caps, marked with the insignia of Earth, and thick black utility belts wrapped around their waists with datapads and stun batons attached.

"What going on here?" asked a gruff-looking, gray haired man as the security guards looked about. They moved with the assured nature of men used to being given respect. As they checked the passageways, they came across the dirty and bloodied shapes of Khan and Spartan. Upon spotting the weapons in their hands, they immediately made for them.

"The machines are gone," said Khan in a matter-of-fact tone.

"Is that so?" asked the man sarcastically.

Spartan moved closer to the man.

"Yes, it is so. Now, what exactly are you doing here?"

The man looked up and down at Spartan as if he were nothing more than a common criminal. He refused to answer him and waited until three more of his comrades move in to support him. Now confident of his position, he extended his hand toward Spartan, perhaps to grab him.

Yeah, I don't think so, Spartan thought.

He tilted a few degrees to the left and brought his leg down on the back of the man's knee. His leg gave way instantly, and then he was on the floor, face first. Spartan stood his ground, and Khan growled, that low, deep down snarl that even a fool would avoid.

"Now, what the hell is going on out here? We have machines trying to take over the station, and a Spacebridge that is off-line."

Spartan kicked the man away and then looked to the other officers.

"Where the hell were you, and why didn't you stop the machines?"

The Earthsec officers lifted their stun batons and waited while the man pulled himself painfully to his feet. One leaned over to help, but he shook the other man away, refusing to accept any assistance. His face was bitter, but also more than a little embarrassed. Spartan watched him carefully as he stepped back, and for a brief moment thought it might turn into an all-out brawl.

"You're not from around here, are you?" he said before spitting blood on the floor.

Spartan laughed.

"You only just worked that out?"

The man looked to his colleagues and spoke for a moment before turning back. Before he could speak, an officer flanked by four men in Marine Corps uniforms marched toward them. Spartan was very familiar with the training, organization, and equipment of the Marines, and these men looked very different to what he was used to. All four carried thermal shotguns, a weapon more commonly associated with civilian and security use. Their armor was only partial, covering just their heads and chests in a layer of plastic of some unfamiliar type.

"We're on lockdown here, orders from Earthsec Command," said the officer. "Commander Stanley is coming here for an inspection."

"Lockdown?" grumbled Khan, "What's going on?"

The thin, gray-faced man in an Earthsec uniform pushed to the front, lifting his hands in a conciliatory gesture to both groups.

"Easy now," he said, looking at his own people. He then looked to the two guests.

"This is Spartan, and this one here is Khan, both are former Alliance Special Forces...and our guests."

The man Spartan had cast to the ground reached for Spartan's weapon.

"They are civilians. You know the rules," said the man.

The officer laughed and stepped back to give the man easy access to Spartan. He turned to him.

"If you think you can take them without losing a limb, feel free to try it."

The man stopped, now suddenly unsure. He waited, perhaps considering whether he should try his luck and then moved back, doubt now taking over.

"Good man," said Spartan, "you just saved yourself a lot of trouble."

"And pain," added Khan, tensing his great fists.

The newly arrived officer extended his right hand to shake Spartan's hand.

"You don't recognize me, do you Spartan?"

Spartan shrugged.

"The name's Jenkins, John Jenkins. I enlisted at Prometheus with the same stream as you. My platoon trained alongside yours before we went into that meat grinder on Titan."

Spartan looked at the man carefully. There was something in the eyes that looked vaguely familiar, but he didn't recall spending any real time with the man. A brief glance down showed he hadn't maintained the kind of body or fitness one would expect for a man of so much experience.

"What happened?"

The man gave a modest smile.

"Retirement. I came out here when the first Rift generator station was activated. Earthsec pay good money for ex-military."

Khan grabbed Spartan.

"Enough talking, there are things that need doing."

"He's right," said Jenkins.

The man walked to the row of small windows to the right of them. The stars moved swiftly in the background, as the section of the station was still rotating to provide artificial gravity.

"We're spread pretty thin out here, Spartan. Earth and Mars have less than sixty million citizens between them, with half again spread over the moons. With the Rift down, we've lost contact with Terra Nova and our fleet."

"Wait, what about the Sol Patrol Force?" asked Khan suspiciously.

Jenkins shrugged.

"Force? Is that what they're calling it now?"

Khan and Spartan looked at each other before returning their gaze to the man. He looked different to the others, his bearing was more upright, a hint of his confidence perhaps due to his past in the Marine Corps.

"Look, that force is just one frigate, and it's in about a hundred pieces near the Rift. All we have left are the war barges. There are nine spread through Sol, and they ain't worth a damn."

"That's it?" asked Spartan incredulously.

Jenkins nodded.

"Yes, and they answer directly to Earthsec, not the Alliance."

"What about the Rift station?"

The older man in the unit moved in to interrupt them.

"Look...I don't know who you think..."

He stopped when more men in suits from their interrogation appeared. The one with the bloodied nose smiled when he saw the Earthsec security man clutching a sore arm.

"I see you two have been making friends."

Spartan sensed something in the man's tone though, as if something had changed, and not to Spartan or Khan's advantage. He wasn't entirely sure what it was but was certain he could sense a double-cross. Khan must have felt the same because he tensed and then moved his feet slightly apart as if readying for a fight. From behind these men walked a man in a smart suit, flanked by four more Earthsec operatives, each in their security uniforms but apparently unarmed. Spartan could make out the batons on their belts and that the civilians seemed to move quickly away from him as he approached. Jenkins cleared his throat, and Spartan suspected it was a warning, to him. He then looked to Spartan, but the newly arrived man spoke first.

"Greetings, Gentlemen. Report."

The older man with graying hair spoke first.

"The station is secure, and we've sent the automated orbital barges in to finish off the flotsam in space."

"The docking arm and the T'Kari ship?"

The man nodded.

"Yes, Sir. The ship was infested with machines, same as the docking arm. The barges are pounded it as we speak."

The man still refused to look at Spartan and walked to the window to look at what was left of the arm, far out in space and flickering as gunfire raked the metal structure. He nodded to himself.

"Good, good. Shame about the loss of the docking arm though."

Then he turned about and looked to the gray haired

officer.

"What about the T'Kari? I have orders to bring them to the surface for…discussions."

The man tilted his head, looking at Spartan while waiting for a reply.

"They are safe on this station, Sir."

The man waited in silence, as if he needed the time to digest the information. A couple of seconds might have been manageable, but he dragged it on for so long it became uncomfortable.

"Lieutenant Jenkins," he said before stopping amidst the group. All three groups coalesced into a single mass of Earthsec personnel.

"Good work to you and your staff. The station is secure, and we will be back to normal in no time."

Spartan opened his mouth to speak, but the man lifted his hand and interrupted him.

"Let me introduce myself. I am Commander Richard Stanley. This Earthsec station is under my official jurisdiction."

Spartan was unimpressed at this.

"Then you've been doing a piss poor job, Commander. It came down to me, my friend here, and a single one of your engineers to fix this mess. Where were all your suits and officers when there was real fighting to be done?"

The man looked at Spartan suspiciously, but it didn't stop him from speaking.

"You have a Rift down. That means no communications and no help from the rest of the Alliance."

The man smiled at him, one of those smiles Spartan knew meant anything but good news. He'd met men like this many times before, men whose interests lay in their own advancement.

"Yes, that is very true."

He nodded to one of the men in the suits, and one walked closer. They spoke quietly for a few seconds and then separated. The Commander waited patiently while the other man walked to the side of the passageway and activated a communication panel.

"By order of the Governor of Earth and its colonies, stations, and territories, a state of martial law is being declared. All citizens are to contact their nearest Earthsec center within the next twenty-four hours."

The Commander looked away from Spartan and to the rest of his people.

"I've been saying for the last ten years we needed to become more self-sufficient. With this fighting starting, it is critical that we keep Earth and our colonies out of harm's way."

Spartan stepped closer to him, but two of the men blocked his path.

"Are you insane? We need to open the Spacebridge and find out what's happening?"

Commander Stanley shook his head.

"No, I don't think so."

He indicated for Spartan and Khan to walk with him. Khan refused to move, but a stern look from Spartan forced him to comply. They walked along the passageway until reaching one of the many bulges that extended like pimples from the station. The Commander looked out into space and waited until the blue orb of Earth drifted into view.

"The last information that came through the Rift was that machines were attacking territories throughout the Alliance. It seems they are using the Network against us."

Spartan wasn't surprised in the slightest.

"Makes sense. They've been using uncharted Rifts in the past, and they have servants among different races, including the rebel T'Kari."

"Ah, yes, the Raiders?"

Spartan nodded.

"We've had dealings with them and the Biomechs themselves."

The man studied Spartan for a few more seconds before speaking.

"We are not ready for this enemy, not out here in Sol."

"Then let us open the Rift and get help!" growled Khan.

He looked back out of the window and the view of the stars once more.

"We are not what we were, less than a hundred million souls throughout this system. If Terra Nova or Prime are under attack, then we can expect no help from that quarter."

Spartan pointed to the window.

"Take the station, open the Rift, and send through a scout. If you find trouble, you can close the Rift."

The man looked to Spartan and smiled.

"My friend, I don't think you quite appreciate the situation. We are fully self-sufficient, especially since the arrival of the heavy equipment from Prometheus."

Khan looked back into the passageway. Nothing of note had changed other than the large number of uniformed personnel moving about. It was when a group of civilians and children were stopped and escorted away that he realized what was happening. He turned back to find the Commander looking right at the two of them.

"You're not serious?"

The man smiled.

"We managed alone for a long time before useful contact was re-established through the Spacebridge. It used to take over eight years to send a message to Terra Nova and to get one back. When you had your little civil war, it was over before we even heard about it!"

Spartan wiped his brow and turned to Khan.

"They're going it alone."

He then looked back at the Commander.

"Aren't you?"

The Commander nodded slowly.

"When a diseased limb threatens the host, you remove it from the body. The Alliance is a luxury we can happily manage without. At least, for now."

A whistling sound appeared from the space above them, shortly followed by a holographic image appearing in the center of the passageway. The Earthsec officers stepped back and watched flickering image stabilize to show the form of an aged man with a monocle.

"The Governor of Terra Antiqua," said the Commander in a hushed tone.

Spartan had never heard the honorific title for Earth used before and found it almost absurd.

"Citizens of Sol. Due to incursions from the colonies of the New Alliance, we have been forced to permanently deactivate the Spacebridge. A number of vessels forced their way through and deposited objects onto the Martian surface before our barges could destroy them. But there is no way of knowing where else the decadent taint of Terra Nova has spread."

Khan spat on the floor in annoyance.

"This is…"

Spartan shook his head, encouraging his friend to remain silent.

"…until such time as this Biomech menace is permanently eradicated, it is with a heavy heart that I enact Martial Law throughout Sol."

This sent a murmur of conversation through the

station, even into the sections that couldn't be seen from where they all waited.

"All colony transport and transfers will be monitored via Earthsec border controls."

Those civilians still in the wide passageway started to move away, but the Commander lifted his hand.

"No, listen to this!"

"Earthsec Militia has been activated, and all units are to report to their local barracks."

The holographic image vanished, and a buzzing sound from the Commander's aged datapad drew his attention to his thigh. The man lifted the unit, examined the display, and then placed it back in its small pouch.

"As you can see, we are in a perilous situation out here, so far from the might and power of the Alliance. Governor Trelleck wishes to meet you both."

"Trelleck?" snorted Khan.

"Yes, the Governor of Sol."

"Why?" Spartan asked.

Commander Stanley grinned, but Spartan could see through his expression, and it was one of amusement, mixed with a little arrogance.

"That is between you two and him. I suspect he wishes to seek your counsel with regards to these machines that have landed on Mars. You are the two most experienced warriors in the whole of Sol, after all."

Spartan watched Khan lift his right hand and instantly

knew what he was going to do. Rather than let him get them both into serious trouble, he stepped in his friend's path and nodded politely.

"That makes sense. We have more than a little experience. Perhaps the Lieutenant could join us? He fought in the Uprising as well."

The Commander looked taken aback that Spartan had agreed so readily.

"Of course, why not?" he said, slightly confused.

After a short word with the officer, he moved back to the window, and the shape of Earth appeared once more. He seemed entranced by the shape of the object.

"Earth is more than the home place of humanity, Spartan."

He looked back at the grizzled warrior and his monstrous companion.

"It is the most important planet in the galaxy, and together we will return it to its position of preeminence above all other worlds."

Khan moved alongside them and looked out, just as the planet disappeared from view again.

"So, we're going to Earth?"

Spartan took in a long breath and waited for the object to return.

"It looks that way."

* * *

For the first time in the battle for Eos, the sides were equal. Fourteen of the Alliance's most advanced warships faced off against the deadly Biomantas of the Biomechs. Although they had moved past them on the first pass, this time would be different. As the ships altered course to move to a higher attitude, they effectively slowed to almost match the speed of the Biomech forces. From this height, the ships were now well away from the thin atmosphere of the moon and spread out in wide formations. As before, the Alliance forces were led from the front by the two massive Battlecruisers, with the remainder of the fleet drawn up into two columns behind each ship.

The red nosed fighters accelerated to their maximum combat speed and set a direct course for the nearest of the Biomech warships. Super-heated flames roared silently from their twin engines in the coldness of space. Behind them waited the fleet and the dull orb that was the moon of Eos. Around them two Battlecruisers moved all remaining fighters from the fleet in large groups.

"Now!"

Captain Jim 'The Hammer' Evans hit the button on his fighter. Nothing happened to him, but all around them moved off the shapes of scores of shuttles. Every single one was empty and being operated by remote. He waited until the counter ran down to zero before tapping the next button.

"Alpha group, with me!"

He hit the boost control on his fighter and instantly felt the surge of power as he slid in the back of the fighter cockpit. His Lightning fighter was one of twenty similar fighters that covered the right flank of ANS Royal Oak. They rushed ahead, along with half of the other fighters toward the closing formation of Biomantas. Alpha Group included a small contingent of Maulers, as well as four shuttles equipped with missiles. It was an improvised force that increased the size of the fighter force by almost double.

"Captain, flash message from Captain Harper. They are powering up their weapons."

"Affirmative."

The plan was rough at best, but he still remained confident it would work. They continued to push past the capital ships and on toward the force of Biomantas. Captain Evans looked at the schematic of the closing ships and smiled to himself at the sections indicating damage.

Good work, guys.

The earlier run passing their fleet had caused a number of casualties, but more importantly, they had raked every ship in their force before vanishing off around the moon. Only now did he realize quite how much damage they'd caused. According to the clock, he was just three minutes away from weapons range, yet he knew the Biomech ships could hit him the minute he came into sight.

Why aren't they firing?

He looked at his fighter disposition once more, in case any had gone astray. The swarms of fighters were exactly where they should be, and the decoy shuttles were out in front. One light vanished on his screen, then another.

There, they are taking the bait!

He made direct contact to Captain Harper, his CAG aboard ANS Royal Oak.

"Captain, they've started."

"Good work, you know what to do. The assault wave will launch as soon as you hit the first targets."

"Understood, out."

"All fighters, this is Alpha Leader, move into position!"

It was a short yet simple command and was acted upon instantly. Groups of fighters broke away, setting course for their targets in the middle and rear of the fleet. Unlike before, fighters moved around the flanks rather than attacking directly. This simple change gave the capital ships a clear line of sight to the Biomantas for their surprise. Captain Evans couldn't quite believe what he was seeing when the big guns started their bombardment. Unlike before, the particle beam emitters were being used on a much lower powered firing mode and in a more dispersed pattern, so they could deliver long bursts of energy. Rather than seeing substantial explosions on the targets, there were hundreds of much smaller flashes across half of the Biomanta fleet.

That should keep them busy enough. Now it's our turn!

"All squadrons; start your attack runs."

The fighters moved closer and closer to the predatory Biomech ships. The shuttles were now almost all gone from the repeated defensive gunfire of the enemy vessels, and it was the turn of the actual fighters to take the damage. Two vanished in the first twenty seconds, and then the nearest ship was in range. Captain Evans targeted the damaged locations from the raking attack run and sent the data to his wingmen.

"Fox One!" said the first of the pilots in the formation.

It was a brevity code used to indicate the launch of a semi-active radar guided missile. First one missile launched, and then there were more than thirty, all of them heading directly for the Biomanta. Impacts from the particle beams caused continuous damage and scorch marks to the surface of the ship, and though half were shot down, at least a dozen struck in and around the damage already sustained. The fighters split apart as they traveled past the damaged ship.

"Good work, Alpha Group, onto the next wounded bird."

* * *

Jack gazed out of the window at the side of the Mauler with a look of stunned disbelief on his face. Many more craft moved with them, along with a much smaller group of Biomech fighters that struggled to keep up with the accelerating Alliance vessels. The mixture of marines, Jötnar, and Helion soldiers was bizarre but nothing compared to the look of joy he could see on Gun's face. Jack's body ached from the battle and the battering he'd sustained, yet even after all they'd been through, he couldn't for the life of him see why Gun would be so happy.

"Glad we got out of there?" he asked finally.

"Huh?" muttered the battered Jötnar, "No, not much point in staying behind to die though."

Jack thought he could see something resembling regret on the warrior's face. The craft shook violently, and the alert sensors started to blast. The interior speakers activated to the sound of a worried pilot.

"We just took a major hit. The gun targeting system is offline. We need gunners!"

Another impact shook the craft, and it lurched to the left before the pilot could right it. A patter of rain ran along the hull, a sure fire guarantee of gunfire hitting the thick armor plate.

"She's a strong bird," said Gun with amusement while looking at the marines inside the craft. "Well, maybe somebody should get on them?"

Jack and Callahan were the first to deactivate their clamps and fixed their straps to the rails overhead, in case another impact threw them about. A Navy crewman and a marine from another unit moved to the corners where small hatches led to the gunnery control turrets. Jack pulled himself to the rear starboard turret and clambered inside. The strapping was similar to the seating in the Mauler, and it only took a few seconds to get into position. The gunnery system was based on the tried and tested yoke system, but the computer system was offline.

Great! What about the servos?

He pulled on the yoke, and the entire gun turret mount to his side moved quickly and smoothly.

Okay, that's a start.

The visual display system was also offline, so he pulled on the shutter lever and opened the plating. It revealed the view from the tiny array of thick transparent layers. They were protected from dangerous radiation, but even so were far less useful than using the conventional display system. In the center was a grid marking the angled and distances for type of ammunition.

"Here they come, three targets, seven o'clock!"

Jack swung the turret mount around to find him staring at a pair of Biomech fighters. Both flashed repeatedly as they fired bursts into the flank of the armored Mauler. Jack leaned a little to the left and pulled the trigger. The turret shook slightly, and the quadruple gun system released a cloud of hardened slugs at the attackers. The burst was way off.

Come on, you fool. Hit them.

He took aim once more, and just as one was about to

move from sight, pulled the trigger again. This time a few rounds struck the fighter's engine mount, and he cried out with satisfaction as it split apart into three large sections and vanished into the night.

"Yes!"

The other fighters disappeared from view, and the Mauler shook as yet more rounds clattered into her armored hull. Jack's stomach turned each time they were hit, but none made it through, and he was able to take aim at another fighter moving in to launch a rocket at point blank range. This time he didn't even have to lead the target, and it exploded into a thousand pieces as his hardened shells smashed into the engine and weapons of the fighter. Scattered debris clattered uselessly against the Mauler, and then they were free.

"Good work, people. We're in orbit. Now for the rendezvous."

The passengers cheered, but Jack remained silent. From his position, he had the perfect view of the Alliance fleet. The others might think the ships were waiting patiently for them, but he could see the reality. All around them were the vast shapes of cruisers and Battlecruisers intermixed with Biomanta warships. Fighters screamed about in all directions, and arcs of light flashed all about them. But it was not the ships or the guns that caught his eye, it was the explosion-riddled shapes of a dozen Biomech warships that he couldn't believe.

They fought them head-to-head…and survived? he wondered incredulously.

CHAPTER FOURTEEN

Particle beam weapons were finally used in open battle in large numbers at the battle of Eos. Although a tactical victory for the Alliance, the Biomech warships had demonstrated their parity with the Alliance in terms of firepower, technology, and tactics. For the first time, Alliance ships were able to deal with any foe on equal terms. The reality of these deadly weapons was that battle could be decided in minutes and at impossible ranges. Many predicted this would mean the end of kinetic weapons. Only the great struggle for Helios would answer that question definitively.

Direct Energy Weapons – An Introduction

ANS Conqueror shuddered as a massive volley of explosive shells slammed into her thick armor. The spaced plating did their work and absorbed a large amount of the impact before the damage spread inside the vessel. The weight of gunfire was beginning to show though, and her hull was pockmarked with a thousand small impact craters.

"Roll her and present our underside!" snapped the XO.

Admiral Lewis nodded with satisfaction. The ship was equally protected on all sides, and so far they been struck hard on the topside and right flank of the Battlecruiser. By performing a rotation, they would be able to move the fragile damaged sections out of the line of sight and place fresh armor to face the remaining Biomantas.

"What's our status?" he asked, though the tactical display showed him most of the data he needed to know. He just wanted to hear the words, to know from somebody else's mouth that the battle was going the way it appeared.

Lieutenant Vitelli highlighted the primary ships still involved in the main space battle before speaking.

"Serenity and Olympus are gone, Admiral. The enemy is down to four of the Biomantas and the Ravager. The rest are heading to the surface of Eos in flames."

He should have been happy at the news, but he knew the captains and many of the officers on board those ships. Captain Alyani Tinychai of ANS Serenity had encountered the T'Kari Raider so long ago in T'Karan space, and now he was gone. Admiral Lewis could only hope against hope that enough of the crews had escaped before the ships finally blew. He was down to a dozen ships and nearly half of his fighters were either lost or had landed and were currently beyond repair.

"What about the marine extraction?"

"It's done," said a familiar voice from the side doorway of the CIC."

He turned to see the still armored form of General Daniels enter. He wanted to race forward to greet him, but that would have looked bizarre in the middle of a battle.

"Great work, General." It was the best he could manage while half of the officers in the room whooped with pleasure at the return of the officer. Right behind him followed a handful of marines, as well as Colonel Gun. All had removed their helmets or slid back their visors to reveal their faces. Gun could barely squeeze through the doorway and managed to tear a pipe off the wall as he moved inside.

"What are your casualties?" asked the XO.

The General shook his head bitterly.

"You don't want to know, Captain."

Lieutenant Vitelli highlighted the last four Maulers as they approached ANS Royal Oak.

"Admiral, the last four birds will be aboard Royal Oak in less than three minutes."

"Good," said the Admiral under his breath.

He turned about and stared with his tired eyes at the moon below them. It was a place he'd never expected to see in his lifetime, yet alone fight a series of deadly battles.

"Then it is time to leave this place."

"No!" called out one of the marines.

Admiral Lewis was not accustomed to disagreement and looked about the group before spotting the man. He was lightly built, but the face and the eyes reminded him of somebody he knew well.

"Morato?"

"Private Jack Morato, Admiral."

"Spartan's son?"

Jack nodded.

But there was no time for pleasantries, and he looked back at the tactical display showing the ongoing battle. It wasn't necessary for him to micro-manage the action, but he was determined to maintain a firm grip on what was happening.

"I want that carrier brought down."

He selected the Fleet-wide channel that connected to all captains and fighter controllers."

"Move the fighter squadrons in to protect the frigates and then bring down that carrier. All other ships are to eliminate the remaining Biomantas! I want this battle ended, and quickly!"

Once the responses came in, he turned his attention back to the marines.

"Private, you were saying?"

Jack took a step closer to face him.

"Admiral, a group of Khreenk assisted in the battle. They came back with us on the transports."

Admiral Lewis looked surprised and turned his

attention over to General Daniels, who simply nodded in agreement.

"And?"

"Well, Sir, they said the Biomechs troops are only a short distance from the Helion settlements. Give it another hour, and they will leave the Fort and move on to the next target."

"Really, you know this for certain?"

General Daniels walked to the tactical schematic and tilted it to show the surface of Eos. The main Fort was now completely red with smaller patterns around it. He slid it to the right and pointed at four green areas.

"These are the nearby underground habitation quadrants and industrial sites. As we left, my drones detected elements from the Fort already moving away and heading for these locations."

Gun growled at this.

"They're screwed then. Two marine battalions couldn't hold them back, and you saw how useful the Helion Army was."

The disparaging tone came over as more insulting than he may have intended, but it did its job. The imagery certainly supported the assessment of the marines, and the Admiral didn't like it.

"Assuming we can win this battle, there is nothing we can do to help them. I have orders for us to join the defense force around Helios at full burn with any ship that remains. How long would it take to take on and defeat the Biomechs on the ground?"

General Daniels almost choked at that.

"Defeat? They smashed us on our own ground. We could return and attack their forces in hit and run strikes, but that won't help the Helions. We need to stop them decisively and in less than an hour."

He placed his chin in his hand, considering what they were telling him. He had a long-term requirement to assist at Helios, but the defeat on Eos was a stain upon the honor of the Alliance. Even worse than that, was the potential loss of the moon and all of its civilians.

How can the Helions trust us if we leave their citizens to die as we flee?

"Admiral, Commodore Hampel has started his strike on the carrier," said Captain Marcus.

His stomach shuddered for a moment at the thought. The frigates were much smaller than the heavy cruisers that made up the bulk of his fleet, but what they lacked in size, they more than made up for in short-ranged gunnery and speed.

"Good, let us hope they can help end this before every Helion burns on Eos. I want this battle over!"

* * *

The small force of four frigates moved in a line abreast

formation at a distance of just eighty kilometers apart. In space this was almost on top of each other, but it meant they could provide mutual gunnery support against the swarm of Biomech fighters that moved against them. ANS Spearfish, the lead ship in the formation, inched slightly ahead of the others and made for a direct assault course on the Ravager. Unlike the Biomantas, this ship followed a more conventional design, with no indicators showing a biological component to its twin hull. The multitude of ribs running down its flanks hit the launch tubes for fighters and gun systems. At nearly twice the size of the Biomantas, she was a ship worthy of a Battlecruiser, perhaps even a battleship from the glory days of the Great War.

"Close formation, and watch for fighters!"

Captain Jim 'The Hammer' Evans maneuvered his red-nosed Lightning fighter alongside the freshly arrived X57 Avenger combat drones that had now entered the fray. At roughly the same size of his craft, the Avengers were more heavily armed with a multitude of weapons fitted in their armored hulls. Their shape was something closer to a bat, and the wings contained four small engines on each side, both to propel the fighter and to power the might primary armament. The hull consisted almost entirely of a single weapon system, a quadruple barreled railgun that had been heavily modified from the weapon systems once carried on cruisers.

"All fighters report in," he said calmly.

The drones, of course, said nothing. They were fully autonomous and only communicated directly with the controlling capital ships and the forward controllers in the fighter squadron. A pair of Hammerheads moved closely to the frigates to monitor and give tactical orders to the robotic warriors, and six more drones circled the Hammerheads watching out for signs of missiles or other craft. One by one, the squadrons reported in until he knew the fighter group was ready for the next phase.

"All squadrons, you have your targets. Break and attack!"

Captain Evans was just one of six leaders for the fighter assault, of the six he was the one with the greatest experience. He'd fought pirates, T'Kari Raiders, and now Biomechs fighters. Even he wasn't prepared for the flak corridor put up by the Ravager. It started as a dozen turrets fired scattered shards into space and then extended to more than fifty guns firing almost repeatedly.

"What the hell!" he muttered as a chunk of his left wing tore off, exposing bare wiring. One of his missile hardpoints indicated a system failure and immediately went offline.

Screw this. We're going in!

He hit the boost control and accelerated toward the stern of the massive carrier. His wingmen moved in right behind, the rest of the fighters moving about the carrier like flies.

"Captain, enemy fighters launching!" said Lieutenant Leary, one of the pilots in the squadron moving to the underside of the carrier. No sooner had he said the words than two-dozen Biomech fighters rushed out from the massive ship and into the formation of fighters. Captain Evans spotted the threat indicator right behind his comrade, but it was too late.

"Watch your tail, Green Three."

Gunfire ripped into the fighter and exploded the starboard engine, instantly killing the pilot and sending shards of red-hot metal into the cockpit. The wreck twisted out of control before striking the carrier in a fiery flash. The frigates were now in range, and the tables quickly turned on the newly launched fighters. Like the carrier, they were well equipped to deal with fighters and dispatched half of the Biomech fighters with a barrage of tiny flechette rounds from their point-defense turrets. The frigates also made use of their larger caliber railguns to put barrages of gunfire into the carrier itself. Explosions ran along the length of the vessel even before the volleys of missiles and torpedoes from the fighters did their work. Three sections sustained the worst of it, with most landing near the rear. Missile after missile slammed through the defensive fire and blew out chunks of metal while the Avenger drones sent high-velocity projectiles deep inside the ship.

Captain Evans launched his final missiles before

contacting Royal Oak's CAG.

"Captain Harper, the breaches have been made. She's ready."

"Understood. Evans, get your people out of there. You have forty-five seconds."

The Captain had already sent the pre-determined code, however, and the large groups of fighters circled about, turning on the last of the Biomantas that were still being struck by an overwhelming barrage of wide-band particle beams. He was halfway to the nearest of the ships when he spotted the IFF warnings on the missiles.

Nukes, about damned time!

They tracked quickly from the launch tubes aboard the Battlecruisers as they moved on the carrier. There were only twelve of them, with three times as more decoys launched from the other warships. Three made it through what was left of the defensive gunnery and smashed deep inside the stern of the ship.

Nothing happened.

* * *

Admiral Lewis watched with a bitter expression on his face as one of the frigates took the full brunt of the Ravager's gunfire. The ship had been able to turn its guns away from the retreating fighters, and in less than thirty seconds, the frigate had sustained over five hundred separate impacts from the high-velocity guns.

"What's happened to my atomics?" he demanded angrily.

There was no answer until finally the tactical officer spun about to look at him.

"Admiral, the activation signal has been jammed by the carrier. We can't activate them this far away."

"What? Are you kidding? Burn through it and trigger them."

"It won't work, Admiral. The jamming is coming from the bow of the ship. We need to get right against their stern to get through the jamming."

"What about another volley?"

Lieutenant Vitelli checked his computer for a moment, calling out while keeping his eyes on the screen.

"Three minutes till they're ready, Admiral, but they will have the same problem."

"Then remove the safeties and set them for proximity detonation. That ship is already moving in on ANS Sentry. It must be stopped, now!"

Lieutenant Vitelli almost protested, but the bright flash of ANS Narwhal as it exploded near the Ravager persuaded him otherwise. There were now just three of the small frigates remaining, and he doubted the others had more than a few minutes of life left.

"Aye, Sir, working on it."

General Daniels looked at the disposition of ships and

pointed at the group of Hammerheads leaving the scene of the battle.

"Who are these?"

Admiral Lewis glanced at them before answering.

"They're the controller craft from the drones, why?"

The General knew what he was about to say would consign the crews to their deaths but time was not on their side, and they were the only crew in the area.

"Give them the order."

The Admiral looked at him and then at the flashing marker indicating the craft. He knew it was the right thing to do but hated the General for reminding him of it. He hesitated, but every second that went by saw more casualty reports coming in. He placed his face in the palm of his hand as he picked up the intercom.

* * *

Lieutenant Jim Davidson tapped in the data for the last time into the navcomputer. It was a long shot, but he was damned if he was going to lead his electronic warfare crew to their deaths on a suicide mission.

"Are you sure this will work?" he asked the two engineers sitting inside the transport section of the craft.

"It's on a timer. As long as she gets within ten meters of the ship, it'll work."

The Lieutenant was one of newest pilots in the unit,

but his aptitude for seat of the pants flying had almost got him the top spot in the fighter squadrons. It was only his failure on the gunnery trials that had pushed him back to the support units. Now he was starting to wonder if the fighter squadrons would be safer.

"Okay, the computer is set. Get ready for ejection in ten seconds."

He looked out of the cockpit and at the shape of the Ravager right in front of them. It was a big ship, perhaps bigger than any Alliance ship ever built, and from this distance it might have been a moon. The timer continued to run down until it reached the last digit. His muscles tensed, and he almost panicked, thinking for a second that he'd not fitted his helmet. He reach up and found he was right.

"Oh...crap!" he groaned.

A powerful blast flew him and his co-pilot out of the bottom of the craft at the same time as the crew section detached from the rear mountings. Retro thrusters pushed them down and away from the craft as it continued forward on its course with the massive ship. Lieutenant Davidson kept his eyes and mouth closed for as long as he could manage, but the force of the escape and his own nerves reduced that to just a few seconds. He groaned as he blew out the air to find fresh, clean air coming back.

What?

He opened his eyes to see the compartment was drifting

away from the ship, and his co-pilot sitting directly next to him.

You fool!

In the panic, he'd forgotten the escape sequence blew out the crew modules rather than the individual crewmembers. He knew this, and it made him feel like an idiot that he might have thought otherwise.

"Jim, look," said Jonas, his co-pilot.

Both of them looked out of the window section as the tiny dot that was the Hammerhead crashed into the stern of the ship. It looked like they must have failed, but a tiny red flash appeared and then expanded to engulf the entire rear third of the ship. It shuddered and split as great chunks were blown off the Ravager.

"Yes!" he cried in excitement.

* * *

Jack had only just entered the CIC of the Battlecruiser to find the officers arguing about what to do next. The escape to the fleet had been fast and violent but incredibly, the bulk of the marine rescue craft had made it away from Eos. He'd given his opinions to the Admiral, but it was now out of his hands. Gun and the General were right next to him, and he began to feel like a naughty pupil at school, unsure whether to move or speak.

"They've done it. The Ravager is burning!" said a seated

officer.

Jack turned his head slightly to look at the large mainscreen positioned so most of the officers could see it. The space battle filled the rectangular space, but nothing was more significant than the massive carrier as it was torn apart by a series of micro-atomic warheads that fractured and shattered her hull. Even he found himself caught up in the jubilation as the most powerful ship in the Biomech fleet was torn apart.

"Excellent work, people. How are we doing on the Biomantas?" asked the Admiral.

The ship's XO spoke to a woman before replying.

"Just one left, Admiral, and the fleet is converging on them."

The mood seemed to shift as more news arrived of the shattered Biomech fleet. Only then did General Daniels nod to Jack and Gun to walk with him. The three approached the Admiral and waited patiently. Finally, he turned to look at them. He seemed almost happy, but the look on General Daniels' face halted that.

"General?"

The marine officer pointed to the tactical display.

"Eos? What are we going to do?"

The Admiral nodded slowly and took a single step to close the distance. He used his hands to expand the image, isolating the ruined Fort so recently abandoned by the marines. He looked back at the General.

"What about the insurgents, and these Khreenk?"

"Admiral, the insurgents melted away and back to their inhabited regions. Those are the ones the Biomechs are advancing on."

He could see the look on Admiral Lewis' face, and for a moment thought the man might simply leave it so the civilians would be killed. He opened his mouth to object, but the Admiral spoke first.

"They may not like what has happened on Helios, they might not even like us, but if we let the Biomechs overrun their homes, we will be no better than the machines. This is an opportunity to show them our strength and our solidarity."

General Daniels liked what he was hearing but was still unclear as to what was being suggested. It came to Gun to ask the blunt question.

"We can't save them, Admiral, not in the time we have."

Admiral Lewis gave a half smile.

"I know. Eos is just a moon, a minor world they hit while heading for Helios."

He changed the display to show the projected course for Helios of the comet.

"The only positive point is that that the elliptical course they are on is deceptively unremarkable, probably to give the effect of being a naturally occurring event."

"They may also only have the ability to partially modify their course instead of making radical changes," suggested the XO.

Admiral Lewis considered this for a moment.

"True, in the long-term they can probably make massive changes, but altering the course of something so massive as a comet would require more energy than we have ever had access to."

He looked to the General.

"It doesn't give us much of an edge though. It might be slightly slower than the direct route we could take on full burn, but we're still talking a difference of hours. Nothing more."

He paused, not wanting to say it, but time was moving quickly, and he knew he needed to act fast.

"General, I will leave behind any ships and marine units unable to make the journey, but the rest of us have to leave in a matter of minutes for Helios."

"What about them?"

Admiral Lewis closed his eyes for a second and thought one last time about what he was about to suggest. He couldn't remember a time in the last decades, even generations where the same had been done, but there was nothing else he could think of, not with the time and resource constraints he faced.

"General, the only option is an orbital bombardment with ground-strike neutron missiles."

He watched as the General's eyes widened in shock.

"I know it seems excessive, but it is the only way I

can guarantee our forces can wipe out the bulk of these machines and their servants."

Jack was stunned at the news, but neither the General, nor Gun said anything.

"What about the civilians down there? You can't just nuke the place!"

The General examined the map of the surface before speaking.

"No...he's right. Neutron atomics have a very small blast radius, not much more than the Fort itself. The neutron blast and shockwave will cause far heavier casualties, but if we're smart, the impact should only be felt up to about here."

He used his hands to create a circle around the base and then enlarged it to cover the approximate lethal range of the weapons. It covered all the land around the Fort and a single industrial site to the north.

"That's the only place that could be affected."

Admiral Lewis looked at the site intently.

"Population?"

"Less than a hundred workers plus a few Helion Army guards."

The Admiral scratched at his chin for a second.

"If we're going to do this, it has to be now. What do you think?"

Gun reached out to General Daniels' shoulder and twisted him about to face him.

"This is quick and painless. Wipe out their forces, and then we can send in a few small squads to finish them off."

All of them remained silent for what seemed like an eternity. Jack watched them and then remembered the others they had brought with them.

"The Khreenk, they know the area better than us. Leave them behind and some marines to finish the job. Who knows, it might get a response from the Helion insurgents."

General Daniels shrugged and looked far from convinced. He walked around the display, adjusting it to see the potential blast effects from different angles. He stopped and looked directly to Gun.

"Get a signal to the Helions. Tell them to get underground and fast. There are nukes on the way."

* * *

A day had passed and still ANS Dreadnought moved at a slow, yet steady pace through the storms. Her hull had been lashed by a hundred impacts, though none had caused more than a few scorch marks and burns on the hull. The route through the storms was proving tiring but remarkably free from danger. Teresa had been at her post in the CIC without a break when Captain Vetlaya approached her.

"Colonel, we have a clear route now to Prometheus.

My helmsman estimates no more than seventy-two hours to reach the station."

Teresa let out a sigh of relief. Her body was exhausted from the constant checking and course corrections she'd been forced to feed to the officers of the ship. Although the navbeacons had guided them through the storms, they had still come across more than a dozen Anomalies that only her experience allowed them to pass.

"That's good news," she said happily.

The Captain looked less than pleased about something.

"What is it?"

"Come with me."

The two walked across the CIC to the banks of displays where the Captain usually commanded the ship. On the screen was an image of the Chairman of the Joint Chiefs.

"The General?" she asked.

Captain Vetlaya nodded.

"Yes, there's news from across the Alliance, and it isn't good."

The Captain tapped the screen, and the image burst into life. As well as showing the General, there were multiple feeds from different parts of the Alliance. Images of ground combat on Eos, space battles, and fighting near a dozen Rift stations throughout Alliance space; all contributed to a growing feeling of dread in her body.

"It looks like they've woken up," said Captain Vetlaya despondently.

"Yes," replied Teresa, "and they all seem to be heading in the same direction."

She turned to look at the Captain, but it was Teresa who spoke first.

"Helios."

CHAPTER FIFTEEN

The Fairwater Corporation Secpad was the latest in a long line of personal computer and communication devices that dated back to before the Great War. Based around a hardened shell and a direct connection to the Alliance mainframes, it was a critical component in the digital communication and battle space for years. The technology was far from state-of-the-art, but it did allow all Alliance personnel to stay in permanent contact and acted as a portable computer terminal for medical use, tactical planning, and administrative management on a hundred colonies.

Computer Science 101, 7th Edition

Jack couldn't believe quite what he was seeing as he restarted the video stream. They had all watched the video from the CIC when it had first arrived, but he'd been unable to stop himself from watching it more than a dozen times from the temporary quarters they'd been assigned aboard ANS Conqueror. The room was one normally used by the engineers, but after the battle there were many rooms and quarters freed up due to casualties and deaths in the battle for Eos.

"I can't believe it," said Riku, sitting next to him in her nightclothes.

They were the only two in the room designed for four people in separate bunks, and their small number of holdalls lay in the corner, still unpacked. Jack shook his head bitterly as they looked at the screen. The main video feed showed images from the space battle with an emphasis on the destruction of the Ravager and the Biomanta fleet. There were some scenes showing Alliance ships taking damage, but none showing any losses. It was the aerial feed of Fort Macquarie that stunned them the most. Riku moved closer to Jack to sit behind him and rested her head on his shoulder.

"I know," he said quietly in reply, "The base is gone, just like the other two."

He reached out to the unit to switch it off, but a new window appeared with a flash alert message. He considered hitting the accept icon, but it ignored him and instead brought up the imagery in front of him. It was the face of General Rivers.

"What's happening now?" asked Riku.

Jack could sense the nervousness in her voice. He

looked at her face and the temporary stitches on her cheek from a wound she'd sustained during their escape. He moved his hand to touch her face, but he could see her tense up. The voice of the General burst out from the device, making him turn around. Facing him was the smartly dressed Chairman of the Joint Chiefs, the highest-ranking military officer in the Alliance, and a good friend of his parents.

"Men and women of the Alliance Armed Forces. It with great regret that I must announce the atomic bombardment of enemy forces on Eos, the primary moon of the Helion planet Gaxos."

"Atomics?" said Riku under her breath.

The image changed to show a view from high orbit over Eos. The imagery was slightly blurred and occasionally shook. A dozen white flashes, followed by large fireballs and clouds of dust marked the impacts on the surface.

"This was a strike of last resort, following the Fort Macquarie Massacre. Alliance ground forces are already working alongside fresh Helion Army units to reclaim Eos."

The imagery moved to show the fleet of Alliance ships around the moon. Jack instantly recognized several he knew to have already been lost in the space battle. It gave the impression more ships were at Eos when he knew only three remained, and they were those unable to continue the chase to Helios.

"As prophesied by the Helions, T'Kari, and countless other races, the Biomechs as we call them are here. Many have been found lurking on planets and moons, but most are hidden within the confines of the so-called Doomsday Comet."

Jack was all too familiar with the object. It's coming had been talked about for weeks throughout the battalion. It was the first time he'd heard of it discussed so openly though.

"By order of the President, all Alliance forces are being mobilized to defend our allies and ourselves against this Biomech threat."

The video feed of Eos changed to show the vast structure of the Alliance, with its many stars, planets, moons, and colonies.

"Biomech forces are attempting to break through our Rift networks, as well as the Anicinàbe and Byotai."

Jack shook his head as he listened.

"All of these forces are heading toward a single point, one objective they are intent on capturing or destroying."

Jack turned away from the screen and looked at Riku. The scar running down the side of her face always seemed to become more prominent the more upset or stressed she became, and it was clear to see.

"They want Helios, don't they?" she asked.

He opened his mouth to speak, but a triple beep from the display indicated a priority message. He looked back and tapped it to see the encrypted seal from Colonel Teresa Morato.

"Your mother?" asked Riku.

The contests of the message were heavily encrypted and would take some time for the system to decipher. It was the header that went with the message, and as Jack looked at the screen, he felt a trickle of water drip down from one eye. Riku saw it and leaned in.

"It's okay," he said, now worried she was about to panic.

"What is it?" she asked.

He turned to look at her.

"It says that Spartan, my father, has been found."

Both were silent at this news. Riku had never met the man, but his reputation in the Corps was something bordering on legendary. She also knew the troubled past Jack had gone through growing up in a family where his parents had been unable to spend much time with him.

"Where is he, Jack?"

He pressed a button and waited until an image of a blue world appeared. He knew immediately what it was, but to Riku it was just another planet. The light from the display shone on his face, giving his skin an odd blue tint.

"Earth," he said, his face starting to relax.

Riku noticed his lips moving and ever so slowly a smile formed.

"It says he was found near Earth!"

www.ingramcontent.com/pod-product-compliance
Lightning Source LLC
Chambersburg PA
CBHW031506210626
46816CB00019B/1544